Dead & *Kicking*

ALBY MURDOCH 3

GEOFFREY McGEACHIN

First published by Clan Destine Press in 2025

PO Box 121,
Bittern Victoria 3918
Australia

National Library of Australia Cataloguing-In-Publication data:

Dead & Kicking!

ISBNs: 978-1-922904-96-6 (paperback)
978-1-922904-97-3 (eBook)

Cover design by Willsin Rowe

Front Cover Photo Credit
Camera Lens Insert: Matthew Fraser
Model: Ni Komang Sunianti

Design & Typesetting by Clan Destine Press

www.clandestinepress.net

For Wilma

as ever and always

Chapter One

HUNKERED DOWN IN A SHALLOW DEPRESSION OFF TO ONE SIDE OF THE trail, my position was concealed by a thick layer of branches and palm fronds. While the camouflage protected me from being spotted, it also sealed in the heat and humidity and the cramped space was like an oven. My neck was aching, I was tired and soaked in sweat, and something nasty had crawled up the leg of my combat fatigues and was busily biting me on the bum. I'd have given a million bucks to be anywhere else but I knew I was probably only going to get this one chance and I needed to make every shot count.

The soldier resting on his haunches down the trail in front of me could hear the approaching patrol before he could see it; noisy chatter, the clinking of equipment, a tinny PX transistor radio. The patrol's point man ambled around a kink in the trail and stopped, suddenly. The whole idea of the point man is that he should be far enough out in front of his unit to spot any trouble before it happens. In this case, however, he'd been standing still for barely ten seconds before the rest of the patrol bumped into him.

There were about a dozen men in the group, bunched up, talking, walking close together on the trail. Most of them looked like they should still have been in high school and they started griping and cursing until they saw what the point man was staring at, and then they shut up.

A dozen yards further along the trail, the soldier stood up slowly and faced the patrol. He smiled, showing them his empty hands, palms outward. The point man looked around at the lieutenant, who looked back at the sergeant, who shrugged.

'He ain't shootin',. Lieutenant,' the sergeant said, 'and he's smilin' and ain't no gook so I guess that makes him a friendly.'

The sergeant had the kind of aged, weather-beaten face that said he knew what he was talking about. The tone in his voice indicated that what he'd just said should have been pretty bloody obvious to his superior officer.

The lieutenant nodded and walked slowly towards the soldier. The sergeant followed, keeping the muzzle of his M16 down but pointing forward, his index finger resting on the trigger guard. The soldier casually studied the rest of the patrol as the two men approached. Most of the grunts had their flak jackets gaping open, understandable given the fierce heat of the afternoon, but potentially deadly in a mortar attack. They were still standing bunched together, an easy target for any Vietcong in the area.

The American Lieutenant was studying the soldier. The uniform was different from his, and the man wore a soft bush hat rather than a steel helmet. The weapon slung around his neck and resting across his belly looked like a skinny metal pipe with two wooden handgrips and a skeleton stock. A straight magazine poked out the top and the whole damn thing looked almost homemade. The sergeant saw his lieutenant staring at the weapon.

'Owen gun,' the sergeant said to the soldier. 'Am I right?'

The soldier nodded.

'I remember seeing 'em in Korea,' the sergeant continued. 'Guess that kind of weapon would make you an Aussie.' He pronounced it 'Ossie'.

The soldier grinned. 'Got it in one, Sergeant. Good memory you got there.'

'I watched one of your boys pull one of them things out of two feet of mud, give it a splash in a puddle and fire off a whole damn magazine easy as you please.'

'Good little gun, the Owen,' the soldier agreed.

'If you're Australian, aren't you a little outside your area of operations?' the lieutenant asked.

'Yo, El-Tee,' one of the soldiers in the patrol yelled, 'can we take a load off?'

The lieutenant's face reddened at the familiarity. He glanced at the sergeant.

'Give them ten minutes.'

Before the sergeant could speak, the men were shaking off their packs and moving towards the shade of a clump of bamboo. The Australian soldier gave a whistle and when the patrol looked back at him he slowly shook his head. One of the grunts parted the undergrowth beside the track with the muzzle of his rifle and swore. 'Hot damn! Motherfucking punji stakes.'

Dozens of sharpened bamboo stakes almost certainly smeared with human excrement lined the shaded ditch. The men looked warily at the soldier and one of them pointed to the rice field on the opposite side of the trail. The soldier nodded and the grunts moved slowly into the lush field of rice, still cautiously prodding the vegetation with their rifles.

The sergeant and a couple of the grunts wore faded, stained and torn fatigues. They carried their load of grenades, ammo, flares, Claymore mines, C-rations and canteens with an ease born of long practice. The once-black leather of their combat boots was worn down to a dull, dusty grey. In contrast, the lieutenant and the rest of the men still had some shine to their boots and an olive green newness left in their fatigues, and they handled their cumbersome packs with an awkward clumsiness.

The lieutenant took a long swallow from his canteen and offered it to the Australian, who took a swig and grimaced.

'Kool-Aid,' the lieutenant explained. 'It kills the taste of the sterilising tablets.'

The Australian handed back the canteen with a smile. 'You can say that again.'

'What are you doing out here all by yourself anyway? You're a few clicks outside Phuoc Tuy Province.'

The soldier smiled. 'Actually, you're about three clicks inside our territory.'

The lieutenant stiffened. 'I can't see any badges of rank but if you think I'm -

'Sorry,' the Australian said, 'should have introduced myself earlier. Name's Cartwright. Major Peter Cartwright.'

The lieutenant's face flushed bright red and he straightened up. Cartwright's left hand shot out and stopped the young soldier's right hand as it started moving upwards in the general direction of a salute.

'We don't need any of that parade-ground bullshit out here, do we, Lieutenant? You never know who's watching.'

He pronounced the rank as "left tenant." Some of the soldiers lying closest in the rice field sniggered.

The lieutenant looked at the major. 'Sorry, sir, but we usually don't get too many officers on the ground way out here in the boonies. Are you sure we're in your area?'

Cartwright nodded. 'Where are you supposed to be, son?'

The sergeant unfolded a map and pointed to a grid.

'You and the sergeant there have a disagreement about which way to march earlier?'

'I guess you could say that,' the lieutenant mumbled glumly.

'Take my advice: if in doubt, always listen to your sergeant.'

'Yes, sir,' snapped the lieutenant. Cartwright grabbed his saluting hand just in time.

There was a whop whop whop noise overhead and the shadow of a helicopter passed over the patrol. No-one even looked up. Hueys coming and going were just part of daily life in Vietnam, like yellow cabs on New York's Fifth Avenue, only sometimes with a hell of a lot more blood on the back seats.

Cartwright glanced across the rice field towards the tree line and the setting sun.

'Maybe you'd better get your men back to a good place to lie up for the night. It's getting late.'

'What about you, major?' the lieutenant asked. 'You okay on your own out here?'

Cartwright smiled. 'I'll be just fine. No need for you to worry about me.'

The sergeant got his griping and grumbling charges back on their feet and into some semblance of a military formation and they moved off slowly in the direction they'd come from. The area where the Americans had been resting looked like a rubbish tip. Empty C-ration boxes and discarded cans littered the flattened rice stalks.

Cartwright waited until the patrol was out of sight and the last sounds of the unit's radio had faded. The sun was low now and they needed to prepare their night ambush position. After casually scanning the landscape one more time, Cartwright held his hands out at waist height and slowly raised them, palms up.

Seven men wearing jungle greens and draped in camouflage netting laced with foliage slowly emerged from the rice field, 7.62mm Browning self-loading rifles at the ready. Three of the men had been lying motionless and unseen less than two metres from the resting GIs. Cartwright pointed towards the west and the patrol moved out silently, keeping well apart and well away from the trail.

The Major looked back over his shoulder, right at where I was hiding. It was the moment I'd been waiting for. I took careful aim, framing the major in front, the seven men behind him and the sun setting on the distant tree line. Timing is crucial in this sort of thing and I squeezed off a rapid-fire burst of eight shots. Timed it just right, right when the director yelled, 'Cut! Check the gate.'

Without even checking the LCD display on the back of my Nikon, I knew I had the perfect image for the movie poster. Then I climbed out from under my cover of greenery, turned, caught my foot on a tree root and fell flat on my arse in front of the whole film crew.

Chapter Two

Vietnam 2003

Falling flat on your arse in front of a film crew can be embarrassing, but everyone was too busy, too tired or just too over the whole damned business of movie-making to notice. On the plus side, landing on my butt crushed whatever had been biting me. I scrambled to my feet, casually checking my camera and trying to look cool and unconcerned while all around me the organised chaos that is filmmaking continued.

A hair stylist and the make-up artist fussed over the actor playing the Australian major while assistant directors, both Aussie and Vietnamese, lined up the supporting actors and the gaggle of backpacker extras hired to play American soldiers, just in case we had to do one more take in the rapidly fading light.

The scene of the meeting of the Aussie major and the yank patrol would take up about three minutes in the movie but we'd been on location in the heat and humidity of Vietnam's Mekong Delta since just past dawn and it was now pushing sunset. Those three minutes of screen time would be made up of various wide shots, mid shots and close-ups, plus things called reverses to show people talking back and forth, and it all took time to reposition lights, change camera angles and rehearse the action. Back in Australia, film editors would cut all this footage together, and hopefully their talent and the skill of our cinematographer would disguise the fact that the sun was to the right of the soldiers when they rounded the bend and on their left when they marched away an apparent couple of minutes later.

While I dusted myself off, the camera crew behind me were 'checking the gate' on the big Panavision movie camera, making sure there were no 'hairs' - minute slivers of film negative - or pieces of grit caught in front of the film that might ruin the image. When the focus puller called, 'Gate clear,' Damien, the first assistant director, glanced over towards a balding, intense young man sitting under a big umbrella in a black canvas director's chair with 'Director' stencilled in white paint on the back.

This was our director, a talented veteran of four gruelling years of film school, three video clips and a TV commercial for pet food where he'd forced an actor with thirty years' experience and three AFI awards to repeat the line, 'It's Woof-A-Licious' seventy-four times until he felt the poor bastard had the intonation and delivery just right.

The director conferred intently with someone with a clipboard, nodded a couple of times, looked up at Damien and announced, 'We'll go with that take. I think I'm happy.'

And about bloody time, I said to myself.

Damien glanced at his watch and announced, 'The gate is clear, boys and girls. We have a print-take, finally, so that's a wrap on location photography for Lost in Action.'

There was scattered applause from the exhausted crew, along with a few whistles. We'd been at it for five weeks now and everyone was totally knackered from early starts, late finishes and shooting six days a week.

The scene we'd just finished was actually the opening of the film, but for logistical reasons movies are often shot out of sequence. It was also the location wrap shot, meaning cast and crew could now take a much-needed break and then reassemble in Queensland for another few weeks of filming.

'Crew call for interior photography is at Warner Bros. Roadshow Studios on the Gold Coast in two weeks,' Damien continued, 'so enjoy the break. Wrap party tonight in the terrace bar of the Hotel Indochine

Luxe Royale. Grips and gaffers will please wear pants. And if anyone missed our stills photographer, Mr Alby Murdoch, falling into that hole I'm sure he'll be happy to do it one more time - with feeling.'

The crew laughed and whistled some more and then set about the business of packing up the production. The lights were quickly loaded back into trucks by burly blokes wearing shorts, work boots and tool belts; rented electrical generators were shut down for the very last time; army uniforms and equipment were collected by the wardrobe department and prop guns by the armourer. In less than an hour there'd be no sign we'd ever been at that location, apart from crushed vegetation and the odd paper cup, cigarette butt and lolly wrapper.

Shooting movie stills was generally a fun gig - taking photographs during production for use in PR and the advertising of the finished film six months or so down the track.

The trick was to make sure I wasn't seen by the movie camera and the click of my Nikon's shutter wasn't picked up by the sound recordist's sensitive microphones. I'd sometimes shoot rehearsals, when the sound of my Nikon wouldn't be intrusive, but on 'takes' or the actual filming of a scene I had to use a soundproofed camera housing or choose my moment carefully. If I got my timing wrong, and fired off a burst of shots at the wrong moment, a headphones-wearing sound recordist would look up from his Nagra digital recorder and glare at me.

I didn't get it wrong too often, though - I'd learned not to.

In my other job, the one nobody is supposed to know about, if you got it wrong the result could be a lot worse than just a nasty look from a sound recordist. It could get you hurt, and hurt bad. In fact, it could sometimes be downright fatal.

Chapter Three

My other job, working for D-E-D, also involves getting the necessary shots without being sprung. The Directorate for Extra-territorial Defence is a top-secret Australian government intelligence-gathering department whose agents operate undercover as globe-trotting news photographers for the totally legit WorldPix International Photo Agency. Around 10 per cent of WorldPix snappers are spies, and the rest of the photographers and everyone else at WorldPix are unaware of the double life led by the undercover bods, or Dedheads, as we like to be called.

Setting up the WorldPix photo agency to provide cover for D-E-D operatives had been my idea. The inspiration came from an early undercover assignment I'd done for D-E-D in Afghanistan in the eighties, when I'd posed as a freelance wildlife photographer. Not only did I get my assigned shots of the Mujahedeen guerrillas using CIA-supplied Stinger anti-aircraft missiles against the Soviet invaders for the first time, I also snapped a series of pictures of mountain goats that was published internationally in the geographic magazines and made me a nice little pile of money.

It took some spirited arguing, but eventually those in charge in

Canberra realised that not only could a picture agency be useful cover for D-E-D, it could also potentially pay its own way and perhaps even make a small profit. As it turned out, our talented photographers, spies and non-spies alike, began making very large profits right from the get-go.

Since WorldPix had become an unqualified and highly lucrative success story, every bureaucrat in Canberra, including my new boss, the Honourable Gwenda Felton AO, and our ultimate boss, the Minister for Defence, was anxious to bask in its glory.

Gwenda Felton, Director-General of D-E-D, was a living, breathing demonstration of the law of physics which states that light travels faster than sound. At first sight she appeared to be a normal, if somewhat fashion-challenged, human being. When she opened her mouth, however, it was instantly clear that Glenda's grasp of reality was tenuous at best.

My recent shouting match with Gwenda, and subsequent suspension, had resulted from her suggestion that the government consider severing all ties between D-E-D and WorldPix, and just run the WorldPix side of things as a purely money-making operation. She would take over as chief executive, while the D-E-D operatives, myself included, would be chucked out to fend for themselves in a very cold world.

The idea was breathtaking in its short-sightedness and stupidity, and I'd made the mistake of saying so. Gwenda may have been a political appointee with limited powers of reasoning but she had plenty of friends in high places, and I didn't stand a chance. I was suspended from D-E-D and she'd even pulled me from the WorldPix shooting roster. There was a brief moment when it seemed appropriate to punch her lights out, but I'd been brought up never to raise my hand to a lady, or even to someone like Gwenda.

A recent change of government had forced Gwenda to put her privatisation plan on the back burner, as she, like all political appointees of the former government, was busy ducking for cover and frantically figuring out ways to save her skin. But I was still on suspension since I had very few friends in high places and Gwenda Felton really knew how to hold a grudge.

When my mate Boxer heard about my suspension he made a few phone calls and landed me a job shooting stills for a feature film he was about to start working on in Vietnam. Byron Oxenbould was a much sought-after sound recordist and the film's producers were happy to go along with his suggestion.

After all, I had an international reputation as a photographer, I was available, and I'm always more than ready to hop on a plane to any place in the world that has great food.

Which was why I was in the middle of the chaos of a film crew wrapping one last location somewhere in the Mekong Delta. I was tired, hot and sweaty, and looking forward to a shower and a couple of weeks of doing absolutely nothing. I'd just finished packing my cameras and lenses into their cases when Jack Smart yelled, 'Hey, Murdoch, fancy a lift back to the big smoke?'

Ho Chi Minh City might be better called the Big Smog but the thought of getting there pronto, into some air-conditioning and scrubbing off the dirt under a hot hotel shower sounded just great. My lift back to the city would be in a sixties-vintage Huey helicopter, the same chopper that had zoomed low over the patrol earlier, right on cue, flown by Jack's mate Van Tuan, or VT. A man would be crazy to say no to an offer like that.

Jack Smart was the film's military advisor, the bloke who made sure all the actors and extras playing soldiers saluted with the correct hand, pointed the business ends of their rifles at the enemy in fire fights and kept hold of the pin and chucked the hand grenade, rather than the other way round.

Jack really was an ex-soldier and Vietnam veteran, as advertised, but there was a wee bit more to him than the rest of the crew knew. He was actually Jack Stark, an Aussie who'd been conscripted in the sixties, gone to Vietnam and risen through the ranks, got himself a battlefield commission and been promoted to major before being chucked out in disgrace for unspecified reasons.

The behind-the-scenes reason for this well-publicised dishonourable discharge was to provide cover for a government false flag operation, in which Stark was set up as a bitter and deranged anti-government activist known as the Mad Major, living inside an isolated, booby-trap-protected compound on a hilltop in Far North Queensland.

Stark, as planned, became a hero for many of the world's emerging terrorist splinter groups, which made it easy for him to infiltrate them.

When he eventually discovered that an extreme right-wing cabal with strong influence inside the Australian government had been using him for their own purposes, Stark jacked up, refusing to play along, and was marked for elimination. He was reported to have died in a massive explosion at his mountain hideout.

The truth was that he now lived in Macau, where along with his mate VT he ran a boutique hotel called the Pousada do Estoril. Jack and the Australian government had apparently agreed to a truce, allowing him to stay dead in peace. I figured this meant that Jack had a lot of embarrassing dirt on some very highly placed people.

The movie we were working on, Lost in Action, was a dramatisation of the life and death of another Vietnam soldier, Major Peter Cartwright VC. Cartwright had gone into Vietnam early on as part of the Australian army training team, serving through to 1969. He'd gone missing, presumed killed, in a hush hush operation up near the border with North Vietnam but his body was never recovered..

Cartwright had been recommended for the Victoria Cross a few months before his death when he'd called in an air strike on his own position as his unit was about to be overrun by the enemy.

'Ballsy move on his part, and not always as suicidal as it sounds,' Jack had explained one night over post-wrap drinks. 'If you're well dug in, and you know what's coming, you stand a hell of a lot better chance than an enemy advancing towards you without cover over open ground. Noisy as buggery though. Pretty scary.'

Something in his voice made me think Jack knew what he was talking about.

Jack had worked with Cartwright for a brief period, and his knowledge of the late major and the war together with his attention to detail had caused some friction on the set. Early on in the production, we'd shot a scene where Cartwright stood in a smoke-filled jungle clearing, valiantly blazing away with his Owen gun into masses of advancing North Vietnamese Army regulars to provide cover for the withdrawal of his patrol.

Jack had a barney with the director about the actor playing Cartwright using a weapon like the Owen gun and standing up in the middle of a fire fight.

'Wouldn't have done it, sunshine,' Jack had argued, 'not firing piss-weak 9mm ammo. I knew the bastard. We covered each other's backs a few times and he wasn't that dumb, not by a long chalk. Maybe we could have him using a cut-down L2A1.'

The L2A1 was a heavy-barrelled, full-auto version of the 7.62mm standard-issue Oz Army's self-loading rifle. The SAS chopped off the barrel, ditched the flash suppressor, stuck in a thirty-round mag and nicknamed it the Bitch. When you squeezed the trigger, you got enough flame and noise to scare the crap out of everyone within a couple of hundred metres, including the person doing the shooting.

'But the Owen gun is such a pretty-looking weapon, Jack,' our 25-year-old wunderkind director had argued, 'and you have to understand that looking good is what the film business is all about.'

'It's your show, mate,' Jack had answered with a shrug. 'No skin off my arse.'

Up to that point in filming VT had been happy to fly the director back from location when the shoot wrapped for the day, but after that conversation there always seemed to be some kind of mechanical glitch that kept the helicopter grounded until after the director left on a long, hot and painfully slow drive back to the city.

The Huey was waiting in a clearing, the rotor blades slowly turning and VT in the pilot's seat. We instinctively ducked our heads as we sprinted under the blades and Jack grabbed my heavy cases and easily hefted them into the chopper's open rear cabin. He might have had silver-grey hair and been pushing sixty hard, but I reckoned he must have been almost as trim and fit as the day he first arrived in the Nam in '67.

After securing my cases to the Huey's deck, I strapped myself into one of the frayed webbing seats in the rear cargo area while Jack climbed into the co-pilot's seat and pulled on a helmet. As VT opened the throttle, the whine of the jet turbine engine increased in pitch and the massive rotor blades turned faster and faster. VT glanced back to check that my seatbelt was fastened and I gave him the thumbs up.

There wasn't too much about flying a Huey that VT didn't know. He'd been a top helicopter pilot for the South Vietnamese Air Force during the war. Just before he pulled up on the control stick to get us airborne, he reached over and squeezed Jack's thigh. Jack smiled and returned the gesture. VT had been Jack's partner for the past thirty-five years.

'Ain't love grand,' I said to myself, and then the Huey's skids cleared the temporary landing ground in a choking whirlwind of dust and chaff and sticks and stones. Below us I could see the director and his personal assistant running towards the departing chopper, waving hopefully. I waved back as we climbed higher and they grew smaller and smaller.

Since filming was finished in Vietnam, and the rented ex-US military chopper had to be handed back to the government within the week, it was odds-on that VT wouldn't be able to resist one last chance to show me what a Huey could do.

I tightened my seatbelt and ten seconds later I heard his voice in my headphones yelling, 'Hang on, Alby. Here we go!' And then my world turned upside down.

Chapter Four

The Hotel Indochine Luxe Royale had more words to its name than it had elevators, but was a nice place to shack up during the shoot. It had been built in the 1930s and, according to the brass plaque in the lobby, it was one of the many hundreds of hotels in Saigon where Graham Greene had stayed exclusively while researching The Quiet American. Restored to its original Art Deco glory in the 1990s, the hotel was centrally located, sedate and comfortable, and actually did have quite an interesting history.

'Bugger me, the old Luxe Royale,' Jack had said to me when we met a couple of days before filming began. 'Biggest knocking shop in Saigon, back in the day.'

I'd glanced around at the wood-panelled and plushly carpeted lobby with its rattan armchairs and potted palms. 'Really? This place was a brothel?'

'You better believe it, mate,' Jack had said. 'That plaque should read "On this site more GIs contracted the clap than in any other place in South-East Asia". I think they used to have a giant, flashing neon sign up on the roof advertising penicillin.'

My fourth-floor room had a small balcony opening onto a public square, a great spot to unwind with a G & T after a long day. I was really going to miss the joint. Any bullet holes left by drunken American soldiers had long been papered over, along with those made by the Vietcong when they'd briefly taken the hotel during the '68 Tet Offensive. Today's guests enjoyed king-sized beds, air-conditioning, 24-hour room service - now limited to food and booze only - and big marble bathrooms with plenty of hot water.

I took a long shower while my images from the day's shoot uploaded and down linked to our production office on the Gold Coast and to MB&F, the movie's marketing and PR people in New York. By the time I had towelled off and poured myself a whisky, my knees had stopped shaking from VT's moves in the Huey. It made you wonder what the bloke could manage in an up-to-date attack chopper like an Apache or Super Cobra.

There was an email in my inbox from Julie Danko, currently in the US attending a counter-insurgency seminar at the Battle Command Training Center at Fort Leavenworth, Kansas. 'Congratulations on not getting suspended, demoted or fired for four straight weeks, Alby,' the email read. 'Is this a new record?'

Julie worked with me at D-E-D and had been my 2IC during the demoralising six-month stint I'd recently spent as acting Director-General. I had learnt a lot during that time, including the fact that I wasn't cut out for management. I'd also learnt there was a lot more to Julie than met the eye - never mind that what met the eye was pretty agreeable.

After carefully packing all my serious camera gear into travelling cases and my spare clothes into a suitcase, I phoned reception for a porter. My cases would be shipped back to the Gold Coast studios, along with the rest of the production's equipment, but with a week or two to kill I planned on staying on in Vietnam. I'd travel light, with just a passport, a backpack, a compact Nikon DSLR and a couple of lenses in a small camera bag, plus a tiny digital Leica D-Lux camera in my pocket.

When I wandered into the cocktail bar of the hotel just after nine there was a string quartet playing. Neatly dressed guests were sipping champagne and grabbing canapés from passing waiters. The producer, director, screenwriter, various money men and the usual studio bods and hangers-on clocked me, immediately recognised that I wasn't anybody important and went back to their networking.

'Let me help you with those, sport.' Pinching a silver tray of deep-fried spring rolls from a passing waiter I kicked open the French doors leading out to where the real action was. 'Cha gio, anyone?' I yelled. 'Get 'em while they're hot.'

'Love Her Madly,' by The Doors was blasting out over an open marble terrace packed with crew and actors, local production office people, girlfriends, boyfriends and assorted camp followers. A film crew on location usually sorts itself into a number of temporary relationships, most of which don't survive past the end of the shoot.

My time in Vietnam had been romance-free, which Jack impolitely attributed to a lack of desperation on the part of the unattached female members of the crew. I'll admit my track record with women hadn't been too impressive lately.

There'd been the stunning Major Grace Goodluck, who'd claimed to work for the US Justice Department and had loved me and left me after shooting our local CIA chief full of holes. And there'd been Lieutenant Clare Kingston, a US Navy weapons specialist who'd been kidnapped almost out of my bed to arm stolen nukes for a wealthy conservationist who had a bone to pick with the Japanese about whaling.

Then, of course, there was Julie, who'd recently come between me and a dozen submachine gun bullets fired by a psycho ex-paratrooper named Chapman Pergo on a rocky island off the Tasmanian coast. Her bulletproof vest had saved us both and I'd blasted half a magazine from Julie's MPSK in Pergo's direction before SASR troopers had taken him out. After an incident involving some mouth-to-mouth resuscitation, I was still trying to figure out exactly where I stood with Julie.

In the middle of the crowded terrace I found Damien, the first assistant director, with Megan, who was doing make-up on the film. Megan and Damien were chatting with Brett Tozer, one of the film's associate producers. The old film-industry gag defines associate producers as people who are morally bankrupt enough to associate with the producer. In reality, no-one in the film business cares if anyone is morally bankrupt as long as they fiscally liquid enough to kick in some cash.

Brett's employer, the New York PR and marketing conglomerate Markham. Barkin & Fargo, had done just that, securing Brett his slot on the production. He seemed like a nice bloke, for a Yank, and we were getting along. He was wearing a suit I hadn't seen before.

'Not more new threads?' I said, as he helped himself to a couple of the spring rolls.

Soon after arriving in Saigon I'd introduced him to a local tailor who'd run me up a couple of very nice retro safari jackets, just like the ones all the butch war correspondents had worn in the 1960s. The bloke could also whip up an excellent made-to-measure business suit in less than three days. This had come in handy for Brett after he'd discovered on-set film catering is a never-ending feast and a real temptation for people with not much to contribute to the actual filmmaking process.

My tailor friend was probably well on his way to owning a couple of new houses thanks to Brett's constantly expanding waistline.

Just behind Brett, my mate Boxer was sitting at a table sipping a cocktail and drinking in the adoring looks of a couple of local extras. With Boxer, girls always seemed to come in pairs, which I could never figure out. Who knew that a bloke who had the build of a Greek god, chiselled good looks, blond hair, blue eyes, a dry wit, charm and the air of a bad boy plus the glamour of a job in the film industry would attract women?

'Heading back to Sydney soon, Boxer? To be with the wives and kids?'

One of the local girls gave him an angry look.

'Ignore him,' Boxer said, slipping his arms around both women. 'He's just a sad, jealous little man. Trust me, I only have eyes for you, babe, and for you too?'

The angry looks were redirected towards me, and Boxer grinned and winked. Bastard.

I spotted Jack and VT standing at the edge of the terrace, which was a great excuse for making myself scarce.

The Luxe Royale's terrace fronted a brightly lit square, noisy with street vendors, pedestrians, cars, motor scooters and the odd cyclo, the Vietnamese version of the three-wheeled pedal-powered bicycle taxi. The raucous din of engines and car horns, the humidity, the smells of street food, sweat, incense and leaded petrol fumes all added up to my favourite word: Asia.

A tall, slender Vietnamese woman wearing a diaphanous white silk Áo dài was standing with the two men. The Áo dài a high-necked, long-sleeved, ankle-length tunic split at the sides and worn over matching trousers, has got to be the sleekest, most graceful and sensual national dress going.

I guessed the woman was in her late twenties, almost my height and nicely curved in some excellent places. A small white flower was tucked behind one ear and long, glossy black hair was swept up, framing the most beautiful face I'd seen in a very long time.

'Alby, Mr Murdoch,' VT said, 'I would like to present Miss Nhu Hoang.'

Miss Hoang was gorgeous. She smiled and held out a delicate hand with long elegant fingers. As our skin touched, I felt an electric tingle shoot up my arm, run across my shoulders and down my legs, all the way to my toes. I knew instantly I was about to get myself into a whole lot of trouble.

Chapter Five

'I'M VERY PLEASED TO MEET YOU, MR MURDOCH.'

Miss Hoang spoke perfect English, with just a slight hint of an American accent.

Jack took a sip of his champagne. 'Miss Hoang is the granddaughter of VT's sister,' he said, giving me a look that I read as a warning to behave myself.

'Miss Hoang is an officer with the national police,' VT said, his voice giving me the same warning.

I reluctantly released her hand. 'Some of my best friends are coppers Miss Hoang and believe me, none of them could wear a dress like that, not even the women.'

Taking two glasses of champagne from a passing waiter I offered one to Miss Hoang, who accepted it with a smile.

'Miss Hoang is also the national police pistol champion,' VT said.

It was game, set and match in the warn Alby to behave himself stakes.

I looked Miss Hoang up and down. That Áo dài was one hell of an outfit.

'You don't appear to be armed at the moment, Miss Hoang,' I said. 'I mean, not as far as I can see.'

She smiled. 'Looks can sometimes be deceiving, Mr Murdoch.'

I knew that to be a fact from bitter experience.

'I hear from Uncle you are interested in the cuisine of our country, Mr Murdoch.'

I nodded. 'I've got a couple of weeks to kill so I'm planning to go wandering, hit some markets and maybe take a few cooking lessons.'

'Please just ask if there is any way I can be of assistance.'

Jack gave me that look again.

'You and VT still planning on heading north?'

'Probably. The production has the chopper leased till the end of the week so we've got clearance to fly up that way to visit some of VT's relatives near Hanoi. Then we thought we might take a quick side-trip out to have a squiz at Dien Bien Phu. The joint was a bit out of reach last time I visited Vietnam.'

Jack was a military history buff and Dien Bien Phu had military history in spades. The valley near Vietnam's north-western border with Laos was where the French colonial government had built a massive and heavily fortified base in 1954. They'd crammed it full of Algerian and Vietnamese soldiers and the elite of the French Foreign Legion, daring Ho Chi Minh's Vietminh rebels to bring it on. Bad call. When the smoke finally cleared, the fortress was pretty much obliterated, along with most of the men inside it. The majority of those who survived the catastrophe died in captivity.

The music suddenly cut out and there was a murmur of voices behind us. When we turned towards the terrace door-way, the film's producers and stars had joined the party and someone was tapping on a wine glass with a spoon to call for silence.

'Bugger me,' Jack said glumly, 'speech time.'

With exquisite timing, Nhu excused herself. 'I have some police matters I need to attend to. Have a safe trip, Uncle.'

She smiled at me. 'Perhaps we shall be able to get together before you leave my country, Mr Murdoch Do you perhaps have a card?'

'I look forward to it,' I said, handing over my WORLDPIX business card and getting another warning glare from Jack as I found myself watching her disappear into the crowd.

Thankfully, the speeches were short and to the point. Mention was made of the fact that it had taken over twenty years to finally get Lost in Action into production. The Peter Cartwright story had seemed jinxed from its inception, with insurmountable legal, logistical, political or financial problems always popping up at the last minute. In fact, the project had broken the spirits and emptied the bank accounts of a large number of very experienced film producers over the years. Yet somehow the production was given the green light six months back and, almost unbelievably, given government permission to actually shoot some important scenes in Vietnam.

As the producer wound up his speech Jack turned around and looked out over the busy square, glass in hand. The moon, just on full and sitting low in the sky, had come out from behind a cloud and the square was bathed in soft light. The two men standing together made a great picture: VT, his arms folded while watching the speaker, Jack facing the busy square with his back towards me. I took the tiny Leica from my pocket and carefully framed them against the action.

Behind me, the producer finished by thanking the cast and crew for their efforts on a difficult location shoot, and said how much he looked forward to us all meeting again in a few weeks on the Gold Coast. Then he proposed one final toast to the man who had brought us all together on this terrace in Saigon. 'Ladies and gentleman,' he said, 'I give you the late Major Peter Cartwright VC, Lost in Action.'

There were murmurs of 'Peter Cartwright VC' from the crowd on the terrace, and as I gently pressed the Leica's shutter button I saw Jack stiffen and heard a barely audible, 'Bugger me dead.' He turned back and emptied his champagne glass in one gulp.

'Problem, Jack?'

'Not sure, mate' he said quietly. 'You just take a picture?'

I nodded.

'Let me see it.'

I brought up the image on the Leica's crisp, bright viewing screen. It was a good picture, I thought, nicely composed with the two men on the left of frame, the moon shining and the hustle and bustle of the crowded square below filling the right half.

'Can you blow it up?'

'We can't see your face, Jack. The viewer will just have to assume that you are ruggedly handsome.'

'Not me, you dill, that cyclo,' he said, pointing to a pedicab with a red plastic roof that was on the edge of the frame.

I pressed the magnify button a couple of times to make the picture bigger on the screen, toggled the cyclo to the centre of the frame and then used the magnify button again to make it as large as possible. The passenger was a man, European, maybe in his sixties. He'd been looking up towards the terrace as I'd pressed the shutter. There was something vaguely familiar about that face.

'Friend of yours, Jack?'

'Used to be, Alby,' he said, staring at the image intently. 'If I'm not going crazy, and I don't think I am, then our movie's hero, Major Peter Cartwright VC, dead and gone for thirty some years, just went past sitting up like Jacky in the back of that cyclo.'

Chapter Six

Back in my room I fired up my laptop and downloaded the picture from the terrace. Using Photoshop, I cropped it down to just the cyclo, driver and passenger, then sharpened and tweaked it as much as possible before printing out a hard copy.

Jack studied the photograph for a long time before speaking. 'Could be the bastard,' he said, taking a swig of the outrageously overpriced Scotch from the mini-bar.

Thanks to the excellent optics of the Leica's lens, the faces of both the driver and passenger were surprisingly clear, even though I'd focused on Jack and VT and the shutter speed was slow'ish due to the low light levels.

'Last time we saw each other was over thirty years ago. Cartwright dragged me down into a shell hole and out of the line of fire of a couple of companies of stroppy Vietcong who'd taken exception to us calling in an artillery strike in the middle of their smoko.'

'Was that where Cartwright got his Victoria Cross?'

Jack nodded. 'We were cut off, surrounded and running low on ammo when he shot his way into our position, rallied the boys, formed a perimeter and then, after making sure we were all dug in, he got the radioman to call in that air strike right on top of us.'

'What were you doing while all this was happening?'

He smiled. 'Bleeding. Cartwright lay on top of me in that shell crater until it was all over and then waved goodbye as I was flown out in a medevac chopper. He was reported missing presumed KIA a month or so later, probably before he heard about the medal.'

That explained why Jack had wanted to work on the movie and why he hadn't been impressed with our director's habit of changing history.

I opened a manila folder marked 'Photo Reference' that I'd borrowed from the film's art department. Inside were dozens of press clippings and photographs from the sixties, including shots of soldiers from the Australian task force on patrol, in action and relaxing off-duty in South Vietnam. There were some shots of a very young Peter Cartwright, and it looked like Jack was right. The bloke in the cyclo was a dead ringer for the major.

'Even if it is him, Jack,' VT said, 'it's a very long time for someone to play dead. What about his family?'

'Cartwright was an orphan,' Jack explained. 'Grew up in a series of foster homes, some good, some not so good. He was a very smart kid but a bit of a hooligan. Back then, magistrates offered bad boys the choice of joining the army as an alternative to a spell in the clink, and as it turned out Cartwright and the army were made for each other. Some bright spark spotted his potential as officer material and he was on his way; career army, in it for the long haul. If he hadn't got himself killed I reckon he'd have been chief of the defence force by now, and all set to retire and write his autobiography.'

'Instead of dead and kicking in a cyclo in downtown Saigon,' I said, and after a pause, 'or maybe getting blown up on a mountaintop in far north Queensland.'

Jack picked up the photograph of the cyclo once again and was studying it closely.

'I had my reasons for playing dead and if that's really him I imagine he had his.'

'Something murky you reckon?'

'Not the Cartwright I remember. I did hear rumours just before he died that he was mixed up in something dodgy, but I didn't give them much credence. As far as I know he was a straight shooter.'

Jack glanced over towards VT, who was out on the balcony smoking a cigarette.

'Hey, VT - you mind if we put off heading north for a day or so? I want to have a sniff around town to see if I can track this bloke down, or the cyclo driver at least'

VT smiled. 'It's fine with me, Jack. I've still got a lot of gifts to buy for my family in the north - Nhu reminded me I have more nieces and nephews than I realised. What about you, Alby? You going with Jack to keep him out of trouble?'

It was more of a request than a question.

'I guess I can spare a morning, but I'm pretty sure Jack can look after himself.'

'VT likes to worry,' Jack said, laughing.

'Saigon's a big city. You don't think finding a cyclo with a red canopy might be like looking for a needle in a haystack?'

'Let's find the haystack first,' Jack said, pointing at the person in the photograph who was driving our mystery man.

Chapter Seven

Next morning, bright and early, Jack and I were up and looking for a cyclo. They aren't all that hard to spot in Ho Chi Minh City, but we wanted a specific cyclo. Luckily we had a photograph to help us.

We also had the help of the government, which was trying very hard to limit the number of cycles by restricting the areas they could work in and the roads they could travel on. Eventually, they would go the way of the rickshaw in Hong Kong, now reduced to just a couple of examples parked outside the Star Ferry terminal in Central, the bored operators giving short, expensive rides to tourists or charging to pose for photographs.

It took us a couple of hours of hailing cycles to get a name and then another couple to get a confirmed last sighting. Jack spoke reasonable Vietnamese, which came in handy.

We eventually found the cyclo we wanted parked near a food stall down an alleyway, its driver sitting on a small plastic stool slurping noodles. It was close enough to lunchtime by now, so we pulled up a couple of stools and joined him.

I ordered pho bo, a Hanoi dish of beef soup with rice noodles, while Jack had the same as the driver, which appeared to be the offal special, featuring beef tendon, liver, kidney and other assorted tasty bits. It was no surprise the bloke could pedal all day in the tropical heat with a dish like that inside him. The driver was no spring chicken, and the sinewy sun-browned legs poking out of his faded shorts looked a bit like some of the things floating in his soup.

When the driver had finished off his meal, Jack passed him over a packet of cigarettes and the photograph. The man nodded as he accepted the cigarettes and then laughed when he saw the photograph. He said something to Jack, who also laughed.

'He reckons a million tourists must have taken his picture, but this is the first time he's actually got to see one.'

The conversation went back and forth while I finished off a second bowl of soup. I couldn't help myself. Simmered for hours, and rich in colour from charred onion and ginger, the clear beef stock was bloody delicious, spicy and salty-sweet at the same time. Thinly sliced beef, rice noodles and crunchy bean sprouts filled the bowl, dressed with ngo gai, sawtooth coriander leaves, the purple basil called hung que and hung lui or spearmint, a popular northern addition. Adding a final squeeze of lime brought a tart edge to the complexity of the deceptively simple dish.

Jack filled me in on the conversation while the old man smoked his cigarette.

'Our mystery man hailed him near the airport and wanted to go to a street by the river. He reckons the bloke spoke almost perfect Vietnamese but with a Hanoi accent. Told him he hadn't been in a Saigon cyclo for years.'

Jack spoke to the man, who nodded.

'We're on,' Jack said. 'I asked him if he could he show us this street by the river. In exchange for the photograph, he promises not to overcharge us too much and I think there was a less than subtle hint in there that we should pay for his lunch.'

Five minutes later we were in a couple of cyclos negotiating the horror that is Ho Chi Minh City's road system. Jack was in the lead with the old man, while I was in the second cyclo following behind. On some cyclos the driver sits in front and pulls his passengers along by pedal power, but on this one the driver was behind me, pushing. You knew it had to be hell on his calf muscles but right now I had my own little hell going on. With the driver sitting behind, there was nothing between me and the rest of Saigon, and the rest of Saigon was coming at me full throttle.

Chapter Eight

THE BEST WAY OF COPING WITH TRAFFIC IN ASIA IS TO IGNORE THE stink of leaded petrol and diesel exhaust fumes, the roar of engines and the noisy squawking of scooter and car horns, and not look too closely at what's ahead of you. I concentrated on the passing faces of bewildered backpackers and tourists standing almost catatonic with terror on the kerb, wondering how they were ever going to be able to safely ford that manic never-ending stream of vehicles.

If pedestrians find negotiating Saigon traffic difficult, for cyclo passengers it feels like a cross between ballroom dancing and a boxing match. The driver's aim is to bob and weave smoothly in and out of the oncoming, overtaking and merging onslaught of trucks, buses, cars, scooters, carts, cyclists and pedestrians. You can only live in hope that your driver is watching out for the one-two punch of anything bigger and heavier than you.

Honking scooters and motorcycles zoomed noisily by us with pretty girls riding pillion or whole families perched on every possible roost. Taxis were drifting lazily left and right across the front of my frail little cyclo, passing so close that I could almost reach out and touch the driver or passenger. The local men, women and children were unfazed and wandered casually through the chaos, going about their business.

We cruised past shops and cafés, and roadside food vendors hunched over charcoal stoves or tending wicker baskets of colourful fruit. The streets were bustling with women wearing trendy dresses or designer jeans and others in Áo dài or peasant pyjamas and conical straw hats. Shopping malls and boutiques featuring Gucci, Chanel and Louis Vuitton competed for trade with vendors pushing bicycles laden with brushes, brooms and home wares, or goldfish in water-filled plastic bags.

Multistorey glass office towers festooned with flashing signs and posters for expensive watches, mobile phones and cognac were jammed up against older two- and three-storey colonial buildings hung with banners or the yellow-starred red national flag of Vietnam. The city renamed in honour of the great revolutionary leader Ho Chi Minh looked like it was stuck in one last battle with decadent Western consumerism, and things weren't going all that well for the revolution.

The combination of stifling exhaust fumes and this visual and aural kaleidoscopic assault was numbing, so it was a relief to come to a stop outside a large four-storey factory building near the river. It had a nondescript façade of crumbling rendered concrete, barred windows, a steel security shutter over what appeared to be a delivery dock, and rolls of rusty barbed wire around the balustrade on the top level. There wasn't a welcome mat out in front of the locked main entrance but there was a CCTV camera.

'Seems like the right sort of joint for a dead man to come calling at late at night.'

There was a brass plate with Vietnamese writing next to the buzzer by the front door. Jack waved the cyclo driver over and pointed to the sign.

'I speak Vietnamese better than I read it,' he explained.

After a brief conversation and a pantomime of wavy hand movements and then a rocking motion, Jack finally seemed to understand.

'Something to do with baby fish, or little fish, I think. Fish, anyway?'

Jack paid off both our drivers and then rang the doorbell.

A crackly intercom conversation with a woman ensued, and five minutes later the door opened and a man in a white lab coat stepped out into the sunlight. He was about thirty-five, I guessed, handsome with a face that had a more Eurasian than Vietnamese bone structure.

'My name is Peter Tranh,' he said, handing each of us a business card. 'How can I help you today?'

Tranh had a hint of an American accent and his card told us that he had a PhD from the University of California at Berkeley and was the research director of Tranh Fisheries and Aquaculture Enterprises, which was based in Hanoi.

I let Jack do the talking. He explained we were trying to trace a man who had been dropped off outside the building last night.

'I was here till midnight, all by myself,' Tranh said, 'and we had no visitors. Perhaps the man in the cyclo was looking for another address, or the driver made a mistake about the street.'

Jack showed him the photograph. 'So you don't recognise this bloke?'

Tranh shook his head. 'I'm sorry I can't be of more help but no. Now, if you'll excuse me I have to get back to my work.'

'This place doesn't look like any fish farm I've ever seen,' I said.

Tranh smiled. 'We don't farm the actual fish here. We do research, and hatch and raise fingerlings - the baby fish.'

Jack smiled. 'Well, it sounds like our cyclo driver must have made a mistake. We'll let you get back to your work. Sorry for disturbing you.'

Tranh smiled. 'No worries. I hope you find what you're looking for.'

The steel door slammed shut behind him with a very solid bang.

I turned around to look for a taxi but Jack was already dodging traffic and crossing the road towards an alleyway, where our cyclo driver was sitting under an awning having a beer. We joined him and Jack ordered a couple more 333 beers.

Jack handed the driver the photograph and they chatted back and forth. The driver became quite animated and pointed emphatically across the street to the concrete building several times. Eventually Jack nodded and smiled and bought the driver another beer.

'What's the scoop?' I asked.

'It's the right building. Not only that, but young Peter Tranh was waiting outside and he and the passenger got into a right little barney before they went inside. They were speaking English so the driver couldn't understand what was said. He came over here for a beer and a snack, and after about half an hour a big Merc with tinted windows pulled up and took our mystery man away. But not before he gave Tranh a big farewell hug.

Jack took a swig of his beer. 'You saw the similarity?' he asked. 'I mean between Peter Tranh over yonder and the late Peter Cartwright?'

I nodded. 'There's certainly a resemblance to Cartwright in some of those old photographs.'

Jack took another swig. 'And did you happen to notice what young Peter said when we were leaving?'

I nodded. 'No worries - not exactly the kind of phrase you might pick up at UC Berkeley.'

'Too bloody right, mate,' Jack said, 'too bloody right.'

Chapter Nine

JACK LEFT ME AT THE HOTEL AND HEADED OFF TO TRY TO FIND OUT AS much as he could about the fish-raising business we'd visited, and to see if and how it related to Major Peter Cartwright. I'd taken a snap of the brass nameplate by the door of the factory building that I figured might help so I made him a quick print.

Since I now had some welcome time off in an exotic city, I decided to leave Jack to it. For once in a very long time, I wasn't sticking my nose in where it wasn't wanted, and nobody wanted me dead because of it. My plan was to have no plan, just to toss my camera bag over my shoulder and head out picture hunting.

Brett Tozer was sitting in the lobby reading the International Herald Tribune. He waved as I stepped out of the brass-caged elevator, so I walked over to speak to him after I'd dropped off my key at reception.

'A couple of the picture editors in New York have been making complimentary noises about your most recent snaps, Alby,' Brett said. 'They're comparing them to Tim Page's work, and some of Don McCullin's stuff.'

Page and McCullin were just two of a whole gang of shooters who put their lives on the line daily to graphically show the world the reality of the conflict in Vietnam. At least one hundred and fifty photographers never made it home from the South-East Asian wars, and those that did often shared the physical and mental scars of the combat soldiers.

"Yeah, right,' I said. 'Page and McCullin and the rest of those guys didn't have five-star on-set catering and air-conditioned limos and portaloos. They didn't get to ask for retakes. They had landmines and booby-traps to contend with, along with blokes chucking grenades and shooting actual AK-47s and RPGs in their direction. The blood and guts in their photographs was real, not something poured out of a bottle by a make-up artist.'

Brett put out his hands defensively. 'Hey, I'm just passing on what they told me. Don't shoot the messenger.'

'Sorry, Brett,' I said. 'Touchy subject. Anyway, I thought you'd be long gone by now. Most people can't wait to hit the road when a movie wraps.'

He nodded. 'And I'm one of 'em. Just got to pick up one more suit from my friendly tailor and then I'm on a flight out at three this afternoon.'

'Back to the grindstone in the Big Apple?'

'Yep, for a couple of weeks anyway,' he said, 'until the shooting starts again in Australia. What about you, Alby? Heading off with Jack and VT?'

'No. We're going our separate ways for a bit. I'm planning on hunting down some good food and great pictures. VT's got more relatives to visit up north and Jack's got a bee in his bonnet about our Major Peter Cartwright not being as dead as everyone seems to believe.'

Brett stared at me. 'That seems highly unlikely, doesn't it?' he said. 'After all this time, I mean.'

I shrugged. 'I snapped a picture of someone last night that could have been him. Bloke in the picture looked a bit similar, but it's more than thirty years on so who can say for sure.'

'You have the photograph with you?'

I pulled the Leica from my bag and scrolled through to the picture.

Brett studied the image and shook his head. 'Just looks like your average round-eye tourist to me.'

'You're probably right,' I said, tucking the Leica into my pocket, 'but I wouldn't want to be the one to tell the screenwriter he needs to redo the whole end of the movie. Great hook from a PR angle though - "Dead war hero back from the grave"?

'That could work,' Brett said.

The 'Ride of the Valkyries' began blasting out from his jacket pocket. 'New York calling,' he said, glancing at the screen of his mobile phone. 'Gotta take this, sorry.'

I nodded. 'Have a safe trip home. See you back in Oz.'

As I walked out of the lobby, I heard him grunt, 'Tozer here,' in his best Masters of the Universe voice.

I glanced back through the hotel's revolving glass doors while I waited for the doorman to get me a cab, and saw Brett pacing up and down as he talked on his phone. He seemed agitated, but from my experience walking up and down looking agitated was the associate producer's lot in life, and Brett did it well.

A shiny white Vinasun taxi pulled up and I forgot all about Brett, the movie and the maybe not-so-dead Major C. The cab was clean and air-conditioned, with a meter and a neatly dressed driver who was sitting on the ubiquitous beaded seat cover. Behind me, a young American couple had walked out of the hotel and were waiting politely.

'You guys want a cab?" I asked.

They nodded.

'Why don't you take this one?'

'You sure?' the woman asked.

I nodded. 'Yep, I've changed my mind.'

They climbed in happily and drove off, while I headed down the street on foot, looking for a cyclo. One day soon there'd be nothing but nice, clean, air-conditioned taxis in this town and I figured a bloke has to get his thrills while he still can.

Chapter Ten

Come dinnertime I had sore feet, half a dozen memory cards full of pictures tucked in my jacket pocket and a yearning for something spicy. After snacking and snapping my way through half the back alleys in Ho Chi Minh City, I still figured I had room for a light dinner. Vietnamese pop music and the noisy buzz of happy locals drew me to a brightly lit café opening onto the street. I grabbed a table, ordered a beer and, looking around, found I was the only foreigner in the place.

Ignoring the menu, I pointed to what looked good on other tables and chatted in broken English and bad French with the young woman who owned the joint. I wound up with too much food, all of it amazingly fresh and tasty: rice-paper-wrapped spring rolls filled with shrimp and pork, crab noodle soup, lotus-stem salad, king prawns in tamarind sauce and a rice pancake with shredded pork, mushrooms and fried shallots. The owner's ten-year-old daughter put her homework aside and insisted on showing me how to wrap various items in fragile rice paper and lettuce leaves, and which dipping sauce to use. I don't think she was too impressed with my technique, but at least she was polite about it.

After downing a couple more beers I was feeling content, relaxed and comfortable, so when my cyclo driver tried to kill me it came as a bit of a shock.

It was around nine o'clock when I finished dinner, and an empty cyclo was parked right outside the restaurant, the driver casually smoking a cigarette. He was a lot younger than the cyclo drivers we'd spoken to earlier in the day, but at the time it didn't ring any alarm bells.

I showed him a card from my hotel, since apart from saying dúng to beer and noodles and xin loi không to offers of young girls, drugs or pirated DVDs, the Vietnamese language is pretty much beyond me. The driver looked at the card and nodded, so I climbed in.

It had been raining, and the streetlights flared orange and green against the black night sky and reflected off the shimmering, water-slick roadway. The traffic was mostly scooters now, ridden by young people off doing whatever young people do on a humid Ho Chi Minh City evening. They crossed in front of us, drifting casually from right to left and left to right, almost in slow motion, their headlights and tail-lights blending into hypnotic psychedelic patterns enhanced by the noise of Asian pop songs and the aromas from roadside food stalls.

We passed people standing chatting in doorways, and nightclubs with speakers blaring out modern dance music.

One club, Captain Willard's Bar, blasted out songs from the sixties and inside there were go-go girls, flashing strobes and a crowded dance floor. Middle-aged men with crew cuts and buffed, gym-tight bodies gyrated in camouflage trousers, T-shirts and combat boots, fake US Army dog-tags from Dan Sinh Market jangling around their necks, living out some weird fantasy of a long-lost Saigon and a war they almost certainly only ever knew from movies and TV.

I'd felt so relaxed after dinner that I'd neglected to negotiate a price upfront for the trip, but now I noticed we were on quieter backstreets. It was a bumpy ride right from the start, and just as I was beginning to wonder how long my driver had been pedalling a cyclo, we turned hard left down a dark, narrow alleyway. The headlights of a waiting car flared into my face, blinding me. Then I heard the squeal of tyres as what sounded like a Russian jeep accelerated straight towards us.

The cyclo driver leapt clear as the jeep hit, squashing the frail metal frame of the pedicab into the brick wall of the alley and me with it. I was jammed in tight against the wall, and could feel several people tugging at me, trying to pull my camera bag from my shoulder. I deflected a fist flying towards my face, but missed the boot aimed at my groin. My vision blurred, there were shooting stars and my stomach was up in my throat.

Then loud shouting came from somewhere further down the alley and I could hear boots pounding on the cobblestones as my camera bag was savagely wrenched from my shoulder. Suddenly, with more squealing of tyres, the jeep was gone, taking my attackers, the camera bag and the cyclo driver with it.

My rescuers were two green-uniformed police officers, who helped me from the mangled remains of the cycle and dusted me down with their hands, helpfully smoothing out the wrinkles in my clothes, which was a very odd feeling. When the pain in my nuts subsided a little, I realised the police officers were asking for ID. My wallet was still safely inside my jacket pocket, along with the little Leica and my passport. I handed over the passport and my WorldPix press card.

One of the officers wrote down some details while I slowly walked around in circles for a moment to see if everything was still working. I found I was in surprisingly good condition, apart from some moderate to excruciating testicular discomfort. I downplayed this fact as much as possible, as I was a bit concerned they might offer to helpfully pat that part of me down, too.

The officers walked me slowly to the other end of the alley, where a police motorcycle with a sidecar was parked. I said the words 'hotel' and 'taxi' several times and one of the cops flagged down a bright yellow Vina cab, which was fine by me as I was well over the romance of the cyclo for the time being.

Both police officers saluted me as I closed the door.

I smiled and waved and if I hadn't been so well brought up I would have dropped my trousers right then and there to let the chilled air inside the air-conditioned taxi swirl around my aching nuts.

Chapter Eleven

A NOTE FROM JACK WAS WAITING FOR ME AT THE HOTEL RECEPTION desk when I collected the key for room 427. He and VT had checked out right after lunch and were heading north in the Huey. Jack had tracked down another place with connections to the Tranh fish-farming enterprise somewhere outside Hanoi, and he wanted to look into it. He finished by saying he'd keep in touch.

When I travel I've got a bit of a reputation for keeping a rather messy hotel room, but even by my standards room 427 was a real pigsty. Ransacked is such an evocative word, and if my room was anything it was well and truly ransacked. Drawers had been opened and their meagre contents dumped on the floor, the mattress had been pulled away from the bed and my portable printer was broken into bits. A quick hunt around revealed that my laptop was missing. Also missing, and obviously jimmied away from the wall, was the room's small electronic safe.

It been in Saigon for five weeks, staying in this hotel the whole time, and suddenly tonight I get mugged and robbed and my room gets tossed. I was mulling over the implications of this with the assistance of my mini-bar and the wonderful people from the Glen Fiddich distillery, when there was knock on the door. A glance through the peephole revealed it was the cops, or one cop in particular. I opened the door.

'Miss Hoang, this is most unexpected.'

'Mr Murdoch,' she said, 'according to a police report, a man named Alby Murdoch was attacked and robbed earlier this evening. I doubt that our city is playing host to two men with that name so I decided to see if you were okay.'

She was wearing a sky-blue Áo dài embroidered with a delicate floral pattern over white trousers. It was just as stunning as her last outfit, maybe more so, and I still couldn't spot any concealed firearms.

'May I come in?' she asked.

I opened the door wide. 'The place is a bit of a mess, I'm afraid. I was going to call housekeeping, but I didn't want to spoil someone else's evening as well.'

Nhu ran a copper's well-practised eye over the place.

'The door to the room was not forced?'

I shook my head.

'The safe in the wardrobe is gone?'

I nodded.

'Were you keeping anything of value inside?'

'Inside a hotel room safe?'

She nodded. 'Most wise.'

I closed the door behind her.

There were a couple of light cotton hotel robes in the open closer and she handed me one. 'Perhaps you should take a long hot shower to relax your muscles. It will make you feel better. I will phone in a report so that you can claim for any valuables on your insurance.'

I really didn't have anything to claim for, apart from my laptop and printer, as everything else had been packed up and collected for shipping back to Australia. I decided to follow Nhu's suggestion about the hot shower, and she was right. I let the water run over me for a good fifteen minutes and it did make me feel better.

After towelling off and running a brush through my hair, I pulled on the bathrobe and walked back into my room. Nhu had used the time to neatly remove all evidence of the break-in. I'm sure the people from CSI Miami or New York or Broken Spoke, Wyoming, wouldn't approve, but this was Saigon and it was her city. The mattress was back in place, the bed made up, the drawers returned to their appropriate positions and my few clothes were hanging neatly in the closet. As was Nhu's Áo dài .

The lights in the room had been dimmed and she was waiting for me on the bed. Besides baguettes it looked like the French had also left the Vietnamese an excellent legacy of fine silk lingerie.

The figure-hugging Áo dài tends to reveal the lines of under-wear, unless said underwear is also quite figure-hugging, and Nhu's certainly was. It was also quite see-through in a couple of spots that I didn't even want to think about, given my recent altercation in the alley.

'Miss Hoang,' I said, 'or should I call you Nhu?'

She stood up and walked slowly around the bed towards me.

'This may seem strange, but I very much like the way you call me Miss Hoang, Mr Murdoch.'

It did seem a bit strange, but then she stood up on her tippy-toes and kissed me. And I have to say I very much liked that.

'Miss Hoang, in the alleyway . . .' I started to say, but she put a finger up to my lips.

'The report of the robbery was quite detailed, Mr Murdoch. I am aware of the circumstances of the assault and I assure you I will be gentle with you.'

And she was.

Later, when she was sleeping, her long dark hair tossed over the pillow of my once-again rumpled bed, I sat back against the headboard, finished off the whisky and looked at her. Nhu's skin was soft and golden and she had the most exquisitely beautiful, delicate feet I'd ever seen. Having a woman like Nhu in bed next to you made a man glad to be alive.

I *was* glad to be alive, and bloody lucky, too. When those coppers had pulled me from the crumpled cyclo it had been too dark for them to notice the bullet marks freshly scored into the alley's crumbling brickwork. The only reason I'd seen the flashes that had flared from inside the jeep was because the muzzle of someone's silenced pistol had been pointing almost directly at me when they'd fired.

'Silenced' is the wrong word because silencers don't actually silence weapons. What they really do is suppress the noise. In this instance, the noise of the vehicle accelerating away had worked with the suppressor to almost completely muffle the sound of the shots, but luckily for me the movement had also spoiled the shooter's aim.

Right now I knew for certain that someone wanted more than just what was in my camera bag. Someone also wanted me dead. And if those two cops hadn't shown up just thirty seconds later, I probably would have been.

Chapter Twelve

I WOKE UP EARLY THE NEXT MORNING, ALL BY MY LONESOME, AND decided to head down to Saigon's old Ben Thanh Market. The city was wide awake and well into its day by the time I arrived. The Lunar New Year, called Tet in Vietnam, was approaching, so the fantastic bustle and variety of a great Asian market was even more frenetic than usual. Being a photographer, it made sense that I was constantly looking around, searching for the next great shot. Of course, what I was also doing was keeping a careful eye out for anyone who might want to take a shot at me.

Ben Thanh is a visual feast for the photographer, and an actual feast for anyone with an interest in food and an empty belly. I was in serious need of a good breakfast; dicing with death followed by some good lovin' will do that to you. I wandered the crowded aisles for a while, grabbing shots with the Leica and marvelling at the displays of spices, exotic fruit, garden-crisp vegetables and masses of clucking, croaking, splashing and slithering creatures that would be someone's lunch or dinner before the day was over. I'm with the Vietnamese: fresh really is best.

There were branches of yellow and pink blossoms to decorate the home for Tet, and specially prepared food for the celebration. Stalls offered banh tet, square packages of sticky rice, mung-bean purée and seasoned pork wrapped in banana leaves; a range of salty, slow-cooked meat dishes called kho; and gio bo, beef and dill sausages. There were pâtés, pickled shallots and leeks to serve on the side, and nuts and watermelon seeds for snacking, plus masses of garishly coloured candied coconut, melon rind and lotus seeds.

My photo-taking efforts were abandoned when I reached a stall serving breakfast and pulled up a plastic stool at a table. The range of food on offer was unbelievable, but I went for my favourite, pho gai - poached chicken and soft rice noodles swimming in a steaming bowl of spicy broth dressed with bean sprouts, chilli, basil leaves and the usual squeeze of lime. Pho gai beats a bowl of cereal for breakfast hands down, and this one was unbelievably aromatic and tasty. I was contemplating a second helping when my past came up and bit me on the butt.

'Alby fucking Murdoch, as I bloody live and breathe.'

Jezebel Quick was six foot six of dynamism, gorgeous good looks, dangerous curves and pulsating sexual energy packed into a five-foot-nothing frame. A shock of shoulder-length curly blonde hair framed her face, her blue eyes sparkled and those red lips were as inviting as ever. Her diaphanous blouse and light cotton trousers made sense in the tropics, but if they'd been any flimsier they'd have blown away in a mild breeze. Jez was an underwear-optional kind of woman, and for a moment I didn't quite know where to look so I looked everywhere.

Jezebel opened her first restaurant at the age of twenty-one to long lines and rave reviews. We'd worked together a lot of years back when I'd shot the pictures for one of her early cookbooks, Jezebel's Quicksnacks. I'd eventually wound up being one of those snacks and I still hadn't recovered from the experience. It was a brief, intense and very tempestuous affair and I'll admit I was a bit relieved when she moved on to fresh fields.

The success of her restaurant ventures and cookbooks had eventually led to Jezebel getting her own TV food series. The show had an avid fan base of women looking for fast, foolproof recipes they could throw together to please their husbands, and husbands who watched every episode desperately hoping Ms Quick would prepare something featuring whipped cream. Jezebel made Nigella look like a homely peasant girl and her whisking technique really had to be seen to be believed. There'd even been one famous spatula-licking sequence that had to be edited out, given her programme's early-evening timeslot. The producers decided it was definitely too hot for the tots.

'Hello Jez. Still got that convent girl's vocabulary, I see.'

"Why don't you go and shove your head up a dead bear's bum, Alby, you prick,'

She gave me a big wet kiss. 'Mmmm,' she said, licking her lips, 'you can really taste the star-anise in that stock.'

Off-camera, Jezebel swore like a Queensland bullocky, one with an extremely colourful turn of phrase. In one famous incident on the set of a TV show, she'd been asked by Gordon Ramsay's personal assistant if she could tone the language down a bit as he was starting to get embarrassed. There was definitely the potential for a high-rating reality TV show about Jezebel's life but you'd probably have to call it "Expletive De-fucking-leted."

'What brings you to Saigon, Jez? And didn't I take out a court order that said you couldn't come within 500 metres of me?'

'In your bloody dreams, lover,' she laughed. 'We're here shooting sequences for my new series and I've tied it in with some personal appearances and one of my "Experience Bloody Gourmet Asia tours."'

I figured Asia with Jezebel would be one hell of an experience, and way too much for me to cope with.

'I've just taken this bunch of filthy-rich foodie wankers to Tokyo, Singapore and KL, and after this it's Hanoi and then Hong Kong. To tell you the truth, Alby, I'm bloody sick to death of the bastards.'

Knowing how Jezebel operated, this meant there were no males in the group young enough, fit enough or good-looking enough to keep her entertained.

There was a sudden ruckus behind us and Jezebel glanced over her shoulder.

'It's that motherfucker Bourdain and his crew trying to screw up my interview with the cock and balls soup lady. Prick. My boys will sort him out.'

The world's most exotic markets and locals-only food stalls were now being besieged by film crews from food and lifestyle TV shows, all competing to find something unique for their viewers. The hunt was becoming brutal, and production companies were actively seeking out ex-military types or people with martial arts training to work as producers and cameramen.

The whole food as entertainment thing was getting way out of hand. I'd recently come round a bend on a jungle track while on assignment deep in the heart of unexplored Sarawak and stumbled across a tiny shack, whose owner was squatting in the mud grilling slices of monkey over a charcoal fire. A laminated card pinned to one of the poles holding up the sagging thatched roof read, '*As featured on Asia's Yummiest Street Snacks - Gourmet TV Network*'.

I noticed a group of police heading in our general direction and assumed they were on their way to handle the TV crew's demarcation dispute, but they stopped at my table.

Usually I'm not all that pleased to see the local wallopers, but this morning I wasn't too fussed. Not when the cop in charge was so good-looking.

Chapter Thirteen

'Good Morning, Miss Hoang. How very nice to see you again.'

Nhu didn't return my smile. 'Mr Murdoch, we need to talk,' she said, 'most urgently.'

'Who's your friend with the nice tits, Alby?' Jezebel asked.

Nhu was wearing a neat uniform of trousers and a crisply pressed shirt with red shoulder boards bearing a thin gold band and three silver stars indicating her rank. It was an outfit that really did show off her curves.

I made the introductions. 'Miss Jezebel Quick, this is Senior Lieutenant Nhu Hoang of the local police. Miss Hoang is the national police pistol champion.

'Interesting,' Jezebel responded. 'Is that why she's showing us her gun?'

It was a good question and I was wondering about that myself. This time I was definitely able to see that she was armed, as the muzzle of a Russian 9mm police-issue Yarygin Pya semi-automatic pistol was pointing in the general direction of my navel.

'Mr Murdoch, I need to ask you some questions regarding your activities last night.'

Something in her dark eyes made me stifle the comment about my activities the preceding evening and her part in them.

'We urgently require your assistance with our inquiries.'

She turned to Jezebel and smiled politely. 'Ms Quick, since this affair does not concern you I suggest you go about your business.'

Jezebel looked at me. 'Alby?'

I nodded. 'It's under control, Jez.'

Jezebel leaned down and gave me a kiss. 'We'll catch up later, okay?'

'Ms Quick,' Nhu said, 'I very much enjoyed your recent book on romantic dinners for two.'

'Then you'll wanna keep your eye out for the next one, Naughty Late-Night Nibbles. Alby here has got his own chapter.'

Jezebel smiled, turned and walked towards her waiting film crew. I think I might have blushed.

'Now, Mr Murdoch, if you would please put out your hands.'

One of the officers snapped a nice shiny set of handcuffs around my wrists. I was glad Jezebel had left since I knew exactly what kind of comment she'd make.

Nhu holstered her pistol. She joined me at the table and ordered a bowl of pho while her officers fanned out in a loose circle around the table, looking outwards to scan the crowd, Last night Miss Hoang had been very, very hot and this morning she was just way too cool.

"Mr Murdoch, please excuse the use of my gun and the handcuffs but it is necessary to show anyone observing us that you are in my custody.'

'Necessary why?'

'Following our investigations, we now feel confident that the incident in the alley last night was more than just thieves wishing to steal your camera. We have become aware that there is a plan to kill you. I believe you would say there is a price on your head.'

I kept my mouth shut, since the rule with cops is to never volunteer any information. Even with a cop as hot as Miss Hoang.

'Any society,' she continued, 'even one such as ours, has its undesirable elements, and certain of these elements have been offered large amounts of money to eliminate you as quickly as possible. Would you perhaps know why?'

I shook my head and from the look on Nhu's face, I sensed there was something else.

'What can you tell me about a man named Brett Tozer, who was also working on the movie with you?'

What did Brett have to do with this? I wondered.

'Mr Tozer is an associate producer,' I said, 'and people with that title don't usually do any actual work. He was flying out to New York yesterday afternoon, as far as I know.'

'Mr Tozer does not appear to have boarded his flight,' Nhu said, 'and this morning the body of a man answering his description was discovered floating in the Saigon River.'

This was suddenly a bit heavy.

'Did he drown?' I asked. 'Was it an accident?'

Nhu said something in Vietnamese and one of her officers produced a photograph from a satchel. It was Brett Tozer all right, no question of that. The photograph had been taken using harsh direct flash, which isn't too flattering at the best of times, but poor old Brett was way beyond caring. He was on his back on a mortuary slab, and he hadn't drowned, that was for sure. He probably had enough lead in him to make swimming difficult, though. The photograph clearly showed five big bullet holes smack in the middle of his chest. Brett hadn't needed to fly all the way from New York to the Gold Coast for the shooting to start again - the shooting had come to him.

'It appears it is most dangerous for you to be in Vietnam,' Nhu continued. 'It is imperative you leave the country immediately. Do you have your passport with you?'

I nodded. 'Zippered pocket inside my jacket.' She spoke to one of the officers, who reached inside my jacket, found the passport and handed it to her. She passed it to one of her waiting entourage with brief instructions. He saluted and left.

'Now, Mr Murdoch,' said Nhu, standing up, 'we will leave this market with you in my custody in full view of everybody. Several streets from here at a convenient location we will remove the handcuffs and you will leave my vehicle. The officer who just left will meet you at the airport with a ticket and boarding pass for the next available flight out of the country. He will also escort you onboard the aircraft.'

It looked like she had everything sorted.

'This way you will bypass all normal immigration formalities,' she continued, 'but there will be an official departure stamp in your passport to avoid difficulties on arrival at your next destination. Please ignore the fact that your boarding pass may be in a name not your own, since you are officially in police custody.'

'My clothes -' I started to say, but she interrupted me.

'Are being collected from the hotel and will be waiting for you at the airport.'

She really had thought of everything.

'I suggest that after you leave my vehicle you go by cyclo to the airport,' she advised. 'Inefficient, yes, but less obvious than a taxi and more difficult to follow without being observed. I doubt anyone will think you would travel this way. One of my officers will travel behind you, discreetly, to ensure there are no ... incidents on the journey.'

This wasn't the way I'd hoped to end my stay in Vietnam, especially after just meeting Nhu. You had to wonder about the whole karma business. Why was it that every time I met a nice girl, someone came out of the woodwork looking to kill me? Was I paying for mistakes I'd made in a past life? Or was it because of some nasty incident I'd been involved in during this one? God knows, there'd been enough of those.

And what about Brett Tozer? Last time I'd seen him alive he was on his phone, which was just minutes after I'd shown him the picture of the bloke who might be Cartwright. Later that night, someone had tried to whack me. I wondered if it was the same shooter in that jeep who'd been a bit more successful with Brett than he'd been with me.

Ten minutes later I was rubbing my wrists and choking on the fumes of Saigon's morning rush hour while sitting in a cyclo with the hood pulled as far forward as it would go.

The trip to Tan Son Nhut International Airport was uneventful but hey, I was just another bloke who was supposed to be dead riding a cyclo through downtown Saigon.

Chapter Fourteen

The next available seat out of Ho Chi Minh City that morning was on a Thai Airways flight heading for Bangkok. Getting deported at short notice severely limits your options for seat preference and I found myself on the aisle in economy, jammed in next to a Japanese bloke about the size of a two-door refrigerator. If it came down to a fistfight over who got the armrest, it was pretty obvious who was going to win.

Bangkok isn't a bad destination if you're a fan of humidity, hot chillies, smog and a freeway system in desperate need of a high colonic. But this time around, Thailand suited me just fine. As a matter of fact, any place where I didn't have a price on my head would have been okay.

Travelling with just a carry-on backpack had me through customs and immigration at Suvarnabhumi Airport in double-quick time. I hit the terminal toilets twice - the first time because it's always smart to use the facilities before getting stuck in Bangkok traffic for an indeterminate period of time, and the second to make one hundred per cent sure I wasn't being followed. Straight in and straight out really confuses a tail who has to do the same thing, and it makes them stick out like dog's balls.

When I was sure I wasn't being followed, I took a taxi to Sukhumvit Road and grabbed the Skytrain to Mo Chit Station in the north of the city. From there, it was just a ten-minute taxi ride to Mo Chit bus terminal.

An afternoon bus for Chiang Rai was just leaving, so I grabbed a ticket with a voucher for a meal at the halfway rest stop. In Asia I'm usually more of a fan of overnight buses, since you can sleep if you're lucky or watch some noisy local sword and sarong epic on DVD. Another plus is that the oncoming traffic and suicidal local driving techniques are moderately less terrifying in the dark. However, I didn't feel like hanging around in Bangkok for another five or six hours.

On the cab ride from the airport I'd talked the driver into selling me his spare balisong, and I now had it safely stowed in my jacket pocket. I'm not crazy about folding butterfly knives, or knives in general, but this one had a nicely honed eight-inch doubled-edged blade tucked inside the handle. My seat at the back of the bus would let me keep an eye on the rest of the passengers for the next eleven hours, and in the event that I needed the balisong, and could get it open without cutting off my own fingers, I could probably do someone some serious damage.

The bus's afternoon departure would put us in Chiang Rai sometime around midnight. The northern Thai province of Chiang Rai is located in the Kok River basin in the Golden Triangle, where Myanmar, Laos and Thailand bump into each other. Its attractions range from magnificent mountain scenery, the ruins of ancient settlements, Buddhist shrines and a bunch of ethnic villages, since the province is also home to a number of hill tribes. Of course, right now there was one thing in particular that made it my destination of choice and that was the presence of the Dutchman.

Once we cleared Bangkok's urban sprawl, the scenery was mile after mile of green rice fields, blue sky and distant mountains. As the bus chewed up the highway, and it appeared less and less likely that one of my fellow passengers was going to come after me with a machete or MAC-10 submachine gun, I made use of the time to do some thinking.

Someone had pressed a very big panic button very quickly and they'd pressed it hard. They'd taken out Brett and it looked like they wanted me out of the picture PDQ. The connection had to be Cartwright. Jack was hot on Cartwright's trail - were he and VT now in danger? And what about the lovely Nhu? She'd poked her delicate little nose into the middle of things to rescue me, and that couldn't be good.

On the flight out of Ho Chi Minh City, I'd considered heading back to Australia but had decided against it. I was still suspended from D-E-D, my movie stills gig was on hiatus for another two weeks, and someone had put a price on my head and I wanted to figure out who. I needed to lie low and work out my next move. If you wanted a place to drop out of sight, you couldn't beat Asia. And if you needed to drop out of sight in Thailand, then the man to see was the Dutchman.

Travelling at what seemed a tad under the speed of light, we passed through a succession of provinces: Angthong, Singburi, Phitsanulok, Uttaradit and Phrae. As with Hong Kong taxis, Thai buses always have their air-con set to Ice Age and the twenty-minute meal stop at the Phitsanulok bus depot, some 450 k's north of Bangkok, wasn't so much to eat and stretch the legs as to defrost. This being Thailand, the food was fresh, good and ridiculously cheap.

We rolled into the Chiang Rai bus terminal close to midnight. I woke up a sleepy cab driver near the night market and gave him the address. Traffic was minimal so we reached the bar in five minutes. After paying off the cabbie I wandered inside. The place was almost empty, and for good reason. You could hear the din a couple of blocks away.

A five-piece ensemble was jamming on a stage at the rear of the small brick and tin establishment. Four of the group were heavy-metal Thais and the fifth was a skinny Dutchman with a crew cut, a gravelly singing voice and a twelve-string acoustic guitar. The combined effect was like an aural train wreck.

'Struth, mate,' I said, during a pause, 'what a nightmare. It's like a sixties Bob Dylan playing live at the Budokan with an eighties Cheap Trick.'

Huub, the Dutchman, looked around. 'And I suppose you'll be the music critic from Rolling Stone we've all been expecting.'

A lot of expats living in Asia get fat from the cheap food and the booze, but Huub apparently lived on adrenaline so he stayed thin. He had sleepy eyes and a slightly bent nose, reshaped by a broken beer glass when he helpfully tried to break up a fight in a pub a few days after he first arrived in Australia. He learned the hard way why they used to call certain Melbourne hotels blood houses way back then.

Huub told the band to take five.

'Let me guess,' he said, after shaking hands and studying me briefly, 'it's just on midnight, you've got bugger all luggage, no cameras and you look like shit. Someone's trying to kill you, right?'

I nodded. 'Story of my life, Dutchman.'

'Maybe you should do what I did, Alby, get yourself a new one.'

'Mate, I bloody wish,' I said.

Chapter Fifteen

Huub lived in a big rented house on the edge of a small lake inside an old military base. His landlord was an army general who was redeveloping the place into a secure housing estate and he had armed, off-duty soldiers keeping an eye on things. Having someone else keeping an eye on things suited me fine.

I slept till about three in the afternoon, which was really no surprise given my long hours on the film shoot, the recent attempted homicide, testicular trauma, short-notice deportation and a long-distance Thai bus ride. Chuck in my unexpected night of passion with Miss Hoang, and I was surprised I woke up at all.

When I finally surfaced and climbed out of the shower and into a Burmese sarong called a longyi. Huub had breakfast ready out on the balcony overlooking the lake.

'I'm temporarily between love interests and housekeepers, so there's just fruit and toast and coffee. Probably some eggs in the fridge, too, but you can sort that out for yourself. And do your own bloody dishes.'

'Coffee's fine for now.'

It was good coffee, locally grown and roasted.

Huub headed off somewhere to do whatever expats in Thailand do and I wandered around the house. Everything on display dated from Huub's arrival in Thailand a couple of years back. The Dutchman's past was a bit shadowy, with periods in Oman on the Persian Gulf, Réunion Island off the African coast near Madagascar and some time living in Indonesia. He'd also spent fifteen years in Australia, where we'd met, and had links to oil companies, international shipping and God knows what else.

When Huub decided to retire from whatever it was he didn't say he did for a living, he claimed it was a toss-up between a pricey studio apartment in Woy Woy and curried sausages at the local RSL or an unbelievably cheap three-bedroom house with maid's quarters on a lake in the tropics, where freshly cooked pad Thai noodles and a couple of beers in a local café set you back less than two bucks. I sipped my coffee and decided the Dutchman had made the right choice.

Huub had set up a home recording studio to practise his music plus he was involved in a number of volunteer tourism-development projects amongst the hill tribes and refugees up near the Thai-Myanmar border. The Dutchman reckoned he was so busy being retired that he might have to think seriously about putting on staff.

I made a fresh pot of coffee and sat out on the balcony for the rest of the afternoon. Dragonflies and birds flitted around, and there was a four-thirty torrential downpour followed by a short tropical twilight. I thought about fit young blokes steering cyclos into alleyways full of waiting assassins, my ransacked hotel room and Brett Tozer getting cut down in a hail of bullets. None of it made any sense.

The sun had set, the last of the coffee had long gone cold and a column of hungry mosquitoes was circling above my head when Huub reappeared. If I could figure out a way to attract women the way I attracted mosquitoes, I'd be a happy man.

'You feel like some dinner?'

I nodded. 'But a whisky might be nice first, a double.'

'Think that's a smart move on an empty stomach?'

He had a point. 'Maybe I should have a beer to start, then.'

Huub smiled. 'Spoken like a local. I know a friendly little bar down by the river. The sexy owner and all the gorgeous young waitresses have the hots for me.'

'They must have heard about the size of your pension plan.'

'Remind me again why I'm your friend, Alby.'

'Because with friends like me you don't need enemas?'

Huub smiled again. 'I figured there had to be a really good reason.'

Asia is full of friendly open-air bars where expats congregate, and this one was pretty typical. All you need to start one up is some bamboo and thatch, a fridge to keep the beer cold, a tank of propane to keep the wok hot, a CD player for a bit of nostalgia and some smiling locals. The smiling locals and the restaurant staff, mostly female, gave the Dutchman a boisterous welcome.

The bar was squeezed in between the river and a roadway but, being late in the day, the traffic wasn't too horrendous.

We grabbed a booth by the entrance and Huub ordered us a couple of Heinekens and something crunchy to snack on. The crunchy things were deep-fried and had multiple legs and remnants of wings but were pretty tasty.

We had more beers and ordered an excellent red duck curry, which was sweet rather than hot, and an innocent-looking pawpaw salad that set my mouth on fire, and then more beers. Huub chatted to the waitresses in appalling Thai and they laughed a lot, which is what girls with mothers and grandmothers and brothers and sisters to support do when the rich farangs say pretty much anything. Of course, all over the world rich men have no problem getting good-looking women to laugh at their jokes.

At Huub's request Ry Cooder was on the sound system, and we pretty much had the place to ourselves. The owner and the girls were in the kitchen making dessert and giggling about something or someone when a spray of lead from a submachine gun displaced the gaggle of mosquitoes circling above my head.

The shooter was perched on the back of a red Honda motorcycle stopped out on the roadway. I grabbed Huub and dragged him off his seat and down onto the floor. Luckily for us, the gunman was an amateur. The muzzle climb of a short-barrelled submachine gun firing full auto lifted the weapon upwards, and most of the contents of the shooter's thirty-round magazine blasted into the restaurant's roof. The thatched ceiling disintegrated in the stream of bullets, raining all sorts of bugs and spiders and crap down on top of us as we sprawled face down on the tiled floor.

The motorcycle screamed away, leaving us in dead silence except for the sound of Ry Cooder's slide guitar and some whimpering coming from the kitchen. The Dutchman lifted a lump of thatch off his head and looked at me.

'Godverdomme, Alby,' he gasped, 'you really are a dangerous bugger to know.'

I didn't really feel I could give him much of an argument on that.

Chapter Sixteen

HUUB MADE A COUPLE OF PHONE CALLS FROM THE RESTAURANT WHILE I helped the owner and waitresses clean up the mess. Surprisingly, the damage was minimal and the smiles and laughter were back after about ten minutes, but neither Huub nor I felt in the mood to party on. The bill for the food and booze came to less than ten bucks, but I left a hundred to cover the repairs.

My mood improved a little when we got back to the Dutchman's housing estate and found security had been beefed up and a dozen heavily armed men in uniform were watching the main gate. Huub waved to them as we drove past.

'This is where having a general for a landlord really pays off,' he said.

The Dutchman decided to call it a night, but I was still pumping with the adrenaline rush from the near miss in the bar. I snapped on the TV in the living room and had the usual viewing dilemma of a thousand channels and none of them worth watching. Chiang Rai locals made regular cross-border forays into Myanmar to buy black-market Viagra and discount satellite dishes, though I always wondered what the hell you'd need a TV for if you were gulping down Viagra on a regular basis.

I settled down on a comfortable couch with the curtains drawn, lights off and the sound on the TV turned down, and channel surfed with the remote until my thumb fell asleep and the rest of me followed not too long afterwards.

According to my trusty old Omega it was just after ten in the morning when I woke up. There was no sign of the Dutchman so I made a pot of coffee and some toast and scrambled half a dozen eggs straight out of the local free-range chooks.

I didn't really expect to find any cream in Huub's fridge but there was butter and milk, and with chopped fresh chilli, coriander and ground black pepper the eggs came out okay.

The TV was still on in the living room, and when I wandered back in from the balcony a news broadcast out of Vietnam was showing an aerial shot of a smoking patch of heavily wooded hillside. There was some grainy old footage of a Vietnam-era Huey, the footage of the smoking hillside again and then they showed a couple of passport-type pictures - of Jack and VT.

Huub walked in from the recording studio.

'Jesus, Alby,' he said, 'you look crook. Something you ate?'

I shook my head. 'Something I saw.'

'You sure you don't need a Stemetil or some Imodium?'

'Nope, but what I do need is some time on your computer.'

'It's in my bedroom - don't look in any of the files marked "Don't look in this file."'

After tracking down several news reports on the crash in English I pulled up Google Maps to get an idea of the location. The helicopter had just taken off from the small airport at Dien Bien Phu when it was seen to crash and burn on a heavily wooded and difficult-to-access hillside. Aerial reconnaissance had shown no sign of survivors, and strong downdrafts and an impending storm had ruled out any attempt at a landing near the site. A ground party would be sent in to recover the bodies but given the location it was likely to take up to a week.

Huub was in the living room when I finished.

'What I need now is that little package you've been keeping for me.'

Huub went into his office and came out with a sealed buff envelope. There were similar envelopes collecting dust with friends all over the world. I ripped it open and dumped the contents on the table: a couple of thousand US dollars in used notes, a passport, a dozen passport-size photos, a driver's licence and a credit card. The passport was issued in Fiji, as was the driver's licence. Both documents were current and had my photograph on them. The licence and passport were in the same name as the credit card - Barry Jones.

'What does Mr Jones need in the way of visas if he wants to get to Luang Prabang?' I asked. 'And then cross over the border into Vietnam near Dien Bien Phu.'

Luang Prabang was the old royal capital of Laos and the closest city with an airport to the Vietnamese border. I could get a direct flight to LP from Chiang Mai, in the next province.

Huub scowled. 'Mr Jones is a real pain in the arse. But what else is new? You can get a visa for Laos at the port of entry easily enough, but Vietnam is trickier. They're not keen on visitors showing up unannounced.'

'Tell me about it. I'm starting to get a bit that way myself. What about a green visa?'

A green visa was a fifty or hundred US dollar bill folded inside a passport.

Huub shook his head. 'Personally, Alby, I wouldn't risk it. You might get the visa but you also might get some serious jail time or a bullet in the head for the rest of what's in your wallet.' He picked up the passport, a couple of the small photographs and several hundred dollars. 'I might know a bloke who knows a bloke. Let me see what I can do.'

I made a fresh pot of coffee and went out onto the balcony to think things over. There was a beautiful view of the lake, but right now all I could see was that patch of smoking hillside in Vietnam. VT was a hell of a pilot, and he knew the Huey inside out, but sometimes even a great pilot might find himself with more grief than he could handle.

But it was the sequence of events - me being on a hit list, Brett Tozer turning up as a floater, and now Jack and VT going down in a chopper - that was really disturbing.

Jack and VT and I had become good friends over the five weeks of the film shoot, but our connection went much further back. I wasn't sure if they remembered our previous meeting, and I hadn't brought it up. It was on my first overseas assignment, when I was posing as a press photographer while working undercover for D-E-D.

I was young, impetuous and pissed as a cricket when I went to the aid of a female Swedish reporter in a Bangkok bar full of bored, boozed-up Aussie newspaper correspondents covering the latest half-arsed military coup. Maybe it was a language problem, but it really hadn't been a good idea for her to walk into a joint like that wearing a tight T-shirt with the word 'PRESS' stretched invitingly across her chest.

The last-minute intervention by an Aussie ex-special forces type who was drinking in the bar with a Vietnamese bloke was the only thing that stopped me from being beaten to a pulp. The two of them had jumped in boots and all, dragged me clear of the scrum and dumped me outside in the street. My kidneys ached, my right eye was blurry and my cheek felt wet.

'You gotta learn to pick your battles, sunshine,' the Aussie had said.

He knelt down and wiped some blood off my eyebrow with his thumb. 'See if you can find a local quack to put a couple of stitches in that. I think you'll live to snap another day. You can tell the ladies the scar's from a near miss from a commie AK-47. With a story like that, I reckon you'll be getting your leg over big time.'

The two men had walked away laughing while I'd sat in the gutter trying to stem the flow of blood with a handkerchief. That scar was the first of many, but like a first kiss or a first love it was the one that stuck in my mind. And now Jack and VT were missing, quite probably dead, and I wanted to know why.

Logically, the place to start looking was where the chopper had gone down. I wasn't ready to give up on Jack and VT just yet, not until I saw the bodies. I held on to the thought that they might have survived the crash, even though I knew that was probably a long shot.

Huub got back a couple of hours later with the news that the visa would be ready first thing in the morning. I was getting gun-shy, literally, about eating in restaurants so I rummaged through Huub's cupboards and fridge to see what I could come up with for lunch.

While I sweated down some shallots, garlic and chillies in a wok, I was thinking about Major Peter Cartwright VC. The bloke was supposed to be long dead and gone, and now it appeared that anyone possessing evidence to the contrary stood a very good chance of winding up six feet under themselves.

Chapter Seventeen

After collecting my passport and visa, the Dutchman and I made the three-hour road trip from Chiang Rai to Chiang Mai. Huub had suggested I could make the journey on the back of his motorcycle, but I figured I'd already done enough dicing with death in the last few days to last me a lifetime, so we drove.

A Lao Airlines ATR turboprop was warming up on the tarmac when we arrived at Chiang Mai Airport, ready to take me over the border and into the Lao People's Democratic Republic where Thai baht and US dollars turned into kip and 'sawaddi turned into 'sabaai-di and the smiles just kept on coming.

The twin-engined ATR has a high wing so the views from the big cabin windows were spectacular. Six thousand metres below us, the wide brown expanse of the mighty Mekong River cut through the countryside on its journey to the delta where we had been filming only a few days before. It was hard to believe that the lush green jungle passing below us was the most heavily bombed piece of real estate on the planet.

Back in the sixties, while the war in Vietnam was getting all the publicity, a secret war was raging in Laos with the Soviet and North Vietnamese-backed Communist Pathet Lao holding the lowland areas and CIA-backed Lao and Hmong hill tribes occupying mountaintop strongholds that were secretly resupplied by Air America flights. In the meantime, the American Air Force was bombing the crap out of everything that moved in an attempt to stop supplies getting through to the Vietcong via Laos. The Pentagon logged almost 600,000 missions over the country, and given that around 30 per cent of the bombs that were dropped failed to explode and were still lying about, it wasn't a great place to go wandering off the beaten track.

As we started our descent, the landscape beneath us began to change. The riverbank was dotted with red-roofed houses and golden temples appeared on the hilltops. As we dipped lower, closer to the airport, bigger buildings and roads busy with traffic filled the view. Then we were thumping down on a runway grimy with black skid marks from hundreds of landings and I was one step closer to finding out what had happened to Jack and VT.

Any other time Luang Prabang would have been a great place to rest up, but I was in a hurry. The joint has a UNESCO World Heritage listing, some great guesthouses, lots of interesting places to eat, museums, night markets and, of course, temples up the wazoo. And Buddhas - more Buddha's than you can shake a stick at. Plus enough saffron-robed monks to make shaking sticks at the local Buddha's seem like a very uncool idea.

I took a crowded and battered back roads minivan to Oudomxay and then another on to Muang Khua, trying to maintain a low profile by keeping my head down and my mouth shut. Maintaining a low profile also meant suppressing the urge to stick the pointy end of my balisong into the kneecap of every pissy backpacker who complained about the overcrowding and the heat. Give me screaming over whining any day. It made me think of my late colleague Harry, who used to snarl, 'If you can't stand the heat, stay out of the tropics.' He generally added, 'Dipshit.'

Located on the banks of the Nam Ou River overlooking a ferry crossing, Muang Khua has a bit of an American Old West border trading post feel to it, or it would have if you chopped down the jungle, whacked in some cactus and replaced the local Yunnanese, Vietnamese and Lao inhabitants with Mexican vaqueros.

From Muang Khua it was just one final long ugly sixty-five kilometre journey along an overgrown and deeply rutted dirt track in a local truck to the tiny border crossing point at Tay Trang. The geriatric Soviet Gorky truck I hitched a ride on may have had springs at some stage in its life but those days were long gone, along with its paint job and most of the tread on the tyres.

By the time we reached the Lao-Vietnam border, my spine felt like it had been compressed by a good six centimetres.

My visa passed muster on the Vietnamese side of the crossing and after an hour's wait I managed to grab a ride in a battered Russian jeep with a local who was heading back to Dien Bien Phu after dropping off some Pommy back-packers. The driver had heard about the helicopter crash and he let me off in the general vicinity of where it had happened. This left me standing on a muddy track in the middle of nowhere, with only a vague idea of which direction to head in. The light was just starting to fade when the old man wandered by.

I nodded and smiled. 'Chao ong,' I said in greeting, and then, 'Anh co khoe khong?' which I was pretty sure meant, 'How are you?'

'Bonsoir, vous êtes français, monsieur?' he asked.

I shook my head, 'Non, je suis Australien.'

The man was old, how old I really couldn't guess, and he had the look of a farmer. He was limping, barefoot, dressed in a tattered black shirt and loose mud-stained black trousers, and his skin was tanned and leathery. He had squinting eyes that twitched constantly from too many years spent working in the blinding sun.

I had an uncle, a farmer, with that same twitch and the leathery skin. He had a finger missing, casually plucked off by a potato-harvesting machine in a moment's inattention.

My uncle's eyes had also held a hint of things seen and best forgotten, and when I was older and learned he had been in New Guinea, at Isurava, fighting the Japanese Army, I began to understand why. This farmer had that same faraway look - a look journalists in Vietnam had called the thousand-yard stare.

'Monsieur,' I said, using up the rapidly dwindling reserves of my schoolboy French, 'dites-moi, avez-vous vu un accident d'hélicoptère?'

The farmer nodded. He had seen the crash. He looked west, towards the sun sitting low on the mountaintops, and asked, 'Ong muon uong gi khong?"

I gave him the internationally recognised quizzical look and tilt of the head to show I didn't understand.

'As-tu soif,' he said, making a drinking motion with his hand.

I nodded. That bit I understood. I could use a drink too.

He led me further up the hill towards a small shack. It was a pretty steep grade but even limping he outpaced me. After a couple of minutes he stopped to admire the view, which was a polite way of letting me catch up. As we caught our breath, I pointed to his dodgy leg.

'Un accident?' I asked.

He pulled up the left leg of his floppy trousers and smiled.

'Une femme,' he said.

It must have been some woman. Between his knee and hip there was a hole in his thigh big enough to put my whole fist in. The wound was all scar tissue, with no sign of stitching or any medical treatment. It looked like a chunk of his flesh had been ripped out, and he'd been left to heal or die.

'Une femme Française?' I asked.

He nodded and smiled. 'Beatrice,' he said, and continued up the hill.

Beatrice was the codename of one of General de Castries' five hilltop outposts at Dien Bien Phu. Defended by French Foreign Legionnaires, it was attacked on the first day of the battle and fell just after midnight following some very fierce fighting. My farming buddy had somehow survived the battle with an untreated wound that should have been fatal, General Giap's troops being a bit light on for medical units. No wonder the old bugger could outpace me going uphill - he was one tough cookie.

The interior of the shack was a jumble of clothes, bedding and farm tools. The old man picked up a battered teapot and smiled at me. I shrugged. He reached under some empty sacks and pulled out a bottle. It was unlabelled with a clear liquid inside. Probably ruou can, locally brewed rice wine. I nodded. That was more like it.

There was something else interesting under those sacks and the farmer saw me looking. He tossed back the covering and handed me the weapon. It was an MAT-49, a French submachine gun. Produced by the Manufacture Nationale d'Armes de Tulle and adopted by the French Army in 1949, the MAT-49 is a lovely-looking gun, with a wire stock and shrouded barrel. This one was pitted with corrosion and looked like it hadn't been used or cleaned for over half a century. I wondered if the original owner had fired his last burst into an oncoming Vietminh on a hill named Beatrice, but I didn't ask.

Chapter Eighteen

THE FARMER LED ME A HALF MILE OR SO DOWN THE HILL TO A ROCK ledge overlooking the valley. We sat together and watched the last rays of sunlight kiss the mountain peaks surrounding Dien Bien Phu goodnight. Looking down into the valley, you had to ask yourself what kind of military genius had decided to pick this place for a showdown with the enemy, a place where from day one you had yielded the high ground. But that was fifty-plus years back, vegetation now covering most of the remaining evidence of that debacle between the French Union forces commanded by de Castries and the Vietminh under Giap.

We passed the bottle of hooch back and forth. I managed not to swallow too much of the booze since I wanted to keep my wits about me and save my throat from the burning liquid. As we drank and watched the moon rise, in a jumbled mix of broken French and charades I heard what the old man knew about the helicopter crash.

The farmer mimed the chopper flying quickly up the valley, keeping low and then disappearing into the heavily wooded hillside. Afterwards he'd heard an explosion and saw flames and smoke. He pointed to a position up the valley, but I couldn't see anything.

I pantomimed the two of us walking to the crash site, and he laughed and shook his head. It seemed it was on the side of a very steep hill and almost impossible to reach. It looked like the crash site had become just one more pile of burnt-out wreckage in a landscape with more than its fair share.

It was getting cold when the wine was done and I was glad I had a liner for my sleeping bag. We staggered to our feet. The old man pulled down the front of his trousers and pissed a mighty stream over the side of the mountain and down into the valley. He hitched up his trousers and suddenly yelled something out into the darkness. The only word I understood was 'Français'.

Sensing a moment for international co-operation and understanding I took a guess at what he was saying and joined in, yelling, 'Fuck you, Frenchies!' as loud as I could.

When we got back to the farmer's shack it turned out I wouldn't be needing my sleeping bag after all. A couple of heavy-set Vietnamese blokes in suits were waiting for us and each of them was holding a nice little TEC-9 submachine gun. They appeared out of the darkness when the hut and the hillside were suddenly lit up by the headlights of a big four-wheel drive.

We stopped for a moment, but since there was nothing but open ground around us and nowhere to run, I figured we should just keep walking. As we approached, a third man came out of the shack. Unlike his companions he was wearing hiking boots, black trousers and the thick, rough linen indigo-dyed jacket favoured by northern hill tribes. He was holding the farmer's MAT-49.

I'd managed to get my butterfly knife past airport security back in Chiang Mai, but even if the MAT-49 was rusted beyond use, the other two blokes had me well and truly out-gunned. As if they'd been reading my mind, one kept me covered while the other quickly frisked me and pocketed the balisong. The third bloke just watched and smiled and then he casually tossed the MAT-49 back into the hut.

'There were a hell of a lot of those left lying around after the French buggered off,' he said, in Australian-accented English. 'Vietnamese armourers modified them to fire Red Chinese 7.62mm ammo - cranked up the rate of fire from 600 to 900 rounds per minute.'

'Nice,' I said.

'Not if you were standing on the other side.'

'I guess you'd know a thing or two about that, Major.'

The late Major Peter Cartwright VC smiled. 'I suppose I would,' he said

Being dead obviously agreed with the major. He was slim and fit looking, slightly tanned, with steel-grey close-cropped hair. If he was a politician you'd say he was 'TV ready. What else he was ready for was another question.

I was kind of sorry I'd got the old farmer involved in all this. Peter Cartwright, it seemed, was intent on staying dead and it looked like he had no compunction about eliminating anyone who might think otherwise.

The headlights on the vehicle snapped off and left us standing in darkness. It would take a moment or two for everyone's eyes to adjust to the moonlight, so it was probably the right moment to make a run for it, but I didn't want to leave the farmer in the lurch.

'The old bloke really doesn't know what's going on here,' I said. 'Why don't you let him go? He's so pissed he won't remember anything in the morning anyway.'

Cartwright looked at me. 'Let him go where? He lives here, doesn't he?'

'Looks like it,' I said, 'so why don't you and I and Heckle and Jeckle there take our business off somewhere down the hillside?'

'And exactly what business might that be?' Cartwright asked.

'Seems like you could be tying up loose ends.'

'Loose ends?'

'I took a picture of you in Saigon a few days ago and now it looks like pretty much everyone who saw it is dead. Except for me. Not for lack of people trying to do the job.'

'You got a name there, sport?' Cartwright asked after a minute.

'Barry Jones.'

He smiled and shook his head. 'I took a dekko at Mr Jones's passport in your backpack and something doesn't smell kosher. Wanna try again?'

'Murdoch, Alby Murdoch.'

'The photographer, right? I've come across some of your snaps in the magazines in my dentist's waiting room.'

'I'm seen in all the best places.'

'Not really. My dentist works in a bamboo shack and he fits me in between the swine gelding, the fertility rites and the exorcisms.'

'Bet he still charges like a wounded bull though - they all do. So why were you in Saigon?'

'You know, mate,' Cartwright said, 'for a photographer you ask a lot of questions and have a decided lack of camera equipment.'

'Maybe I've got a new job - finding out who killed my friends and wants to kill me.'

'Sounds fair enough; Cartwright said. 'Who might these dead friends be, if you don't mind me asking?'

'A bloke named Jack Stark and his mate VT, a helicopter pilot. I saw a story on TV about their chopper coming down somewhere around here. Stark told me you and he had a connection in another life.'

'I saw the same story on TV,' Cartwright said. 'That's why I'm here, too. Funny, but I heard Stark died in an explosion a few years back. Ain't life just full of surprises.'

'I'm with you on that,' I said. 'But it looks to me that whatever happened to Jack Stark and VT, and to a bloke named Tozer, all happened because Stark recognised you in Saigon.'

'And you think it was me who wanted them taken out? And this Tozer character? And you as well?'

'Stark spots you, the word gets out you might not be dead, and next thing people start shooting at me, Tozer dies from a severe case of lead poisoning and then a chopper carrying Stark and his mate VT goes up in a fireball. As far as I can figure it, you were the trigger for all this.'

'I might well have been the trigger,' Cartwright said, 'but believe me I didn't have anything to do with any of the killing.'

'Okay, so if it wasn't you, then who?'

The moon was fully up by this stage and I could see Cartwright's face clearly. He seemed to be thinking this over.

'You got your heart set on spending the night here?'

I shook my head. 'I've stayed in worse places, but I'm easy.'

I'm always easy when I'm outnumbered and out-gunned.

Cartwright said something to one of the men in suits, who made a quick call on a mobile phone. Five minutes later a second shiny new Toyota Landcruiser pulled up.

I looked around for the old farmer and saw him sitting by the doorway of his shack, mumbling quietly to himself. Even as pissed as he was, you had to wonder if all these guns were bringing back memories he'd rather not recall. And maybe, like me, he'd been wondering if it was all about to end out on this hillside tonight.

Cartwright said something to one of his men, who went round to the rear of the second vehicle and came back with a couple of bottles of Martell cognac. The man put the bottles down next to the farmer and then pulled a wad of cash from his pocket. The old man accepted the money with a smile but it was easy to see he was a lot more interested in the cognac. He already had the top off one bottle when I walked over to say goodbye. I got the impression he wasn't going to be sharing this little windfall.

The two men with the TEC-9s climbed into the first Land-Cruiser and Cartwright and I got in the second. The doors closed with a very heavy thud and I tapped the window glass. The doors and windows on the vehicle would probably stop anything short of a .50-calibre bullet.

'Expecting trouble?' I asked.

'Always,' Cartwright said. 'How do you think I've managed to stay dead this long?'

Chapter Nineteen

Our two-car convoy headed down to the main road and then turned towards Dien Bien Phu township.

'Cheese.' Cartwright was looking out of his window back towards the valley.

'Cheese?'

'Early on in the battle for Dien Bien Phu, Vietminh artillery barrages scored a direct hit on a major supply dump. It was a devastating blow to French morale.'

'Ammo?'

'Cheese,' he said. 'And condiments.'

'Not the bloody Dijon mustard?'

He nodded. 'At one stage later on during the siege, a group of French Foreign Legionnaires fought their way out through the perimeter and destroyed an enemy bunker. It was only after they were decorated for bravery that the brass discovered the real objective was to recover a load of army-issue wine concentrate called Vinogel that had been dropped by parachute and landed outside the wire.'

'Dehydrated plonk? They send dehydrated water to go with it? Seems like a pretty weird way to fight a war.'

Cartwright smiled. 'The French do things their own way. The Americans handled it all a bit differently, of course. They choppered in hot meals to their troops in the field when it was possible, and the larger bases had all the comforts of home with burgers and steaks and ice cream and cherry pie. The Vietminh and the VC usually just carried rice and ate whatever they could beg, borrow or steal. When you're hungry enough, rat and rice and some fish sauce is quite palatable. It's the freedom-fighters' diet.'

'From what I know about Dien Bien Phu,' I said, 'those freedom fighters did a lot of their heroic advancing knowing that if they turned around to retreat, they'd get a bullet from their own officers or cadres.'

Cartwright shrugged. 'The soldier on the ground, the Digger, the Tommy, the Poilu, the GI rarely understands the big picture. Just as well, too - it's so easy to become disillusioned.'

'That what happened to you?'

'Perhaps,' he said.

Ten minutes later, Cartwright got a call on his mobile phone. He spoke for a couple of minutes in Vietnamese then ended the call and spoke to the driver, who nodded.

'It's still several hours' drive to our destination so perhaps we should stop for some food at the next village.'

Twenty minutes later the vehicle in front slowed down, flashed its indicator and pulled up outside a small roadside café. The place had a thatched roof and no walls, and the noise of a soap opera playing on the TV carried out to the roadway, Cartwright's bodyguards jumped out of the first Landcruiser and gave the joint the once-over before beckoning us to climb down.

A bloke sitting on a small Yamaha motorcycle appeared to be waiting for us. He spoke briefly to one of the bodyguards and pointed into the café. The bodyguard handed over a wad of notes, which the waiting man pocketed before starting his bike and riding off.

The café had a dirt floor, an open kitchen and a decided lack of Michelin stars. The tables were plastic and most of the seats were overturned beer crates. It looked like we were the only customers, apart from a couple of blokes who were hunched over bowls of noodle soup.

I walked over to their table and said, 'Are these seats taken?'

One of them glanced up and scowled. He looked exhausted. His shirt was ripped and muddy, and his face and arms were covered in scratches and nasty-looking welts.

'Bugger me,' he said, 'a man almost gets blown up in a chopper and then spends a couple of days slipping and sliding down the side of a bloody mountain and getting bitten by mosquitoes and chewed on by leeches and ticks, and then he can't even get to sit down to a bowl of noodles in peace.'

Peter Cartwright walked up behind me. 'Hello, Jack,' he said, 'you look like something the cat dragged in.'

'At least I'm alive, which is apparently more than we could say for you for quite a long time.'

'I heard the same thing about you.'

Jack smiled. Yeah, well a serious case of sudden death tends to keep the bad guys off your tail.'

'That was my plan, too,' Cartwright said.

Jack gestured across the table. 'This is my mate, VT.'

Cartwright and VT shook hands. VT was in the same battered condition as Jack.

'How's the soup?' I asked.

'Not bad,' Jack said. 'This is my second bowl and then they've got half a bloody water buffalo on the grill for us. Why don't you blokes pull up a pew and join us?'

The only problem with sitting down to dinner with three dead men is you just know you'll be stuck with the bill.

Chapter Twenty

Jack and VT slept in the back of the lead Land Cruiser for the rest of the trip and I snoozed in the second with Cartwright.

Around two in the morning we passed through a prosperous-looking village and then detoured up a paved side road and stopped at a heavy-duty security checkpoint manned by half a dozen very alert sentries and a couple of German shepherd guard dogs. Cartwright and the bodyguards got out and had an animated conversation with the men.

While I waited, I studied the chain-link fence topped with razor wire that ran off into the jungle on either side of the checkpoint. In a couple of spots, rectangular metal boxes about the size of a hefty paperback were wired to the fence.

'The Claymores are a nice decorating touch,' I said when Cartwright climbed back into the Landcruiser.

He laughed. 'We used to call 'em VC TVs.'

The curved front on the boxes did give them the look of a small television set, but the only programme they showed was a lethal anti-personnel blast of hundreds of steel ball bearings.

'They're not armed,' Cartwright continued, 'we just stuck 'em there to let people know I'm serious about my privacy. Okay, let's go.'

On Cartwright's order, we drove through the heavy metal gates, past the floodlights, the armed guards and the barbed wire, and continued up the hill. It was another ten minutes before we reached a large two-storey stone building with a wide verandah. Even in the dark, I could see the joint wouldn't have been out of place in rural France. The masonry walls appeared to be a couple of feet thick, which would help keep out the heat of the day and the chill of the night, and probably even slow down the odd rocket-propelled grenade.

As Cartwright and I walked across the verandah, I noticed the plaster façade had been patched in a number of places. The patches were of varying colours and age.

'In the old days this place was shot up on a regular basis by the Vietminh, the French, the Vietcong, the North Vietnamese Army and even the American Air Force on a couple of occasions,' Cartwright explained.

There were a dozen or so white plaster patches around the front door. I rubbed one and it crumbled slightly under my fingers.

'Plaster takes over forty years to dry in the tropics, I guess.'

Cartwright smiled. 'Upkeep on an old building like this is a constant headache.'

The slamming car doors and barking dogs had woken our sleeping passengers and there were numerous servants waiting to corral the visitors, leading them off to guest rooms with offers of late-night snacks or coffee. I passed on everything but a bed, and found myself in a simply furnished upstairs room with a four-poster bed with mosquito netting, an en-suite bathroom and French doors opening out onto a balcony.

From the balcony I could see moonlight shimmering on water and hear a constant splashing. I figured whatever was out there was still going to be there in the morning and decided to take a long hot shower and then hit the sack.

While the water ran over me, I thought about the faint smell in the air I'd noticed as we'd climbed out of the Toyotas. There was the perfume of flowers but also something else, something more familiar. I guessed there could be a chance someone had been letting off fireworks in the major's garden earlier in the evening, but those fresh plaster patches around Cartwright's front door and the sentries on high alert made me think maybe it had been fireworks of another sort.

Chapter Twenty-One

Around ten the next morning I found Cartwright downstairs on a screened terrace overlooking the hillside in front of the farmhouse. He was sitting in a cane chair drinking coffee, the two bodyguards positioned at either end of the terrace, just out of earshot. A servant poured boiling water into a small metal container sitting on top of a cup, which he placed in front of me.

'Sleep okay?' Cartwright asked.

I nodded, waiting for the hot water to drip slowly through the tightly packed coffee grounds and down into the sweetened condensed milk in the bottom of my cup.

'Sound of the water didn't bother you?'

I shook my head.

Stretching down the gently sloping hillside and off into the distance were huge circular ponds, each with a fountain gushing in the middle or quickly spinning paddlewheels attached to a floating pontoon. From time to time there was a silver flash and then a splash as a fish jumped clear of the water.

'The fountains and paddles oxygenate the water,' Cartwright explained. He pointed to a sideboard. 'We've got fresh croissants and pain au chocolat, baguettes and cold meats, cheeses, yoghurt and fruit. Or the cook can do you eggs, bacon or whatever. And if you want grilled fish, we've got plenty!'

'The coffee's fine until I wake up,' I said.

I looked at the view and sipped my coffee. Both the caffeine hit and the view were pretty spectacular. There were hills on every side of us, not quite as dramatic as those surrounding the valley at Dien Bien Phu, but still impressive.

'So what was it like hearing they were making a movie about your life? Must have been a bit weird.'

Cartwright shrugged. 'I'm a bloke who's been awarded a posthumous Victoria Cross, so weird is all relative. Reckon it's going to be a good film?'

'You can never tell at this stage. Apparently when money got tight the producers offered the cast and crew working on the first Mad Max film a profit share in lieu of wages and got laughed off the set. The picture took over a hundred million bucks worldwide, so that should tell you something. It'll either be good or it won't - that's show business.'

'I always thought Mel Gibson should play me,' Cartwright said, 'back when the idea for the film first came up. Much too old now, of course. What's the bloke they're using like? He looks the part, I'll give you that.'

'You've seen him?'

'Not in the flesh. I've been checking out your stills on the internet.'

'He's an actor, what can I say. Intense, dedicated, committed, neurotic, psychotic, self-focused, self-obsessed, self-loathing, egocentric and gentle, caring and kind. Pick any two, except the last three.'

'Not a poofter, is he?'

This was an interesting conversational turn. I shook my head. 'Who knows? He's got a wife and a couple of kids back in Australia, and if you'd had the local cops in Saigon dust most of our female extras for his fingerprints I doubt they'd have come up empty-handed.'

'Still, you never know, I guess,' he said. 'I mean Jack Stark and VT... that was a bit of a surprise.'

I had a feeling I knew where this was going and I didn't much like it.

'That's right,' I said, 'you never know. And people tend to use the word "gay" these days in polite company, just so you know. You fancy another coffee? I'm having one.'

Cartwright shook his head. I walked over to the sideboard and helped myself to a croissant and some more coffee. I'd hoped it might be a good way to change the subject, but it didn't work.

'VT is a good bloke,' Cartwright said, after a pause, 'and he's still a good-looking bastard. Must have been drop-dead handsome when he was younger. It's a bit of a shame, don't you think? It just doesn't seem right, somehow.'

I took a deep breath and turned around, but just before I opened my mouth to set Cartwright straight on a few things, I caught the twinkle in his eye.

'I mean,' he said, 'you'd bloody think VT could have done a whole lot better for himself than a rough nut like Jack Stark.'

It was a nice little ambush and I'd walked right into it.

Cartwright was smiling and seemed very pleased with himself.

"You bastard.'

'Had you going for a bit, didn't I?' he said. 'And I've changed my mind about that coffee, if that's okay.'

'It's great coffee. You grow it around here?' I asked, handing him a cup.

Cartwright nodded. 'It's local, from up on the hillside. This whole place was a coffee plantation in the old days. French planter built the original house in the 1920s.'

'And you put the fish ponds in?'

'Nope, they came courtesy of the United States Air Force back in the seventies. A B-52 strike took out a lot of the coffee plantation but left all of those nice round craters.'

'What were they aiming for?'

'God knows, probably the ground since there was nothing here but coffee bushes. Might have been someone in trouble making a run for home, back to Andersen Air Force Base on Guam or U-Tapao in Thailand. Jettisoned their bomb load after getting hit by a surface-to-air missile over Hanoi, maybe.'

'Well, it's a lovely place, no matter who did the digging. And it looks like the fish side of things is booming.'

He smiled. 'Fish farming was the wife's family's business. They started with a couple of carp in a wooden bucket a few hundred years ago and now we own fish farms like this one all over Vietnam.'

'Nice little earner.'

'We have an excellent management team who are the public face of the business and I like it that way. I've always enjoyed the isolation, and after my wife passed away I found fewer and fewer reasons for leaving the place.'

I understood the sentiment. Sitting on that terrace day after day, seeing nothing but the ponds and the mountains in the distance and the constantly changing sky, could become addictive.

"Going to Saigon was a mistake.'

'Why did you go?' I asked.

'I had to see a man about a fish.'

"Was your son, Peter, the man you were seeing?'

Cartwright nodded. 'Peter's a biologist, specialising in aquaculture. Smart bugger, too. Nothing about the fish-breeding side of the business he doesn't know. But being spotted in Saigon was unfortunate. It seems to have set off a chain reaction.'

'You got that right. Any idea why?'

'Maybe. How's your barbecuing technique?'

Chapter Twenty-Two

'Napoleon had it wrong when he said that an army marches on its stomach.'

As comments go, it was a real barbecue stopper, especially if you were standing in the middle of a bunch of ex-soldiers.

Jack and VT had finally surfaced after twelve hours' sleep and they looked a lot better for it. Jack's first move after having a coffee was to take the barbecue tongs off me. Now he stopped, holding the marinated half-chicken he was turning in mid-air.

'Okay, I'll bite,' he said, carefully putting the chicken back over the coals with the rest of the meat.

'An army marches on its feet,' Cartwright continued,' and those feet need to be in boots and you need socks to go with them. And to stay alive you need a rifle and ammunition and a bayonet and a helmet. On day one at any military boot camp they don't just give you a haircut and a ham sandwich - they give you the gear, all the crap a soldier needs to be a soldier. And all that gear they give you comes from where?'

'I'll give it a shot,' Jack said, 'the quartermaster?'

Cartwright nodded. 'Correct. And with all the millions of pieces of gear coming and going at any one time, an officer in the Quartermaster

Corp with their own private agenda has ideal cover for all sorts of mischief. In '69 1 was called in by the US Army to get close to a quartermaster who someone thought was looking a bit dodgy.'

'And was he?' I asked.

'Depends on how you define dodgy, I reckon. Being in bed with a Hong Kong gangster in an operation to process opium from the Golden Triangle into heroin in a mountain village with its own laboratories and airstrip, and then shipping the heroin via military transport aircraft into Hong Kong and the US could probably come under that definition.'

'Could do, I suppose,' I said.

'I got roped into the situation by a US military investigator - I did counter-insurgency training with his brother at a camp near Vung Tau. The thinking was that since I was from outside the Yank military, and had a bit of an awkward history with the police before I joined up, they could sell me as someone who might be into making some money on the side, no questions asked.'

'And it worked?' I asked.

'Smooth as silk,' Cartwright said. 'They set me up to bump into the Chinese gangster - a guy called Peng - while I was on R& R in Honkers and I managed to get a lot of good background, including the location of the village where they were running this opium-refining operation. I was moving in with a company of Vietnamese Rangers to raid the village and gather evidence for a court martial when the quartermaster somehow got wind that his cover was blown.'

'How'd that happen?' Jack asked.

'I never found out, but somehow he must have twigged and decided it was time to pull the plug.'

Which involved?'

'My men had the village staked out, doing surveillance on the operation, taking photographs, all the usual stuff. One afternoon a bunch of Hueys and a couple of C-123s flew in from Saigon. Place was chock-a-block with bad guys for what looked like a high-level management meeting. Everyone was there, apart from this quartermaster geezer and the Chinese gangster.'

'Which was pretty convenient for you,' I said.

He nodded. 'Almost too good to be true. Everyone together in a neat little package and all I had to do was tie up the bow. I guess I should have seen it coming. An hour later, the village, the couple of hundred people in it, the heroin-processing plant, the bad guys and my rangers were all gone.'

'Gone?'

'Off the face of the earth. You can't see or hear B-52s on a high-level strike and a three-plane cell can dump over three hundred 500-pound bombs in one go. One moment it's all kids laughing and playing, women hanging clothes out to dry, dogs barking, pens full of pigs and chickens, and the next it's hell on earth and you're praying to God to take you somewhere, anywhere else.

Apart from the sound of the water splashing in the fish-ponds, there was silence.

'From what I was able to piece together,' Cartwright continued, 'the rock formation under the mountaintop was limestone and the concussion from the first bomb hitting the village cracked open a fissure. I dropped straight into it, and out of harm's way, mostly. I don't know how far I fell but I had a broken shoulder and a couple of cracked ribs, or so they told me.'

'You were the only survivor?'

Cartwright nodded. 'I staggered out of the hills about a week later and I guess I was a pretty scary sight - naked, sunburned, still half-deaf, covered in dried blood and talking gibberish. A boy washing his buffalo in a creek found me and led me back to his village. The people there could have easily turned me in to the NVA but they'd already lost most of their young men, conscripted by the South Vietnamese Army or the VC, and I guess they figured they could patch me up and use me as a workhorse. They turned me over to a young girl whose husband had been conscripted by the ARVN and killed somewhere down south.'

'Lucky break,' I said, 'for you I mean, not him.'

'Definitely was, as it turned out,' Cartwright said. 'I was totally off the planet for a long time, shell-shocked, I guess, and it wasn't until a year or two later that stuff started to slowly come back. By that time the Americans were already scaling back their involvement and the writing was pretty much on the wall. And there I was a dead man in a tropical paradise with a bit of a weak shoulder, in love with a beautiful woman who was in love with me, and with a kid, a dozen fishponds, a comfortable hut and my very own water buffalo.'

'Sounds like heaven. So no interest at all in going back to your old life?'

Cartwright smiled. 'None whatsoever. I was pretty happy with what I had going so I stayed. It was home. First real one I'd ever had, outside the army.'

You couldn't argue with that.

'Plus there was a complication. The army investigator who'd organised for me to infiltrate the quartermaster's drug operation, and knew what was going on, had got himself shot dead in a cyclo outside the old Continental Hotel in Saigon a couple of days after the bombing.'

'Those cyclos can be bloody dangerous,' I said. 'But that sounds like a convenient coincidence.'

'For the bad guys maybe, but not for me,' Cartwright said. 'The military inquiry into the shooting concluded it was a random VC assassination. But in any event, the bloke wasn't around to back up my story of what I'd really been doing, if anyone wanted to start slinging mud.'

'So you decided to let sleeping dogs lie.'

'In the case of these particular dogs, it seemed like a good idea. Peng and the quartermaster, a man called Captain Crockett, went on to bigger and better things.'

'Would that be Peng of the Peng casino interests in Macau?' Jack asked

Cartwright nodded. 'You know him?'

'VT and I live in Macau,' Jack said, 'and you hear the Peng family name a lot there.'

'Old Peng, they called him,' Cartwright continued, 'even back then when he was young, because he was the head of the clan. A seriously nasty piece of work was Old Peng, let me tell you. People who crossed him usually lost a finger or a hand or their head, depending on the level of the transgression. Bastard moved into Macau, using his drug profits to bankroll a casino. A few decades on, he's rich and respectable and revered for his charitable good works, support for the arts and the spectacular all-you-can-eat buffets in his casino.'

'Story going around Macau is that Old Peng had a major stroke a while back,' Jack said. 'He's stuck in a wheelchair and pretty much off with the pixies, I've heard, which is some kind of justice I suppose.

His son Playford is running the casino now. But what happened to this Captain Crockett character?'

Cartwright laughed. 'It's all about American upward mobility. Captain Vaughan Crockett left the military and used his share of the loot to build himself a nice little empire in construction and transport - what people now like to call logistics. In the eighties he got himself elected to the US Congress for a couple of terms, which was reasonably easy for a guy with no scruples, a ton of money and a chest full of medals, even if they were for clocking-in on time and meritorious distribution of Kool-Aid and toilet paper.'

The medals bit sounded about right. I'd actually met a Yank soldier who'd been tasked with printing a unit newspaper when his CO in Vietnam found out he'd been a graphic designer before being drafted. The bloke ordered a printing press, which turned up in its own shipping container with a ton of ink and paper, plus a complete darkroom with cameras and film and chemicals. So he ordered three more presses and when they showed up he linked them all together and set to work. This bloke actually earned himself a medal for being the first soldier to produce a full-colour newspaper in a combat zone.

'War is hell,' Jack said, 'and sometimes very, very weird.'

'Crockett bailed from government service two steps ahead of some awkward questions about his involvement with lobbyists, and used his contacts to expand his construction and transport empire. He also set himself up a contracting business, supplying mercenaries called the Black Falcon Group. Did very well out of Iraq.'

'And this would be the same Vaughan Crockett...?' I asked.

'Yep. The Honourable, or I guess not-so-honourable to those in the know, Vaughan Tyrone Crockett, United States Ambassador to Australia, and according to rumour on several political blogs, a possible candidate for vice-president to the next occupant of the White House.'

'That would seem to be a man with many, many things to hide,' VT said.

And he'd need to hide them well. The vetting process for a potential US vice-presidential candidate entails his own party ripping his life apart, looking for anything embarrassing - like did he pay his taxes on time or bonk the nanny or smoke dope and molest sheep or his roommates while in college? Then, once he was nominated, the media would get stuck in, looking for even the slightest hint of scandal - not, of course, in the interest of the American voter's right to know and make an informed choice, but rather because scandal is guaranteed to increase circulation and raise ratings.

'Crockett has become very adept at hiding things over the years,' Cartwright said. 'Anyone who gets even close to the real story is taken down by his spin machine at MB&F.

'Markham, Barkin & Fargo handle his PR?' I asked.

'Yep,' Cartwright replied, 'and they're bloody good at it. Crockett actually owns the operation. MB&F haven't met a tin-pot despot, crooked politician or corrupt corporation they didn't like. And if you threaten any part of Vaughan Crockett's idyllic little life or his business interests, the fine folks at MB&F will dig up a twenty-year-old parking ticket and creatively infer you got it when you left your car illegally parked for five minutes while picking up some hookers, drugs or kiddie porn. Or all three.'

'Nice people,' I said.

'Plus, for the things that MB&F can't manage to spin there are a lot of other people on call to do Crockett's really dirty work.'

'I would guess we've met some of them recently,' Jack said.

I nodded. 'I think that's right, Jack, and I think I may have been the one who arranged the introductions.'

Chapter Twenty-Three

Over lunch, I filled in Jack, VT and Cartwright about my encounter with Brett Tozer in the lobby of the Indochine Luxe Royale.

'I guess he mentioned our conversation to head office, and someone decided the best solution was to make the problem go away, permanently, starting with Brett.'

'Poor bastard probably never knew what hit him,' Jack said. 'Talk about shooting the bloody messenger.'

'Yeah, literally,' I said. 'I figure Brett was looking out for Crockett's interests on the film and reporting any unusual developments back to MB&F, without really knowing why. Cushy job for him - a month on a movie set in Asia and then Australia with excellent catering, accommodation and a nice per diem.'

'Lousy termination package, though,' Cartwright said.

'You've got that right. Then around the time Brett gets eliminated, I find a bunch of goons waiting for me down a dark alleyway in a Russian jeep, a 45-calibre welcoming committee in Chiang Rai, and Jack and VT have problems in the Huey,'

Cartwright nodded. 'Plus my recent nocturnal visitors.'

'That new plasterwork by the front door?' l asked.

'So VT and I weren't the only one who'd noticed,' Jack said.

Cartwright smiled. 'Last night while we were out looking for you, three men with submachine guns and an RPG launcher came visiting. They got through the perimeter wire without being spotted but the bastards didn't make it closer than a hundred yards to the house. My people took care of that.'

'Did Crockett send them?'

'They didn't say, Alby. Didn't say much of anything, really, and they're not talking now. They're somewhere out in the coffee plantations fertilising next year's harvest.'

I'd been about to get myself another cup of coffee but I changed my mind.

'As I said,' Cartwright continued, 'a man with Crockett's connections has a lot of people to do the real dirty work, like late-night visits or bringing down a chopper.'

'And speaking of that,' I said, 'from what was on the TV news, that crash didn't look like something you guys could've walked away from. What happened?'

'Booby-trap,' Jack said. 'Some bastard blew up a perfectly nice chopper, and almost took us with it.'

VT put down his knife and fork. 'We went north from Saigon in short hops, necessary given the Huey's limited range. Our plan was to hand the helicopter back to the People's Air Force in Hanoi and then rent a car and drive down this way, Jack was determined to track you down, Peter, and he had discovered that this place was listed as the headquarters for Tranh Fisheries and Aquaculture Enterprises.'

'But when we hit Hanoi we still had a day to spare,' Jack added, 'so I figured we could fit in a quick side-trip to check out Dien Bien Phu valley.'

'But we got to Dien Bien Phu Airport late,' VT continued, 'so we decided to spend the night in town. I went through the shutdown checklist and then made sure the ship was tied down securely for the night. I also had the fuel topped off as we intended to make an early start next morning. During the evening my sister's granddaughter, Miss Hoang, you remember her, Alby? The policewoman..'

I nodded. Boy, did I remember Miss Hoang

'. . .she called me,' he continued, 'and told me what had happened to you and suggested that we be cautious. It was cold the next morning, and as I did my pre-flight checks I could smell fuel. I noticed some spillage around the fuel filler cap, like an overflow. Then, when I crawled under the ship to use the tap that bleeds off any water condensation from the fuel lines, I found this.'

He pulled a shiny metal object from his shirt pocket. It was a circular piece of steel, like a large key ring, and there was a split pin attached to it. He handed it to Cartwright.

'Safety pin,' Cartwright said, 'from a hand grenade.'

VT nodded. 'We Vietnamese became very adept at improvising weapons and making booby-traps. It comes from a long history of fighting off powerful foreign invaders using very limited resources.'

Jack nodded. 'An old favourite was securing the spring-loaded handle of a grenade with duct tape or a heavy elastic band and then pulling the pin and dropping the grenade into a fuel tank. The grenade is armed, but the tape keeps it safe.'

'Until the fuel eats through the elastic or dissolves the adhesive on the tape and releases the handle,' VT said. 'The fuse is activated and four or five seconds later...'

Jack smiled. 'KA-BOOM!'

'At which time,' Cartwright said, 'if they've used the right amount of tape or a thick enough elastic band, I'm guessing you blokes are at 1500 feet over some piece of trackless jungle?'

'That's the drill,' Jack said, 'and an explosion or fire in a helicopter at 1500 feet isn't something you want to deal with 'cos there ain't no bloody place to go. Some chopper pilots in 'Nam made pacts with their co-pilots that in the event of a hit and high-altitude fire, whoever was still functioning would shoot the other person and then themselves.'

Nobody said anything. There really wasn't anything to say.

'So,' Jack continued, 'this type of booby-trap is very hard to time accurately, so we assumed someone gave a signal by telephone or radio to drop the grenade into the rank just as we approached the airfield. It was the displaced fuel overflowing that tipped off VT. Saved by Archimedes' principle you could say.'

'So what did you do?' I asked.

'Well, there were a bunch of goons hanging around trying to look like mechanics and failing badly, so we reckoned they had a Plan B if we twigged to Plan A. Plan B had to be just as nasty and we weren't armed so we took a punt on having a safety window of at least ten minutes and took off, keeping low. I figured it would be better to put her down in a hard-to-access area, so we'd get a good head start on someone looking for bodies to confirm the kill. I don't think either of us took a breath until we were on the ground.'

'From what I saw on the TV it didn't look like you could land a chopper in the middle of all that jungle.'

'VT's the man,' Jack said. 'He picked a grove of bamboo and dropped us down into the middle of it with the chopper blades tearing through the foliage. It was like flying a gigantic whipper snipper.'

'That works?'

'The rotor blades on the Huey have heavy counterweights on the tips,' VT explained, 'and if the vegetation isn't too thick and you have a clear slot for the tail rotor, you can chop your way through.'

'And if it's too thick?'

'That's a whole 'nother ugly story,' Jack said, 'and if it had happened, we wouldn't be here telling you about it. But VT got it right and we grabbed our backpacks and hit the frog and toad as soon as those bloody skids touched the dirt. Excellent timing, too. Probably didn't get more than a couple of hundred feet away before the whole thing went up. Big bang, heat, concussion and we both got blown arse over teakettle and woke up several hundred yards further down the hillside.'

'And nothing was broken?'

Nope. We were bloody lucky. Apart from the obvious scratches and bruises, I've got a couple of ribs that feel a bit ordinary and VT twisted his knee pretty badly, which is why it took us all that time to get down the mountain and find a friendly local to give us a lift to the nearest noodle shop, where you found us.'

Jack looked at Cartwright and smiled. 'Quite a coincidence,' he said.

I remembered that phone call in the Toyota and the bloke waiting on the motorcycle outside the café pocketing a wad of cash. I guessed Cartwright's people had put the word out that they were looking for a couple of blokes who'd recently fallen out of the sky.

Chapter Twenty-Four

After lunch, Jack and VT got ready to head back to Macau while Cartwright gave me the full guided tour, with Heckle and Jeckle and their TEC-9s following at a discreet distance. If you discounted the security fences, the bodyguards and all the firepower, Cartwright's joint was an oasis of calm. Chickens were scratching about, the trees were heavy with fruit, the air was clean and staff were feeding the fish or checking the water quality in the ponds. You could see why a bloke wouldn't want to leave.

We took a breather out of the midafternoon sun in a small tile-roofed gazebo in a bamboo grove. It looked like it had been recently built on a landscaped area between two of the big ponds. A fresh pot of jasmine tea was waiting for us in a wicker basket.

'This was the site of Pond 27,' Cartwright said, handing me a cup. 'I thought it would make a nice spot for a bit of contemplation and reflection.'

'Pond 27?' I said, looking around. 'Given the lack of water, I guess the Yank bomb that hit this spot was a dud.'

'There was a pond here but I had it filled in.'

'Any particular reason?' I asked.

'What do you know about fish, Alby?'

'Fresh is best,' I said, 'don't overcook it and don't order it in a restaurant on Mondays. And it's probably wise to serve it with white wine to a purist like Jack.'

He smiled. 'Right now, the world is in a fish-farming frenzy. I've got pilot projects growing Finnish rainbow trout in the central and northern highlands. You can grow them up to one and a half kilos in just twelve months, with a projected yield of up to thirty tonnes per hectare. Other people are working with sturgeon from Russia.'

'Really?' I said, 'I had no idea it was that intensive.'

'Here in Vietnam we do catfish, shrimp, even shellfish. And carp. The Vietnamese love carp, grow them in their rice paddies as well as on fish farms. They grow fast, too, Probably grow more carp than all the fish raised by aquaculture in Australia, but you can't give the bloody things away to Australians - they don't like the taste, reckon they're muddy.'

'Guess it's all in how you prepare them. I've had carp in Japan and Spain, and even salt-roasted in Baghdad, and it was pretty damn tasty.'

'People might just have to get used to eating all sorts of fish,' Cartwright said. 'Aquaculture has become the great hope for a planet with empty oceans. But one of the reasons the world's stocks are almost depleted, apart from a century of mechanised overfishing, is that we have been scooping out fish from the oceans to make fishmeal to feed to farmed fish.'

'That doesn't seem to make a whole lot of sense.'

'Exactly, especially when it can take up to five kilos of fish-meal to put one kilo on a farmed salmon. There are researchers working on this problem all over the world. They're making fishmeal out of corn and soybeans and testing different qualities and quantities for different stages of the growth cycle. All well and good, I suppose, but now that corn is also used to make sweeteners and bio-fuels, other food crops are being displaced to feed this growing market.'

'And your son is working on the problem?'

'From a different angle. Peter wasn't interested in better fish food: he was interested in a new and better fish.'

'We don't already have enough to choose from?'

'What the world really needs is a robust, tasty, fast-growing fish that will eat almost anything and put on condition on the basis of a kilo of weight per kilo of food.'

'I'd like to see that.'

'So would I, Alby, but so far no-one has. However, it looked for a while that Peter might have been on the right track with something we were calling Project PB. We hoped it would become the world's farmed fish of choice - a real coup for Vietnam and an economic boon for this region in particular. These people have been good to me, and they kept my secret for thirty years, so I owe them a lot.'

'Can we whack one in a steamer with some ginger, soy sauce and spring onions and have a taste?'

He shook his head. 'I'm afraid not. The first batch should have been reaching plate size by now, but unfortunately there were ... complications'

'Complications?'

Cartwright nodded. 'Nine months ago Pond 27 was home to the pilot batch of PB, but we drained it, incinerated all the young fish with flamethrowers, filled in the pond, and the gardeners made me this spot to relax.'

Jesus, mate, flamethrowers?'

'You'd be amazed at some of the stuff the Americans left behind, Alby.'

'Sounds a bit drastic,' I said. 'Did they taste that bad?'

It wasn't the taste of the fish that was the problem. It was their appetite... 'he paused for a moment,' ... and their attitude.'

'You raised fish with attitude?'

Cartwright refilled our teacups before he spoke. 'Project PB was all about producing the perfect genetically engineered fish, and it took us almost five years. We based this new fish on wild barramundi for their desirable taste characteristics and because they're euryhaline.'

'Meaning?'

'Meaning they can live in both fresh and salt water which increases the farming options. We also made them more temperature tolerant so they could be raised as far south as Tasmania. Peter combined these positive attributes with the omnivorous and vigorous eating habits of certain members of the South American *Characidae* family, found mainly in the Amazon and Orinoco Rivers. *Characidae* are more generally known as piranha.'

I knew the piranha is a little freshwater fish with very big teeth and an even bigger appetite. South American folklore is full of stories of people or animals being attacked in rivers and creeks and winding up as a pile of bones in a matter of minutes.

'And this particular barramundi-piranha combination didn't really work out?'

'You could say that. Peter was working with the *Serrasalmus rhombeus* variety from Suriname in the northern part of South America, between French Guiana and Guyana, and it may not have been the wisest choice. What he finally produced was a large, fast-growing and delicious fish, but unfortunately also a savage and extremely aggressive one. They move in packs rather than schools, and apparently found us as palatable as we found them.'

Jesus! How big are these things?' I asked.

'We calculated that they could have grown up to a metre in length, but the damn things were aggressive right from hatching. One of our researchers unthinkingly dangled his hand in the water of Pond 27 from a boat and was nearly dragged in. The man lost his right arm up to the elbow. The flesh was stripped down to the bone in less than thirty seconds.'

Despite the tropical afternoon heat, I shivered.

'I cancelled the project immediately, of course,' Cartwright continued, 'and ordered the destruction of all our stock. Fish farming in this country is a labour intensive enterprise and to my mind it wasn't worth risking the life of the workers.'

'Smart move. Pity though. It sounds like your super fish could have been the answer to the world's food problem.'

'Some people say the problem the world faces today, Alby, isn't a shortfall in food.'

'Really?'

'There are some who feel the problem the world actually faces is a surplus of people.'

I thought of the science-fiction film from the seventies in which Chuck Heston discovered the government was feeding an exploding population by secretly mincing up the dead, the elderly and the anti-social elements before adding a splash of food colouring and stamping them out as a tasty snack bar named Soylent Green.

'Then maybe your Project PB was the solution, after all,' I said. 'We could have simply chopped up all those surplus people and fed them to your piranha-cum-barramundi.

He smiled. 'One possible solution, but probably not something that would be palatable to the politicians.'

Or to the punters lining up at the fish and chip shop - might have been a bit of a problem serving up a fish that could have been fattened on the homeless or their old Aunty Gwen.'

Chapter Twenty-Five

'IF YOUR PROJECT WAS CANCELLED, AND ALL THE FISH DESTROYED, WHAT got you down to Saigon?'

Cartwright said he had something he wanted to show me in the main house, so we started walking back in that direction.

'You've heard of ANL Fischer Seafoods, right?' Cartwright said.

'The big fish wholesalers?'

He nodded. 'ANL Fischer is a major importer of farmed seafood into Australia and the US. I picked up rumblings on the aquaculture grapevine that their CEO, Detlef Fischer, was expanding his business into fish farming through a new company called Fischer Aquaculture Industries. And when I began hearing rumours that he had a new fast-growing, great-tasting wonder fish out of Vietnam, I got a bit concerned!

'You think Fischer somehow managed to get his hands on a batch of your Project PB fish?'

Cartwright didn't answer.

'If he did, couldn't he breed more of these wonder fish to his heart's content.'

Cartwright shook his head. 'Characteristics built into genetically engineered fish that make them suitable for pond rearing could be a problem if the fish escaped and managed to breed with their wild cousins, so farming fish like ours are always deliberately bred sterile.'

'And so the people who own the genetic blueprint can make an ongoing profit selling the actual fish for food and the fingerlings for restocking'

'Exactly,' Cartwright said.

'Same as those genetically modified grain crops where the poor bloody farmer has to buy new seed every year.'

'It took us five years of hard work and a major investment to produce Project PB, Alby, and we deserve a return on all that time and money. But after the accident I instructed Peter to destroy all the records and samples of the fish so that no more could be bred.'

'But if Fischer was planning on farming these things, he'd need a guaranteed source of supply for the fingerlings.'

Cartwright nodded.

'So was that what the blue outside your place in Saigon was all about?'

'I told Peter about Detlef Fischer and the wonder fish rumours and asked him if he was involved. He denied any knowledge and things got a bit heated between us, I'm afraid. I wanted to believe him, but I'd made some inquiries and learned that Fischer had been visiting Saigon on a regular basis over the past six months.'

We'd reached the house and Cartwright led me into an office on the ground floor. It was all wood panelling and heavy antique furniture and looked very last century, apart from the computer on the desk. Cartwright nudged the mouse on the desktop to wake up the computer.

He clicked on a bookmark, and a web page for ANL Fischer Seafoods appeared on the screen. Cartwright clicked through the pages.

'Lot of boring bumph about the history of the company and what they're up to. Nothing about fish farming, though. Then I found this.' He clicked the mouse again. 'You've heard of Jezebel Quick?'

I nodded, trying not to look surprised. 'I've seen her TV show.'

There was a photograph of a smiling Jezebel with her arm around a bloke wearing a dinner suit. He was in his early thirties, I figured, blond-haired and blue-eyed with a demeanour that said private school, rugger bugger, trust fund and I can buy and sell you out of petty cash so fuck off. It was the kind of look that you just knew made valet parking attendants want to urinate in the ashtray of his Lotus Elise.

In the picture, Jezebel was wearing a dress with a plunging neckline that appeared to stop just short of her ankles. The caption said it was taken at a charity event with an auction where Fischer had made a winning bid of fifty thousand dollars for a private dinner with Jezebel. Dinner to be cooked and served by her in her penthouse apartment in Melbourne's swish waterfront Docklands development. The picture was dated about six months earlier.

'So what's the connection?'

'I heard she and Fischer became an item after that dinner, so I Googled her.'

Cartwright typed in Jezebel's name and her website came up - jezebelshotstuff.com. The welcoming image was of a smiling Jezebel leaning forward and offering the viewer a plate of succulent deep-fried ricotta-stuffed zucchini flowers and a fantastic view down her cleavage.

'The lady seems to lead with her tits,' Cartwright said.

He had that right.

He clicked on a link to her blog named 'Watch This Space'.

This page featured a picture of Jezebel posing in waders and holding a fishing rod. It was next to a short, recently posted item cryptically referring to big news that was coming soon about something that would knock the socks off fish lovers - a great-tasting and affordable farmed fish that was going to revolutionise the seafood market.

'I heard she was going to be in Saigon, so after I spoke to Peter I figured I might try and track her down and ask a few questions, to suss out if there was a connection between my son and Fischer.'

'Did you manage to catch up with her?' I asked.

He shook his head. 'The day after my meeting with Peter he emailed me a photograph from the video surveillance camera outside his building, showing two men who had come asking questions. I recognised Jack immediately, but I didn't know who you were. The smart course of action was to make myself scarce again. It was all getting a bit dicey and I didn't want to blow my cover.'

'Unfortunately, it was a bit late for that.'

'In any case, I figured if Fischer had somehow managed to get his hands on a batch of Project PB fingerlings it wouldn't take him long to discover the bloody things weren't worth the risk.'

Bloody things' seemed like an apt description.

'But I can't imagine that your son would have turned the results of five years of hard work over to someone like Fischer,' I said. 'Was Peter short of money? Did Fischer have anything on him?'

'You have any kids?' Cartwright asked.

I shook my head.

'It's always been hard for Peter,' he said, 'being a child of one of the invaders from the American War. Military occupations and civil wars both tend to engender bitterness that runs deep and lasts for generations.'

Anyone who'd spent time in the American South could vouch for that. One hundred and forty years on, there were still a lot of people grumpy about Abraham Lincoln and the War of Northern Aggression.

'And his mother's death also hit him pretty hard. People handle these pressures in different ways. Some drink or take drugs or womanise. My son, I've recently discovered, likes to gamble.'

'I'm guessing you don't mean a few bob on the Melbourne Cup once a year.'

'Over the several years Peter has been spending a lot of time in Hong Kong, which is, of course, just a short ride by jetfoil from Macau and its casinos.'

'So?'

'I believe Detlef Fischer has a backer behind his recent move into aquaculture, a silent partner, someone in the Macau casino business.'

'This Playford Peng character? The son of Crocket's former partner in crime?'

'Possibly?'

'This isn't looking good for Peter,' I said.

'Agreed. He may be in over his head and I'm not sure how to help him. I was thinking of sending him out of the country with some of my people to keep an eye on him.'

'Could be a smart move.'

I scrolled on through the website and came to a link to a page called 'Jezebel's Movements'. I crossed my fingers and clicked, praying it was just about Jezebel's travel plans. Thankfully it was. Most celebrities bitch and moan about their loss of privacy, but Jezebel was a real fame junkie who wanted everyone to know what she was up to, and the press and paparazzi loved her for it.

The page announced that Jezebel would be on a breakfast TV

programme in Hanoi the next day, and in the afternoon she would be making an appearance at the Times Square shopping centre in Causeway Bay, Hong Kong, to promote her new range of cookware.

'I was thinking about heading back to Australia,' I said, 'but maybe I'll take the Hong Kong route to see if I can connect with this Jezebel. Your Project PB and her super-tasty fish do sound like they have something in common.'

'I'd appreciate that, Alby, 'Cartwright said.' Don't put yourself in danger, though.'

'Bit late for that, mate,' I said. 'But I'll be okay. I don't think Jezebel bites.'

That wasn't actually 100 per cent true, but Cartwright didn't need to know the lurid details of my former relationship with Jezebel. He also didn't need to know that I'd noticed a comment on her web page which revealed the lady was looking forward to catching up very soon with someone she called Mister Hotlovin.

I thought back to a time long past when Jezebel had called me Mister Hotlovin.

I felt so cheap.

Chapter Twenty-Six

The ride in to Hanoi's international airport with Heckle and Jeckle watching my back was uneventful and the Barry Jones passport got me through immigration with no dramas.

Things started looking up when the Pan Oriental Airways' A330-300 Airbus had been airborne for about twenty minutes. One of the most beautiful women I'd ever seen walked down the aisle and stopped at my seat. She smiled and handed me a neatly folded piece of paper. The handwritten note simply asked if I was up for a quick shag in the first-class dunnies.

The cabin attendant was tall and slender with perfect skin, exquisite almond-shaped eyes and a face that I guessed might have been Shanghainese. Alby, I said to myself, this is one airline attempting to lift in-flight service to a whole new level.

'It's from the lady in 2G,' the beautiful woman said with another smile.

I leaned into the aisle and in the far-off nirvana that was first class I saw blonde hair and a waving hand.

'Would you like to gather your carry-on articles and come with me, Mr Murdoch.'

Would I what! Two minutes later I was up in the pointy end, ensconced in the magical domain of the well-trained cabin crew and well-heeled traveller. I took the proffered glass of champagne from the flight attendant and glanced at the passenger in the next seat.

'She said there was a lady in 2G, but it's just you.'

'Pig's arse, Alby,' Jezebel said, raising her glass, 'I'm a fucking lady.'

'I'll drink to that,' I said.

Jezebel liked to be comfortable when she travelled, and was wearing black ugg boots and an expensive red cashmere tracksuit. The zipper on her top was at half-mast and I figured we had about fifteen minutes before the pilot discovered who was on board and gave in to an irresistible urge to come and chat to the first-class passengers, or one in particular.

'I guess I should thank you for the upgrade,' I said.

She nodded. 'I saw you hanging about at the gate from the VIP lounge. I gave the purser the old famous international photographer routine and suggested economy was probably awful enough without the other passengers having to share it with a miserable prick like you, plus my arsehole film crew.'

'And I'll drink to that, too,' I said, finishing off my champagne and searching out the cabin attendant for a refill.

It was no accident that we were on the same plane, Using Jezebel's schedule of appearances from her website, I'd looked for the most likely Pan Oriental flight between Hanoi and Hong Kong and booked a seat. Jez had created Pan Oriental's in-flight menu and she flew with them whenever possible, since she got free flights and knew which meals not to order.

I'd figured I'd run into her at some stage, even if it was just collecting our bags from the carousel in Hong Kong, but this way was so much better.

My fully reclining seat was covered in glove-soft leather, the champagne was vintage and the choices on the extensive first-class à-la-carte luncheon menu were quite tempting.

'Try the lobster bisque,' Jezebel suggested, 'and get them to make you the five-mushroom omelette. Avoid that spanner-crab salad like the plague, which it might possibly give you.'

I ordered lunch and then sat back for a chat.

'Meeting up with your food tourists in Hong Kong?' I asked.

She nodded. 'They went on ahead after Hanoi while I picked up some background B-roll footage with the crew. I give 'em the kiss-off after today and about bloody time, too. It's all questions, questions, questions. They must think I'm some fucking tour guide.'

'I'm pretty sure that was what it said in the brochure, Jez.'

'Screw you too, Alby,' she said, laughing. 'So what have you been up to? Having a good time with that lady copper?'

Jezebel's preoccupations in life were Jezebel, Jezebel's sex life and Jezebel's career, so she didn't ask any awkward questions about the goings-on back in the market in Saigon. She mainly wanted to know if Nhu had used her police handcuffs during foreplay. Jezebel didn't think foreplay was worth bothering with unless it involved some rope, a block and tackle, assorted electrical appliances and half a kilo of Normandy butter, preferably unsalted. No bloody wonder I hadn't been able to hack it in that relationship for more than a couple of months.

There was one of those incredibly thin MacBook Air laptops on the table in front of her. 'I noticed you've gotten into blogging recently,' I said, changing the subject and leading her where I really wanted to go.

'It's a way of keeping in close personal touch with my millions of fans,' she said, 'and showing them I'm a caring concerned person. And it also helps me sell a shitload of saucepans and books and other crap through my website. You can even get a tracksuit like this for five hundred bucks.'

'Sounds like a lot of work. Someone do the actual writing for you?'

'I bash out the odd post when I have the time, mostly the stuff on my love-life, but my publisher found this gay guy named Preston who can write just like me and he does the day-to-day and vets the emails for anything interesting. Honest to God, Alby, some of the bloody photographs people send me... I tell you, they give the term root vegetable a whole new meaning.'

'Thanks, Jez,' I said, 'you've just put me off minestrone for life. But I was reading about a new fish surprise you've got coming up.'

'That's all very hush-hush, Alby - Detlef would give me a bloody good spanking if I spilled the beans on that one . . .'

She paused and smiled at me.

'... not that that's necessarily a bad thing,' I said, finishing off her sentence for her.

Jezebel grinned, and I remembered why I liked her. She might have been tough as nails and full of herself but, surprisingly, she didn't have a mean bone in that quite amazing body. Exactly what the hell was she doing in the middle of all this?

'Detlef's the current squeeze, then?'

She nodded. 'He and an old school friend put the deal together but there's one of those very heavy "commercial-in-confidence" contracts attached. All I can tell you is the fish lovers of the world are in for a big surprise. If things go well, yours truly will have her name very closely linked to this finny little miracle and I'm angling to make a motzah in endorsements.'

'Fish, crab, prawns, octopus? What is it exactly? Are we talking krill crackers, catfish kebabs? Give me the dope.'

She shook her head. 'No-can-do, Alby. Let's just say it'll be bloody delicious and plentiful, and leave it at that. Pretty soon the word Barrana is going to be putting the Northern Territory on the map, but for now my lips are sealed.'

She smiled and gave me a look I knew only too well and which still scared the crap out of me.

'Unless, of course,' she said, 'you actually did feel like adjourning to the first-class dunnies for some pre-prandial shenanigans.'

'Thanks for the offer, but not after what happened last time.'

Getting barred for life by British Airways was not one of my finer achievements.

Jezebel smiled again and went back to her writing. I slipped on my headphones and flicked through the hundreds of channels of entertainment on offer on the video screen, while trying to get a handle on our little chat.

The Northern Territory made sense; it was tropical and wet and there was a lot of room for fish ponds. The name Barrana was interesting, too, the sort of thing a marketing person would come up with which to sell a piranha-barramundi cross. It looked like Cartwright's Project PB might still be alive and kicking. And a Jezebel-Barrana combo could make for an interesting advertising campaign - two man-eaters in the one act would definitely grab anyone's attention.

'I've been working on some new recipes,' Jezebel said, looking up from her laptop. 'Tell me what you think of this: a mélange of late-harvest Spanish cannellini beans slow-cooked to a melt-in-the-mouth texture in a thick, rich organic tomato-based sauce, topped with Hungarian Debrecener-style paprika-spiced char-grilled Bangalow pork sausages, served over slices of lightly grilled artisanal San Francisco-style sourdough bread and topped with warmed SwissValais raclette from the Les Haudères valley.'

I shrugged. 'Sounds like beans and franks on toast to me,' and for a moment I thought she was going to call the nice cabin attendant and have me sent back to cattle class.

Chapter Twenty-Seven

A lot of people claim to miss the good old days of landing at Hong Kong's legendary Kai Tak Airport, but I'm not one of them. With its unfortunately numbered Runway 13 sticking out like a long, skinny finger into the harbour, flying in over the water was rather enjoyable. It was the land approach, coming in through the downtown Kowloon high-rises, that was something else. An old 747 pilot told me he could check out what Mrs Kwok was cooking for lunch in apartment 6J through one side window and the racing results in Mr Wong's newspaper through the other.

Four kilometres out, and 300 metres in the air, you came to a chopped-off mountain top with a helpful turn arrow where you hung a hard right, dropped a couple of hundred metres quick sticks and then suddenly you were on the ground with all engines thundering in reverse thrust, both feet on the brakes and 3000 metres of runway going by very quickly. If you came to a stop with dirty brown water up to your chest, a cormorant circling the co-pilot and a couple of fishermen in a sampan looking in through the window, you'd probably misjudged it. This bloke always reckoned part of any pilot's pre-landing checklist for Kai Tak was making sure his life insurance payments were up to date.

Chek Lap Kok, the new airport on the tip of Lantau Island, replaced Kai Tak and is pretty white bread - you fly in over water, you land, you get your bags, you leave. It's ultra-clean and whisper quiet, with automated trains connecting the various terminals, shiny escalators and complimentary luggage trolleys, and when you get to baggage claim and immigration the process is incredibly calm and efficient. Even the white-uniformed and face-masked nurses using heat scanning to check for possible bird-flu carriers look welcoming.

On landing, I tried to keep well clear of my travelling companion in case her legendary hotness set off the scanners and had the medical staff running in all directions. In the main concourse I bought myself a pass for the Mass Transit Railway system while Jezebel rounded up her film crew in her usual style, causing mothers to cover their children's ears and a team of visiting Pommy rugby players to blush.

I gave her a quick goodbye kiss and she told me she'd be staying at the Peninsula, registered under the name Barbara Ganoush, if I fancied a workout. I pointed out that my hotel had its own health centre and gym, and we both smiled and left it at that.

Twenty-five minutes after wheels-down I was in a fast, clean, quiet train heading for Hung Hom on the Kowloon side of Victoria Harbour, on the site of the old Whampoa dockyards. The dockyards were built in the 1860s, and for more than a hundred years they were amongst the largest in Asia. In the 1990s they were levelled and turned into a massive housing development. If nature abhors a vacuum, Hong Kong abhors any space big enough for a housing development that doesn't have one.

The Harbour Plaza on Tak Fung Street was right on the water, with panoramic views across to Hong Kong Island. I liked the fact that the hotel was located in the middle of a neighbourhood of residential high-rises, schools and local shopping centres. For Hong Kong it was pretty laid-back, but still convenient. Central was just fifteen minutes away by Star Ferry and the retail insanity of Kowloon's Nathan Road was far enough away that I didn't even need to think about it.

Hong Kong is a great place for mixing business with pleasure, and with Jezebel already having spilled the beans on the Barrana on the plane, I figured I might squeeze in a couple of days of R and R. Maybe a frantic, noisy, old-school yum cha at the Lin Heung Teahouse on Wellington Street in Central, which offered elbows in the ribs along with your pork buns and dumplings, or perhaps a more sedate, fine-dining experience at a private kitchen like Da Ping Huo, where, after passing through the unmarked steel door, you got exquisite red-hot Sichuan cuisine followed by after-dinner Chinese opera from the lady who ran the stoves. I like a city with options.

After checking in to the hotel and dumping my backpack in the room, I walked down Tak Fung Street to an internet café to grab a coffee and send an email to a photographer mate, Jimmy Yip. Jimmy was the official WorldPix representative in Hong Kong and D-E-D's man on the street when required.

Being on suspension meant my access to the D-E-D databank was blocked, so I asked Jimmy to dig out everything he could on Peter Cartwright, Peter Tranh, Detlef Fischer, the Peng casino interests in Macau and the Honourable Vaughan Crockett, United States Ambassador to Australia. I also set up a dinner date.

Then I ambled back to the hotel for a quick nap and a shower and a shave.

Exactly why five-star hotels consider a phone in the bathroom a necessity is beyond me. I had a face full of lather when mine rang. The phone was on the wall next to the toilet and if I'd had any sense I would have dropped the handset in the bowl and flushed. After I heard who was calling, I almost did.

'Felton here,' the voice on the other end snapped brusquely.

Bugger, I said to myself, this is all I bloody need.

Chapter Twenty-Eight

Gwenda Felton AO had recently started answering her calls with a gruff, 'Felton.' I think she really wanted a codename, like Eagle or Alpha One or Red Dog Leader. Maybe we could call her Sausage Dog Leader, after the psychotic miniature dachshund she kept with her on a leash at all times.

'Murdoch here,' I said, in a clipped voice that I hoped made me sound like a World War II RAF Spitfire pilot. 'Standing by.'

'I've seen your signal, Murdoch, and I want to know what the hell you're playing at.'

You'd think the Director-General of a spy agency like D-E-D would have better things to do with her time than eavesdropping on internal communications, but given Gwenda's style of micro-managing, perhaps that was expecting way too much.

'I'm not playing at anything,' I said. 'Something came up and I just asked for all the background we have on Peter Cartwright, a couple of fish farmers and the American Ambassador.'

'Well, as I see it, Murdoch, you are just wasting the government's valuable time and money. Cartwright died in Vietnam. End of story. And the United States Ambassador, who I might tell you is a close personal friend, is a decorated war hero and successful businessman who also served his country in Congress and is in line to be nominated for vice-president'

It sounded like Gwenda was reading from a press release, maybe one written by Brett Tozer's successor at MB&F

'And Ambassador Crockett has kindly consented to officially open the WorldPix photographic exhibition in Canberra and I'd like you back here for the event.'

The exhibition in question was a collection of some of the best images taken by the WorldPix team over the last twenty years. Sponsored by Nikon and the US-Australia Friendship Alliance, it was scheduled for a six-week showing at the National Portrait Gallery in the Old Parliament House building. I'd helped put the show together, but after the barney with Gwenda I'd figured I'd still be in Vietnam and persona non grata when it opened.

I hadn't been too fussed about missing out on the speeches, the wine, the finger food and the opening-night backslapping I got my buzz from hanging our at exhibitions anonymously and seeing the reactions on people's faces when a really powerful image leapt out and hit them right in the face. And as powerful images go, this show had some doozies.

The WorldPix team shoots anything that moves and anything we can make a profit from. This exhibition, though, was mostly portraits, from potentates, prime ministers and presidents to beggars, orphans, refugees and other people damaged or broken or displaced by the actions of those same potentates, prime ministers and presidents.

The people in power have teams of photographers dedicated to making them look good, and for the rest of us there are the world's photojournalists, risking and sometimes losing their lives to show the ugly reality. The images were being printed bigger than life-size for the exhibition, so you couldn't avoid being confronted by the joy and misery, relief and despair, beauty and ugliness, and the arrogance that the camera can capture so well.

Although only 10 per cent of the WorldPix photographers are covert agents, our work was well represented in the show. To maintain cover, we tend to shoot a lot more World-Pix photos than covert ones and the eternal question for us Dedheads is: are we spies playing photographers or photographers playing spies?

'Did you hear me, Murdoch?' Gwenda snapped.

'Roger, that,' I said.

'Roger who?' Gwenda said. 'Stop fooling about, Murdoch. I'm suspending your suspension and I want you back in the office ASAP'

She pronounced it 'a-sap', like the Yank military characters on TV shows.

'I'm just tying up some loose ends here,' I said, 'and then I'll be on a plane.'

"There are no loose ends, Murdoch, I just told you. I want you on a plane now.'

'Roger, Wilco,' I said.

'Stop doing that Murdoch or I'll...

'Un-suspend my suspended suspension?' I suggested.

'Forty-eight hours,' she said. 'And make sure you fly economy. We're all trying very hard here to demonstrate fiscal responsibility for the new government.'

"Why don't we try for actual competence and really impress people?'

'Forty-eight hours, Murdoch,' she said again, coldly.

'That's a big ten-four. Murdoch over and out.'

Chapter Twenty-Nine

My evening began with a stroll from the hotel to Whampoa Gourmet Place, where some of Hong Kong's best restaurants are clustered together over three levels in a building they share with cinemas, a bowling alley and a bus interchange. Opening a joint in this foodie mecca is by invitation only and one of Hong Kong's top gourmets does the inviting. And unless a restaurant maintains consistently high standards, it gets the elbow. So the standards stay high, the lines stay long, and the longest lines are outside Wing Lai Yuen.

Started by a former Imperial Palace chef who fled to Hong Kong in 1949 after the Communist takeover, Wing Lai Yuen is renowned for its spicy Sichuan Dan Dan noodles. The original restaurant, with its 1950s décor, was in Tai Hom Village in Diamond Hill, and the queues often extended from the shopfront right down to the Diamond Hill MTR exit. Still family-run and maintaining the founder's standards, they'd relocated to Whampoa, where they continued to make eighteen hundred servings of the signature noodle dish by hand each day, limiting portions to strictly one serve per customer.

The Chinese usually eat early, so the queue wasn't impossibly long outside Wing Lai Yuen and I waited patiently as befitted my lowly gwailo status. Jimmy Yip, my dinner companion, was Hong Kong born and bred, and he shook his head sadly when he saw me standing outside the restaurant. After a brief chat with the maître d' we were shown to a couple of empty chairs at one end of a table occupied by a family of five. They smiled politely and went back to attacking what looked to be enough food to feed an army.

Jimmy ignored the offered menus and after a discussion with the waitress ordered for us. I heard the words 'Dan Dan mien' somewhere in his rapid-fire Cantonese so I was happy. A request for Tsingtao beer added to my happiness.

Jimmy Yip was around thirty, and devastatingly hand-some. He tooled around town on a beautifully restored Triumph motorcycle and lived the playboy photographer lifestyle to the hilt. You'd generally bump into him on the street with a camera bag, hanging off one shoulder and some gorgeous young kung-fu movie actress hanging off the other.

It was always the same camera bag, but the actresses changed on a weekly basis. Compulsory gender-sensitivity training at WorldPix had taught me such behaviour was decidedly inappropriate, but my envy went right to the bloody bone.

'No cameras, Alby?' Jimmy asked, as he tucked his Lowe-pro bag under the table.

I took the Leica from my pocket. 'Just the standby.'

I still found it hard to believe a little camera had been the catalyst for so much trouble.

Jimmy pulled a thick envelope from his camera bag.

'Maybe you want to put your head into this before the food arrives. Gwenda blocked me using the D-E-D database for you so I used some outside resources. The Cartwright bloke came up as "Deceased" on the Oz Defence Department records, plus I found some reasonable background info on Fischer through online newspaper archives. Ambassador Crockett comes up so squeaky clean he'd make Mother Teresa look like a part-time callgirl and full-time hit woman for the Mafia.'

The food came quickly, but not before I had time to flick through the pages and study a couple of the photographs.

There was a lot of background on ANL Fischer Seafoods and the founder, Eugene Fischer, Detlef's father, a poor but honest post-war immigrant made good. From peeling spuds in a chip shop, Eugene

Fischer had worked his way up to become the owner of an empire of fish and chip shops and hi-end seafood restaurants. He'd even made enough money to be able to send his son to Fairbrothers, the ultra-exclusive and outrageously expensive Melbourne boarding school.

Fairbrothers was the school of choice for disgustingly rich people who didn't want their sons associating with the riffraff at Scotch College, Trinity or Melbourne Grammar. Fairbrothers offered no scholarships to the deserving poor, on the basis that the poor were getting exactly what they bloody deserved for the sin of being poor. The school had a rugby team known for its bone-shattering brutality and a reputation for bullying amongst the students that made Guantanamo Bay look like a Hyatt resort, without the beach umbrellas and deckchairs.

Detlef had taken over on the death of his father about five years ago, and had rapidly expanded ANL Fischer into a multimillion-dollar seafood-importing empire. His hobbies were fast cars and faster women, so he and Jezebel were a great match.

A waitress appeared with a bowl of steamed Shanghai dumplings wallowing in a sea of glowing red chilli oil and we dug in. The noodles arrived moments later and the bloke sitting on the other side of the table nodded approvingly and gave me the thumbs-up. Jimmy and I entered a non-speaking zone as we savoured the Dan Dan mien's thick and amazingly flavoured broth - sweet, sour, salty, spicy, smoky - with hints of dried shrimp, fermented bean paste, chilli, shallots and garlic, and the wonderfully textured handmade noodles topped with wok-fried minced pork and crushed peanuts.

When our bowls were empty I put down my spoon and chopsticks and brought up the subject of Peter Tranh.

Jimmy took a swig of his Tsingtao. 'Google has a stack of references to his fish-breeding research, which I'm sure you've seen yourself. So I went the other route, digging around on the local underworld grapevine, and I picked up some interesting rumours, but none of them are documented.'

In Asia, the local rumour mill quite often gave you more accurate and up-to-date information than you could get from one of the CIA backroom boys at the local US Embassy.

'Seems like your young Mr Tranh fancied making the odd wager or seven.'

'I'd heard he has a gambling problem.'

'Well, I'd say his major problem with gambling is that he isn't very good at it. Story going round is he was into one of the Macau casinos big-time. Owed the Manchu Palace around five million.'

'Five million Yuan?' A quick mental calculation turned that into about 750,000 Aussie dollars.

Jimmy shook his head. 'I'll bet he bloody wished it was Yuan. It was five million US dollars, and that ain't the kind of money you want to be owing someone like Playford Peng. But suddenly the debt went away and young Tranh was back on the straight and narrow.'

More food started arriving and I was very glad I'd had the noodles before we got on to the subject of massive and suddenly forgiven gambling debts. I really wasn't able to give my full attention to the rest of the meal after I'd heard that little piece of information.

'How old is this Playford Peng character?'

'Early to mid thirties, I'd say. Casino is a family business, but it's not a family I'd like to be related to. The story is Old Peng, the patriarch, made the family fortune on the black market and from pushing junk to American servicemen on R & R in Hong Kong in the sixties and seventies. He eventually used the money to fund his casino.'

'Old Peng still involved?'

Jimmy shook his head. 'Officially yes but in reality not since his stroke a while back. From what I've heard, he just sits around in a wheelchair now, mumbling to himself and dribbling, Totally off the air. Rumour has it the stroke may have been brought on by a combination of fatherly disappointment at his only son's profligate ways and a severe and unexpected blow to the head from one of Playford's henchmen.'

'Sounds like a happy family.'

'I'd steer well clear of them if I were you, Alby. Old Peng is the traditional family name for the senior member of the clan and the buzz is the current Old Peng got the title at the age of sixteen when he encouraged his old man to go for a moonlight swim in Deepwater Bay while connected by chains to a very large steel girder.'

'Charming,' I said.

'The apple doesn't fall too far from the tree and Playford is a pretty nasty piece of work. He's actually Old Peng's second son. Jason Peng, the heir to the Peng fortune and number-one son, was electrocuted in his bath when Playford was about nine. According to the coroner it was an accident involving a faulty hair dryer, but nobody bought that. Fingers were pointed in the direction of young Master Playford, who was sent off to boarding school in Melbourne as soon as the funeral was over.'

'What boarding school?'

'I think it was Fairbrothers, same as Fischer.'

The connections were piling up.

'So Playford is Old Peng in waiting?'

Jimmy nodded. 'He doesn't have the title yet, but since the old man's stroke he's got full operational control. And right now the big money wagers in Macau are on how long it's going to take young Playford to drive the multibillion-dollar Peng empire into bankruptcy.'

Chapter Thirty

In Hong Kong, a nice thing to do after dinner is to take a trip on the Star Ferry across that magical harbour. Then maybe grab a ride on one of the rickety, skinny little double-decker trams on Des Voeux Road out to the terminus and back through Central. A not so nice way to end your dinner in Hong Kong is getting yourself kidnapped.

It was a mild night, the sky was clear and there weren't too many people about, which would make spotting a tail pretty easy. A ferry was just pulling into the Hung Hom pier when I arrived and the wooden gangplank on the upper deck clattered down as I passed through the turnstiles.

Two minutes later, to the noisy warning of an electric bell, the gangplank was hauled up, ropes were cast off and the engine rumbled into action. We left the blazing lights of the mainland behind, heading towards the massive neon-lit skyscrapers rising up out of the throbbing heart of Hong Kong Island. In an effort to help the planet, I'd recently changed over to energy-efficient light bulbs in my apartment at Luxor Mansions back in Bondi, but now I wondered if I should switch to candles to compensate for this energy overkill.

Halfway across the harbour I got a text message from Jezebel. 'FANCY A DRINK?'

Why not? I decided. It was another opportunity to see what I could dig up. I keyed in 'ON FERRY - FCC IN 20 MINUTES.' and hit send.

'Cool' pinged back in around thirty seconds.

The Hong Kong Foreign Correspondents Club was started in the 1950s as a meeting place for journalists covering the post-war turmoil in the region, and it now describes itself as a social, cultural and intellectual melting pot with no rival in Asia. While this is probably true, everyone I know goes for the booze and the bullshit and to see who's hanging out in the main bar.

Ten minutes later, the gangplank clattered down again and I was in Central. From the ferry it was an easy walk over to Queen's Road, up along Wyndham Street past the Fringe Club, then finally looping back down the hill on Ice House Street. I figured on doing the energetic uphill stretch at a pace that would help burn off my dinner.

The footpath was torn up for repair work on the left-hand side of Wyndham Street by On Hing Terrace, where a short flight of stone steps led up to Ivy House. I'd had a studio in Ivy House back in the eighties, and I was amazed that the little five-storey building was still there and hadn't been replaced by a skyscraper. I crossed to the right-hand side of the road and continued up the hill.

The streets were empty now, except for a van parked on the side of the road ahead of me with two men lounging beside it. Just as I reached the van, light flared into the face of one of the men as he lit a cigarette using a chunky gold lighter. The side door of the van suddenly slid open, and I had no time to react before a flying tackle from a heavy-set bloke who came out of a doorway on my right knocked me sideways into the van. There was a bag over my head and my hands were zip tied behind me by the time the vehicle got into second gear.

My kidnappers had been thoughtful enough to put a mattress on the floor of the van and I would have been pretty comfortable if two of them hadn't been sitting on my back.

I listened carefully, trying to hear what they were saying, but it was mostly just grunts in Cantonese. Road noise wasn't giving me any clues as to where we might be headed.

My prospects for being ransomed didn't look all that hot. I'm sure

Gwenda would pass the hat around back at D-E-D, but you had to wonder how much I'd raise.

When I twisted my bound feet to get a bit more comfortable, and brushed against what sounded like heavy chain, I realised that the question of ransom might not actually be on the table. If we were heading down towards the harbour, I figured I was in a lot of trouble.

The van suddenly jammed on its brakes and blasted its horn, and I was shunted forward, bashing my head against something solid. There was the usual post-traffic-accident yelling and opening of doors, and then the noise of a scuffle and the unmistakeable sound of the bolt being cocked on a submachine gun.

The van door slid open and the blokes inside with me were ordered out in coarse Cantonese, with the kind of threats that the Chinese do so well. The driver's door slammed shut and the engine revved up, then someone was in the back with me, the side door was closed with a thud that shook the van and we took off with tyres squealing. Being kidnapped twice in one evening was a new record for me.

What must have been ten minutes later, we skidded to a stop and I was dragged out of the van. There was the sound of water lapping and it looked like I was going for that dip in the harbour after all, but then someone carried me down what felt like a swaying gangplank. I was dumped on a hard flat surface and heard a voice say, 'Get the bow line.' A diesel engine rumbled into life and I rolled backwards as the boat pulled away from the dock.

I was turned over on my face, the plastic tie on my wrists gave way to a sharp blade and the bag was pulled off my head.

My vision was still blurry from the blow to my head and I didn't recognise the Chinese bloke standing over me, but I knew the type. Hired muscle, and the quality stuff, too - none of your bargain-basement street-corner hooligans like the blokes who'd grabbed me in the first place. He was dressed all in black, as was the other bloke standing at the bow.

I got slowly to my knees, and then to my feet. We had just come out of the typhoon shelter and the Star Ferry terminal at Central was coming up on our left. Straight ahead I could see a Star Ferry crossing our path, heading for Central from the Kowloon side. We could easily have throttled back and slipped behind it, but whoever was driving our boat wasn't about to give way. The engines roared, we surged forward and I grabbed a stanchion for support. All I could see was the ferry towering above us, its horn blaring, and then we were under its bow and safely on the other side.

I turned back to the bridge to get a look at the maniac at the helm who was wearing the same outfit as the other two, black hoodie, black pants and black combat boots, but the build was a little less muscular.

'Miss Hoang,' I said, 'this is a very pleasant surprise.'

'Indeed. Have you been keeping well, Mr Murdoch?'

I nodded. 'Much better than you might expect for a man with a price on his head. I've been speaking with your uncle and Mr Stark recently, Miss Hoang, and they're also keeping well.'

'I was aware that Uncle and Mr Stark had survived the incident at Dien Bien Phu, but thank you for the reassurance. It is most kind of you.'

'What brings you to Hong Kong, Miss Hoang?' I asked. 'The food, the sights, the shopping? I believe there's a sale on at Shanghai Tang.'

Shanghai Tang is an upscale Chinese retro hip-chic fashion store on Pedder Street. I could see Nhu in one of their cheongsams or a pair of silk pyjamas - or out of them, for that matter, which isn't a fantasy I have about a lot of the coppers I know.

'I'm conducting an investigation which has brought me here, Mr Murdoch.'

'An investigation?'

'Into money laundering by Vietnamese citizens in the casinos of Macau.'

'And at the moment we appear to be heading in the direction of Macau.'

'A most fortunate coincidence,' she said.

I figured the odds on this being a coincidence had to be about the same as those of a horse with a wooden leg winning at the Happy Valley racetrack. But I wasn't about to complain. And beside I think I'd once seen a horse with a wooden leg win the 3.30 handicap. Happy Valley, they used to say, had the best stewards money could buy.

Chapter Thirty-One

We docked at a marina chock-full of gigantic luxury cruisers that made our runabout look like something you'd find in a bathtub along with a couple of rubber ducks. Nhu had made a phone call during the trip and a Mercedes with tinted windows was waiting for us at the end of the dock. If there were customs and immigration formalities, I didn't see them.

We cruised smoothly over a very big bridge and into downtown Macau, passing ugly casinos lit up brightly enough to be seen from distant galaxies.

I was rubbing thighs with Nhu for most of the trip, which was very pleasant. The driver turned off Avenida Almeida Ribeiro and we drove into the basement of a small three-storey stone building that looked like it was a holdover from the old Macau. A heavy-duty metal shutter came down behind the Mercedes and a familiar figure was waiting for us at the bottom of the ramp.

'Welcome to the Pousada do Estoril,' Jack said as we exited the Merc. 'We have four suites for the discerning, discreet and well-heeled plus five-star fine dining by reservation only on the ground floor. There are no elevators, but if you're rich enough to stay here you can afford porters to carry you up and down the bloody stairs.'

We climbed the stairs without benefit of porters and emerged in a small foyer. VT was waiting and he gave Nhu a hug. He was using a cane so I figured the twisted knee from the chopper crash was still giving him pain.

The foyer was all dark-stained timber, plush carpets and polished brass.

"Very swish,' I said.

'Yeah, not bad for a boy who grew up in a housing commission home in Broadmeadows, eh?' Jack said.

'Not bad at all. You win the lottery or something?'

Jack grinned. 'Something like that. The joint was built as a hotel in the 1890s and refurbished in the late 1920s. We basically knocked her down and rebuilt her back to specs, with the addition of the car park and our penthouse apartment. All the woodwork and fittings are original from the refurbishment but under the skin she's brand-new, with modern wiring and plumbing and so on.'

The restaurant had eight tables for two and one table for four, and a state-of-the-art kitchen. The tables were set with damask napkins, Christofle cutlery and Riedel stemware. The restaurant, like the rest of the hotel, was empty.

'Quiet night, Jack, or did the health inspector shut you down?'

He shook his head. 'Nope, I closed the joint when I took the film gig. My people are off on full pay till I decide to reopen. The place is mostly a hobby anyway so when I get bored I chuck out the guests and turn off the phones.'

'A most interesting business model,' Nhu said.

Jack laughed. 'Works a treat. As soon as word gets out we're open again we have people hammering on the doors - well, they actually get their personal assistants to hammer on the door, but you know what I mean. Never ceases to amaze me how the filthy rich love being treated with total disdain by hoteliers and restaurateurs.'

Jack led us into a small Art Deco bar with an open fireplace and comfortable armchairs. The dark-skinned man who had driven the

Merc to the hotel now stood behind the bar in a crisp white jacket. Jack introduced him.

'This is Mr Rayes. Mr Rayes is Macanese - Portuguese Chinese. If I was a serious wanker I'd say he was our comprador.'

"What's a comprador?' Nhu asked.

'In the old days, foreign trading companies in Macau and Hong Kong employed native-born agents as sort of go-betweens to represent them in commercial transactions with local Chinese. You really couldn't get anything done without them. And we probably couldn't get anything done around here without Mr Rayes. He's extremely discreet, has a black belt in Tae Kwan Do and a Harvard MBA, and I've got a sneaking suspicion he could buy and sell me three times over. He also mixes a mean Manhattan.'

'Sounds good to me, Jack,' I said.

We settled into leather armchairs by the fire. I chose one where I could keep an eye on the bar.

Mr Rayes placed four cocktail glasses on the counter, then filled them with ice and topped them up with water to chill. He noticed me watching and, turning back to the shelf of liquor bottles, selected two and held them up for me to choose. One was a Jim Beam Yellow label and the other was Old Overholt. I nodded towards the Old Overholt and Mr Rayes smiled. A few minutes later four cocktails arrived on a tray, the liquid classically golden red with a maraschino cherry resting on the bottom of each glass.

'Here's to living to fight another day,' Jack said raising his glass.

'I'll drink to that,' I said, taking a sip.

"This is delicious,' Nhu said.

'Proper American rye whisky,' I said. 'Accept no substitutes. Only way to make a real Manhattan.

'Anyone hungry?' Jack asked. 'I can whip us up a quick snack.'

I shook my head. I could feel my body starting to complain about the abuse it had taken over the course of the evening, and I flexed my shoulders. I must have grimaced or twitched at the movement and Jack smiled

'Can't take a couple of kidnappings and a bracing sea voyage all in the one evening, Alby? Struth, mate, you're getting old. Ought to get yourself some exercise. Mr Rayes is available for workouts in the basement gym for those wishing to keep limber,' he continued, looking at Nhu, 'and we can also supply an interesting range of pistols and light automatic weapons for those who like to keep their distance,' he said, looking at me.

'I'm a lover, not a fighter, Jack,' I said. "You know that.'

Jack laughed. 'In your dreams, mate,' he said, and VT gave me one of those concerned-uncle warning looks.

'And speaking of dreams,' Jack continued, 'just grab any key from reception when you're ready to hit the sack. Breakfast will be served on the terrace upstairs anytime you want.'

I finished off the Manhattan and stood up. 'It's been a bit of an interesting day Jack, and I think I need a good night's sleep. And maybe a nice long soak in a hot tub.'

'There's a Jacuzzi in the Lisboa Suite. Mr Rayes can point you in the right direction.'

Chapter Thirty-Two

Reception was unattended, but the door behind it was slightly ajar so I stuck my head in. The brass plate on the door said 'Manager's Office' and Mr Rayes was managing very nicely. He looked up from behind a desk and smiled. Besides the usual computers and office equipment there was a wall of video monitors showing images of every possible approach to the hotel and the building's entry and exit points.

'To let you know when guests might be approaching?' I asked, indicating the monitors. 'So you can break out the bellboys?'

Mr Rayes nodded. 'Mr Stark likes to be aware of the disposition of all visitors at all times.'

That sounded fair enough. I'd had a few unexpected visitors just lately whose disposition I hadn't much cared for.

'And I guess in a classy establishment like this some of your visitors warrant a twenty-one gun salute.'

I was referring to the rack behind the desk that held half a dozen nasty-looking Benelli shotguns.

'We reserve the right to refuse service,' Mr Rayes said, 'and sometimes it is necessary to make the point forcefully.'

I made a mental note not to complain about anything during my stay.

'Mr Stark has suggested I might like the Lisboa Suite,' I said.

Mr Rayes stood up. 'An excellent choice.'

You had to wonder if in a five-star, four-room hotel there was such a thing as a bad choice.

The Lisboa Suite was huge, decorated in a Chinese retro thirties style with antique rosewood furniture, old brass ceiling fans to complement the air-conditioning and a bigger-than-king-size bed. The bathroom had a tub the size of an Olympic swimming pool, which I filled while hunting down some aspirin in a well-stocked cabinet full of razors, after-shave, moisturisers, shampoos and bubble bath. I squirted some bubble bath into the tub, stripped off and lowered myself slowly into the hot water.

I'd turned on the spa jets and was just getting comfortable when Nhu walked in. She was naked; well, almost, apart from the 9mm Russian Yarygin Pya.

She was just as spectacular as I remembered from Saigon - lean, muscular and very, very toned, with a flat belly and the most amazing breasts. I suddenly wondered if the hotel's video surveillance system was confined to the exterior.

'Nice gun,' I said, 'but you won't need it. I've taken some aspirin. I wasn't going to pull the old "not tonight, I've got a headache" routine.'

'It would appear there are still many people who want you dead, Mr Murdoch,' she said quietly, 'and not just in Vietnam.'

My eyes flitted backwards and forwards between the gun and her naked torso. 'Well,' I said, 'that's certainly put a dampener on the romantic mood.'

She put the pistol down on the green jade vanity, pinned her hair up and stepped elegantly into the tub. As her breasts disappeared under the froth, I regretted using so much bubble bath. The toes of her left foot found a rather sensitive part of my anatomy and I sat up straight.

'Is that perhaps bringing the mood back?' she asked.

I nodded.

The next fifteen minutes were a battle between the water jets trying to relax me and Nhu working diligently on having exactly the opposite effect. She used that age-old female trick of doing and saying nothing and just looking gorgeous.

Eventually, Nhu stood up, smiled and stepped out of the tub. That bottom really was amazing. There was a pile of plush white towels on a small table and she tossed me one.

She took the pistol and placed it under the pile before towelling herself dry.

'So I guess I can take it that you don't think I'm in any danger of dying tonight?'

'I think we can say there is little danger of that, Mr Murdoch,' she said, dropping the towel and walking into the bedroom.

But as it turned out she was mistaken. A couple of times before morning I felt like I might have come very, very close.

Chapter Thirty-Three

THE LISBOA SUITE WAS THE BEE'S KNEES. WE HAD KRUG CHAMPAGNE and Godiva G Collection chocolates in the minibar, a real espresso machine, windows that actually opened and no TV with CNN giving us all the bad news all the time. The bed was firm, the lighting was subtle, Nhu was soft and if things got too much for a bloke you simply pressed 9 on the phone on the bedside table for a paramedic with a defibrillator.

Okay, 9 was really for room service, but I couldn't think of anything I needed to send out for that I didn't already have.

At around three in the morning, when the traffic noise outside had died down and the room was dark, I realised I was alone in the bed. A light was on in the bathroom and Nu came out with a glass of water and no gun so I figured I'd been holding up my end of the deal. She handed me the glass and I took a drink.

I watched as she walked across to the window and pulled back the heavy drapes, leaving the semi-sheer diaphanous curtains in place. She was lithe, light on her feet and totally comfortable with her nakedness. In the moonlight she was all soft curves and mysterious shadows. I decided I could watch Nhu walk around naked all night, and all day for that matter.

Even though there was no TV, the suite did have a sound system. Not one of those CD players made to look old in a retro cabinet, but an actual vintage rosewood console record player from the fifties. It looked like something Chairman Mao might have owned. Nhu walked across the room and searched through the collection of twelve-inch LPs next to the player. I decided I could watch her search through LPs all day as well.

The control knobs on the record player were labelled in Chinese characters but she eventually figured things out and gently lowered the needle onto a black vinyl disk. There was a momentary crackle and then the mellow tones of Nat King Cole filled the room, enhancing the romantic atmosphere.

Nhu got back into bed and settled down beside me, looked deeply into my eyes and delicately, subtly and with great sensuality began to pick my brains. I'd been interrogated a couple of times before in my life by people using less subtle methods, and given a choice I'd definitely prefer to go with this technique.

This stunningly beautiful woman who was apparently keenly interested in my hopes and dreams and aspirations was in a rather skilful way trying to find out exactly what I knew about the Honourable Vaughan Crockett.

'How would a Vietnamese police investigation into money laundering in Macau involve the American Ambassador to Australia?' I asked.

'These things are sometimes complex, Mr Murdoch. They are not always as they seem.'

'Too complex for a simple photographer?'

She smiled. 'Sometimes simple photographers are not always what they seem, either.'

I was wondering just what to make of that when Nhu decided to change the subject. The way she did it put her questions and the Ambassador right out of my mind.

When I woke up again around six, the curtains were open, the sky was already bright and the traffic noise out on the street was beginning to build. Nhu was awake, too.

She was standing at the window, naked, her back to me. The soft early-morning light diffused by the semi-sheer curtains accentuated the curves of her body.

'You will be travelling back to Australia soon, Mr Murdoch?'

'Today or tomorrow. WorldPix is launching a big photographic exhibition in Canberra later this week and they want me there.' I paused for a moment and then added, 'The American Ambassador will be doing the honours.'

There was a subtle change in Nhu's body language and I reached across and put my hand on the little Leica camera on the bedside table.

'Please don't make me go and get my gun, Mr Murdoch,' she said, without turning around. I took my hand away from the camera.

Nhu walked back to the bed, scooping up several discarded pillows on the way. She piled them up against the headboard then picked up my camera from beside the bed and pointed it down at me. The sight of this beautiful woman towering over me, naked with a camera obscuring her face, was one of the most striking images I'd ever seen. If I'd had a second camera handy, it would have been a shot worth risking my life for.

'There are people in my department who would give almost anything for a picture of me with my clothes off,' she said.

I could actually help them with that since I'd casually pressed the shutter button when I touched the camera on the bedside table, just as she had warned me off.

'I doubt if they'd be much interested in one of me,' I said.

She laughed and put the Leica down, but not before I caught a quick glimpse of the shutter opening briefly in the lens.

'Something on your mind?' I said, trying to read the expression on her face.

'I was just thinking about breakfast,' she said.

'Want me to ring room service?'

She shook her head. 'I'm certain room service won't have what I had in mind.'

The next fifteen minutes were a strange mix of bliss and discomfort. I jumped a couple of times because Nhu had very sharp teeth, which she used with tantalising effect.

But those pearly white teeth also made me a bit uncomfortable for another reason. I was wondering if Nhu had been lying to me through them ever since we'd first met. I found it somewhat difficult to relax and go with the moment. But only somewhat.

Chapter Thirty-Four

'How's your head this morning, Alby? My old Gran always used to say feed a cold, starve a fever and treat a mild concussion with a big cooked breakfast.'

'Your old Gran wasn't a practising neurosurgeon by any chance, was she, Jack?

It was just after ten and a typical sunny Macau morning, the humidity already building. A breakfast table was laid on the rooftop terrace under a large green market umbrella. There were fresh pastries and rolls, sliced cold meats and cheeses, and a jug of chilled orange juice, along with a bottle of Krug in an ice bucket. Jack was standing over the barbecue while VT made coffees at a rather serious-looking espresso machine.

The cast-iron barbecue plate held bacon, sliced black pudding, thick sausages, lamb cutlets, mushrooms, sliced tomato and thick chunks of potato sizzling amongst nicely caramelised onion rings.

'Bugger all those chefs with their mod-Oz and fusion bullshit,' Jack said, 'believe me, Australia's great gift to the culinary world is the mixed grill for breakfast. How do you like your eggs?'

The breakfast terrace had an amazing view across Macau that was being built out by the rapidly sprouting casinos.

There were just the three of us and the table had only three place settings.

'Nhu not around?' I asked.

Jack shook his head. 'She's done a bunk. Mr Rayes said she left sometime before eight.'

I hadn't heard Nhu shower or dress or leave the room, but then the events of the past week had been exhausting and the overnight erotic activities had left me totally wasted

'She told Mr Rayes she was on an important assignment and had to get back to it,' Jack continued. 'I suppose that could be true, Alby, or maybe you were just seriously crook in the sack.'

VT gave Jack a dirty look before I could answer. Jack whistled and a bleary-eyed beagle wandered out from under the shade of a potted palm. I had a feeling Jack wanted to move the subject away from bedrooms and activities therein.

'Meet Biggles,' he said.

The beagle stopped at my feet, sniffed my shoes and then wagged his tail. I gave his shoulders and neck a brisk rub and he flopped on his back, offering his chest for a pat.

'What a bloody tart,' Jack said.

Breakfast was on the table five minutes later and gone ten minutes after that. My night with Nhu had also left me hungry.

'After you headed off to bed last night, Nhu filled us in on your adventures on the way to the Foreign Correspondents Club. Looks like Crockett's people aren't giving up, so you might want to be a bit careful.'

'That puts us in the same boat,' I said.

'VT and I can take care of ourselves and we keep a low profile anyway. We'll just raise the drawbridge and hunker down until all this blows over.'

'When do you reckon that might be?'

Jack shrugged. 'Maybe when someone makes the American Ambassador an offer he can't refuse. Another cup of coffee, Alby?'

As I sipped my coffee I was wondering what kind of offer that might be. I was also wondering how Miss Hoang knew I was heading for the FCC from the ferry, as I was certain I hadn't mentioned it on the boat ride to Macau. How she'd managed to be in Central at such an opportune moment was a whole other ball of wax.

A few minutes later Mr Rayes walked out onto the terrace holding a silver tray. 'This was just delivered by messenger,' he said.

There was a letter opener on the tray and a heavy envelope, hand addressed to me care of the hotel. 'So much for me keeping a low profile,' I said.

Mr Rayes put the tray on the ground and Jack whistled for Biggles. The beagle gave the envelope a cursory sniff and walked away.

'It's okay, you can open it now,' Jack said. 'All deliveries get X-rayed and then Biggles gives them the once-over. He's a retired explosives sniffer dog. We thought about putting in one of those electronic devices, but I'd much rather have something that likes having its tummy rubbed.'

'Paranoid, Jack?'

He nodded. 'And still breathing, so it's working for me.'

I slit the envelope open and unfolded a sheet of heavy card. The card featured expensive printing, embossing, gold leaf and some extremely elegant calligraphy.

'Apparently, the Manchu Palace Hotel & Casino requests the pleasure of Mr Alby Murdoch's company at seven this evening for some fine dining at the chairman's table in the Eight Banners restaurant.'

'Very nice,' Jack said. 'The Eight Banners does some excellent nosh. Who's doing the inviting?'

I handed him the invitation. 'It doesn't say.'

Jack frowned. 'If it's the Manchu Palace Hotel & Casino and the chairman's table, it has to be Playford Peng.'

'But how the hell would Playford Peng know I was in Macau?' I was starting to get really pissed off that everyone else seemed to know more about what I was up to than I did.

'Beats me, Alby,' Jack said. 'But aren't you supposed to be getting on a plane back to Oz? You said that Gwenda person was threatening to have your guts for garters if you kept dicking around.'

'Gwenda might have to wait. I know there's some connection between Peng, the Manchu Palace Casino, Peter Tranh and the missing fish, and maybe I can find out what it is. The problem is, it says tonight is formal.'

'Don't worry about a dinner suit, Alby, we can fix that' Jack said. 'The real problem is that when you're dealing with the Peng family, formal means a bow tie, no firearms over 9mm and gentlemen will use silencers. Don't say you haven't been warned.'

Chapter Thirty-Five

Modern Macau is a Special Administrative Region of China, and one schizophrenic little city. The former Portuguese colony was Europe's first foothold in Asia, and pretty much a sleepy backwater when compared to Shanghai or Hong Kong. The colony's Portuguese and local Chinese casually intermarried and intermixed their culture and cooking, producing the handsome Macanese and the world's first fusion cuisine, with dishes like sweet curry crab or my favourite, Galinha à Africana, spicy African chicken.

The sleepy backwater part was jettisoned when the decision was taken to open the place up as a gambling mecca with multiple casinos. Macau's low-rise colonial architecture dating back hundreds of years was now overshadowed by high-rise casinos springing up in the city and along the waterfront strip on land reclaimed from the sea. I guess you could describe that part of Macau as looking like Las Vegas, only without its understated good taste, elegance and sophisticated charm.

If over-the-top opulence, blindingly bright lights and cross-cultural train wrecks are what you're looking for in an evening out, you can't go past Peng's Manchu Palace. Speaking for myself, I wish I had. Within thirty seconds of strolling into the glittering foyer, my teeth started to ache. The joint was packed with goggle-eyed mainland Chinese visitors and featured an atrium tall enough to house a Saturn Five moon rocket.

Surprisingly, that was exactly what it held, all 110 metres of it, with an Apollo space capsule sitting on top for good measure. About thirty metres above me, two men in silver spacesuits bounced around on bungee cords in a jerky simulated space-walk.

A beautiful girl wearing a see-through spacesuit over a silver-mesh bikini handed me a leaflet explaining that in honour of the Lunar New Year it was Moon Month at the casino. Various luminaries and retired astronauts from NASA's Apollo space programme would be in attendance and there were also actual moon rocks from the actual moon on display. Moon Burgers served with Space Fries and a complimentary glass of orange Tang - the Astronauts' Drink - were available in the six 24-hour snack bars.

I rode a smooth-as-silk escalator up twenty metres to the restaurant level, where a maitre d' in a dinner suit was standing behind a small desk. I handed over my invitation. The maitre d' ran his eyes down a list on a clipboard, frowned momentarily, checked the invitation again and then smiled.

'Mr Murdoch,' he said, 'we are deeply honoured to welcome you to the Manchu Palace Hotel and Casino.'

He handed me a small black lacquer box embossed with the casino logo.

'With our compliments, should you wish to spend some time at our tables.'

Inside the box were ten poker chips. Ten one thousand US dollar chips.

'And should you wish to avail yourself of any of our other facilities,' he continued, 'please feel free to simply sign for them.'

He handed me another embossed black lacquer box. This one held a fountain pen. A gold Mont Blanc, with my name and the hotel's crest engraved on it.

'Your pen, Mr Murdoch, is solid silver with 24-carat gold plating. It is part of a limited edition specially handcrafted for the Manchu Palace as a gift to its most honoured guests.'

'I'm touched and moved,' I said, 'and I'm glad I decided to dress up.'

Jack and VT had done a great job arranging suitable attire for the evening. Mr Rayes took some measurements, and a quick phone call produced a salesman with a dozen dinner suits, a range of dress shirts and several boxes of shoes. The salesman brought along a tailor for any adjustments that might be needed, a barber stopped by to trim my hair and scare the crap out of me with a cutthroat razor, and by six-thirty I was looking good enough to be critically assessed by two gay men and a straight comprador. Even Biggles had given me a yelp of approval.

'Please follow me,' the maitre d' said.

The restaurant in the Manchu Palace made the State Dining Room at Buckingham Palace look like my local McDonald's. It was the kind of over-the-top opulence where you wouldn't be surprised to find fifty-grand Tang Dynasty ceramic horse statuettes used as doorstops. The place was packed, but most of the action was centred on a massive round table that seemed to have three waiters for each of the fifteen diners. Everyone at the table had one of the black lacquer boxes and a pen in front of them. As I approached, I saw a couple of familiar faces amongst the guests.

One was Fysh Rutherford, twin brother of Graeme Rutherford, a former D-E-D field agent retired from active duty after his cover was blown and he'd undergone some nasty interrogation sessions. While Graeme had gone into the espionage business, Fysh, who had a short attention span and a somewhat tenuous grasp of spelling and grammar, had become an advertising copywriter and made a bloody fortune. On a dollar return per word basis, advertising copywriting has been described as one of the most lucrative forms of writing there is, coming second only to ransom notes.

'No camera tonight, Alby?' Fysh yelled. 'I wanted a snap of me and the missus.'

All Fysh knew about me was my photography work for WorldPix. I shook my head.

'I'm having an evening off, mate,' I said, bending down to give Fysh's gorgeous wife, Jacqueline, a kiss on the cheek. The bloke was a serious foodie so I asked if he was here as part of Jezebel's Gourmet Asia tour but he shook his head.

'Nah,' he said, 'just flew up to meet with our new client. We won the pitch for the Fischer Aquaculture business. We're going to have Jezebel blanketing the media to launch this de'lish new wonder fish, Barrana. Marketed as Jezza Barrana if she gets her way.'

'Jezebel always gets her way,' I said. 'How much background have they given you on the product?'

'Not a lot, mate. It's still in the development stage, and we've signed one of those non-disclosure agreements, but it's apparently some sort of fast-growing crossbreed they're farming somewhere in the Top End.'

I was starting to wonder what people thought the non-disclosure part of non-disclosure agreements actually meant.

'They're supposed to taste bloody Jezza-licious,' he continued. 'We're pushing that for our tag-line by the way, so watch out for it.'

'If I see it coming, I'll run a mile,' I said. 'And speaking of the lovely Ms Quick, is she here tonight?' I asked.

I was wondering if she'd arranged for me to be invited, and then I spotted her.

Jezebel was on the other side of the table, seated between two men - no surprise there. One I recognised from his photograph as Detlef Fischer, and the other was a rotund Chinese guy about the same age or a bit younger. Jezebel saw me at the same time.

'Alby, you old bastard!' she yelled, her voice carrying over the din of the packed room. 'What the hell are you doing in Macau? Get your pasty white butt over here.'

That appeared to take Jezebel off the list of people who might have invited me. When I finally reached the other side of the table I bent down to give her a kiss on the cheek.

'Sorry about missing you for drinks last night,' I said, 'but I was tied up.'

'What drinks? I was stuck all night at a farewell dinner at Felix for my dickwit foodies.'

Felix is the elegant Philippe Starck-designed restaurant and bar on the 28th floor of the Peninsula Hotel Tower. It's popular with the Hong Kong glitterati, and besides the designer food and ambience, one of its many talking points is a men's toilet where patrons piss into jade urinals in front of floor-to-ceiling windows, showing their willies to the whole of mainland China.

But if Jezebel had been at Felix last night, who had sent me that text?

'Jesus, mate,' Jezebel said, looking at my outfit, 'if I'd known you could scrub up this well I might not have given you the arse.'

'I do miss those romantic days we spent tripping hand-in-hand through flower-strewn meadows with packs of gambolling puppies.'

'Screw you, Alby,' she said. 'Let me introduce the boys. On my left here we have Mr Detlef Fischer, who runs a couple of fish and chip shops, and this is our gracious host, Mr Playford Peng.'

Fischer smiled and I was almost blinded by what had to be thirty thousand dollars' worth of cosmetic dentistry. He looked as big a wanker as he did in the photograph Cartwright had shown me. He gave me one of those I'm a good bloke, you can trust me bone-crushing power grips.'

'Nice to meet you,' I said to Fischer, 'any friend of Jezebel's is... probably quite exhausted.'

I bowed slightly to Playford Peng, 'I have to thank you for the warm welcome to your wonderful casino, Mr Peng,' I said, 'and the generous gifts.'

Wash my face, comb my hair, stick me in a dinner suit and you can take me almost any place.

Playford Peng was staring at me with a fixed smile. It was the kind of stare that makes you want to check that your fly is zipped up. Or maybe it was the stare you get when you show up at dinner and the host is wondering exactly who the hell you are and what you're doing there lowering the tone of the festivities.

Chapter Thirty-Six

PLAYFORD MADE A QUICK RECOVERY AND SMILED AS WE SHOOK HANDS. Compared to Fischer's vice-like grip, Peng's handshake was soft and pasty, like one of those Chinese custard tarts.

'Any friend of our Miss Jezebel Quick is most assuredly a friend of mine,' Peng said sincerely, sincerely not meaning every word.

Peng's tuxedo must have cost a bomb and it was cunningly tailored to disguise the fact that he was a short, fat little man. It made him look like a short, fat little man in an expensive tuxedo. His mouth made a shape roughly approximating a smile but his eyes were cold, hard and calculating.

'As to the gifts,' he continued, 'the Peng family, under the sage guidance of my beloved father, believes that generosity is a virtue.'

'Your father is well?'

He shook his head. 'Sadly, since his stroke he is confined to a wheelchair. I have been forced to see to the day-to-day running of the family enterprises.'

'You have my best wishes for your father's speedy recovery.'

Playford smiled that insincere smile again and snapped his fingers.

A chair was placed between Fischer and Jezebel, bowls and chopsticks appeared and a cup was filled with tea for me.

Peng waved to a man who had the look of a bodyguard pretending to be a waiter, and whispered in his ear. The man nodded and hurried away. I sat down and smiled at Fischer.

'Chip shops, eh?' I said. 'You a classic beer-batter man or do you lean towards something in the way of a light tempura?'

He smiled politely. 'It has been some little while since I worked the deep-fryer, Mr Murdoch, and fish retailing is only a small part of my business,' he said. 'I'm actually a fresh fish importer and wholesaler. ANL Fischer Seafoods, you may have heard of it.'

I nodded. 'And there's also a new fish-farming company in the works, I believe.'

'Fischer Aquaculture Industries,' he said

'When I hear the word aquaculture I reach for my grill Pan.'

Fischer stared at me.

'Very good, very amusing,' Playford Peng said.

Now Fischer was staring at him.

'Mr...?' Peng said, smiling at me.

'Murdoch,' I said. 'My friends call me Alby.'

'Mr Murdoch is playfully paraphrasing the Nazi Heinrich Himmler who said, "When I hear the word culture I reach for my gun," ' Peng explained to the table.

He smiled as the smiling guests dutifully applauded his explanation.'

'Or it might have been Hermann Göring,' I said. 'Provenance is bit murky. Actually, I'm paraphrasing a misquote from a National Socialist play by Hanns Johst. The original line is, "Whenever I hear of culture . . . I release the safety-catch of my Browning." '

There was no applause from the table this time. Peng gave me that original icy look and changed the subject.

'So you like fish, eh, Mr Murdoch? My good friend Detlef is in the fish business.'

'I've heard,' I said.

'Detlef and I were at school together, in Melbourne,' he added, 'at Fairbrothers.'

A bloke in a dinner suit appeared at Peng's elbow. He looked a bit out of breath and I got the idea he'd been sent for and told to report on the double. The two men had a hurried private conversation that I had a feeling involved me, and possibly not in a good way. Playford didn't stop smiling, but that didn't make me feel any better.

'Mr Murdoch, let me introduce my accountant, Mr Leroy Fong. Mr Fong looks after my . . .' he paused, '. . . interests.'

Leroy Fong was about my age and height. If he was Playford Peng's accountant, I was a Dutchman. I figured his real job was accounting for anyone who got in Playford's way.

Fong bowed slightly and handed me a business card with both hands, which I took the same way. I know how to play the game.

Waiters placed cut-crystal tumblers in front of Peng and myself.

'A toast to new friendships, eh, Mr Murdoch?'

The waiters half-filled our glasses from matching elegant crystal decanters shaped like smoothly polished river stones.

Then the waiters stood ready with Coca-Cola bottles poised on the lip of each glass.

'Brandy and Coke fine with you, Murdoch?'

I lifted my glass and took a sniff. 'Okay,' I said, 'brandy cokes it is.'

'Jesus Christ, Alby!' Jezebel shouted, knocking the waiter's arm away, spilling bubbling soft drink on to the tablecloth.

'That's fucking Hennessy Ellipse! It costs ten grand a bottle!'

I put my glass down and smiled at Peng, who didn't smile back.

'You don't always want to believe what's on the label, Jez.'

I picked up my teacup and raised it. 'To new friendships, Mr Peng.'

He smiled, but didn't drink.

'What kind of food do you like, Mr Murdoch,' he asked. 'We have separate kitchens specialising in Italian, French and Japanese cuisine, all with five-star chefs, and our Chinese New Year banquet is beginning soon. You like Chinese food, eh? How about some sweet and sour pork or lemon chicken? Maybe some special fried rice? You look like a special fried rice kind of guy to me.'

First the brandy and now this. Playford Peng was set on making me look like a dopey gwailo to his associates. It was a subtle game of establishing superiority that I'd played before and I wasn't all that interested in allowing it to continue - ten grand in welcome gifts or not.

I shrugged. 'Perhaps the kitchen can rustle up some Hakka food? *Ngiong tew foo* or maybe some *kiu nyuk* might be nice.'

Playford smiled coldly and dipped his head slightly.

Round one to Alby.

'You might enjoy our Hakka salt-baked chicken or pork with fermented tofu as well?'

I nodded. 'Sounds great.' I wasn't a big fan of fermented tofu but I was more than ready to force it down just to piss Playford off.

He clapped his pudgy hands and a waiter appeared. Peng rattled off an order and the waiter scurried away.

'You and Miss Quick are old friends?' Playford asked.

When he mentioned Jezebel he smiled across at her. For the first time I saw something approaching warmth and genuine affection in his eyes. The effect was even more disturbing than that cold calculating look I was getting used to seeing.

'Alby and I go way back,' Jezebel said. 'In fact, we flew into Hong Kong together from Vietnam. Alby's been working over there.'

'Mr Fong has also been in Vietnam recently,' Peng said, 'acquiring items for my next big project. The Manchu Palace is staging a free very big outdoor production of Miss Saigon this summer.'

'Sounds impressive.'

'Impressive isn't the word, Alby,' Jezebel said. 'For the final scene they'll be using a real American military helicopter, a vintage Huey. It's going to lift off an exact replica of the US Embassy rooftop in Saigon built right on stage, and then actually fly away. Friggin' awesome. Leroy has been spending a lot of time in Vietnam learning all there is to know about choppers.'

'Is that right, Mr Fong?'

'Yes, Mr Murdoch. Unfortunately, some of those old helicopters are getting to be quite dangerous.'

Fong took a gold cigarette case from his pocket and offered me one. When I shook my head Fong took a cigarette and lit it with a gold lighter. The lighter looked familiar.

'I heard a Huey fell out of the sky a few days ago,' I said, 'near Dien Bien Phu.'

Fong looked directly into my eyes. 'Really? Was it pilot error or a mechanical problem?'

I held his stare. 'Neither.'

Jezebel shuddered. 'You wouldn't get me up in one of those things.

I make it a rule not to fly in anything without wings and a first-class cabin, isn't that right, lover chops?' she said, turning her attention back to Detlef.

'Do you spend much time in Hong Kong, Mr Fong?'

'Please call me Leroy,' he said. 'I am in Hong Kong quite frequently. Why do you ask?'

'I saw someone who looked a lot like you last night on Wyndham Street in Central.'

'I'm quite sure it wasn't me, Mr Murdoch. Besides, don't we Chinese all look alike?'

'My mistake,' I said. 'But believe me, I'll know you next time.'

Fong picked up a glass from the table and raised it in a toast. 'Here's to the next time.'

I raised my teacup. 'I look forward to it,' I said.

Behind us Playford Peng snapped an instruction in Cantonese and we turned towards him. He didn't look happy.

Fong bowed slightly with a fixed smile on his face and left the table.

'Miss Quick tells me you are a famous picture-taker, Mr Murdoch. I'm sorry to say I've never heard of you. Do you do weddings?'

I smiled. He'd have to do better than that. I've been insulted by experts in my time.

'Why? Do you see a wedding in Jezebel and Detlef's future?'

Peng shook his head. 'Miss Quick is not the marrying kind. And Detlef's future is very much involved with his new venture.'

'His top-secret wonder fish? How soon do you think we'll be able to sink our teeth into them?'

'Very soon, I believe.'

'That's fantastic,' I said, 'I can't wait. Just as long as they don't bite back, eh?'

Peng's expression didn't change, but I saw a hard glint in his eye. He stood up.

'Please excuse me, Mr Murdoch. I need to check with my chefs on how our banquet is progressing.'

I had a feeling that Playford was actually going to the kitchen to get his chefs to whip up some extra fermented, extra stinky tofu dishes, and that they'd all be coming my way.

Chapter Thirty-Seven

Mr Rayes buzzed me back into the hotel through the locked security door just after eleven. I was a bloke in a well-fitting dinner suit just back from a night at a casino looking for some hot loving with a dangerous woman between crisp, thousand-thread-count Egyptian cotton sheets. Sipping vintage port with a couple of gay guys wasn't the conclusion to the evening I really had in mind.

How was dinner?' Jack said, putting a third glass down on the table on the rooftop terrace.

'Spectacular,' I said as I pulled up a chair. 'The food at the Eight Banners is as good as you said.'

VT filled the glass from an open bottle. I picked up the bottle and studied the label.

'Trying to get rid of the out-of-date stock, Jack?' I asked.

The port was Warre's, the 1997 vintage - the really, really good vintage. I took a sip. Then I took another. A bloke looking for something to take his mind off the events in the casino, getting dumped by a good-looking woman yet again and having no idea what was going on didn't need to look much further than this. If I was a wine critic, I might have used the words voluptuous or lissom or elegant, but that would only have made me think of Nhu. Dangerous would've worked too, especially if we finished off the bottle, which seemed to be on the cards.

'Figure out who did the inviting?'

I shook my head. 'But I ran into some people I knew and I scored a couple of gifts. One was ten grand in poker chips.'

'Sweet,' Jack said.

I nodded. 'I dumped them into a charity donation box on the way out and almost caused a bloody riot. Plus I got these.'

I took the gold fountain pen from my jacket pocket, along with a small red envelope.

'Mont Blanc, very nice,' Jack said. 'And lai see. You been out mugging little kids for their lucky money?'

I'd been given the little red paper envelope as I was leaving the casino after dinner. Called lai see or hong bao they usually contain small gifts of money and are handed out at Chinese New Year to bring good fortune and prosperity for the coming year. The gift can also be seen as a way of symbolically clearing debts, starting off the New Year with a clean slate.

When I'd left the restaurant there had been a huge crowd gathered at the bottom of the long escalator, the reason being that the Manchu Palace had a lion in the lobby. Not a real lion, though that was something I wouldn't put past Playford Peng, but lion dancers, the traditional and always welcome visitors at Chinese New Year, or on any special or auspicious occasion.

Long strings of red firecrackers were blasting off outside the casino to scare away evil spirits and there was much banging of drums and clashing of cymbals as the two men inside the lion costume pranced through the spectators. This was a southern Chinese lion, and a pretty boisterous one. It had a long, flowing piece of red, black and gold silk for its body and the dancer in front was throwing the fringed, tasselled and elaborately painted wood and papier-mâché head from side to side while winking its eyes and noisily snapping its massive jaws open and shut.

In amongst the crowd I could see an elderly man in a wheelchair. An attractive young woman in an extremely tight-fitting white nurse's uniform was pushing the wheel-chair. From time to time, the nurse would bend down and wipe the man's lips with a tissue. The old man was in a dinner suit and was slumped to one side of the chair, his right arm lying limp in his lap, his head resting on his right shoulder. It looked like Playford Peng still let his father out on special occasions.

Mothers in the crowd were pointing their children towards Old Peng and shoving them forward. Those brave enough to approach were rewarded with a crooked smile and one of the small red envelopes that the nurse took from a bag slung over the back of the wheelchair and placed in the old man's left hand.

The wheelchair was being pushed in my direction, and I was wondering if Old Peng still had enough of his faculties intact to instruct his nurse to wear a uniform a couple of sizes too small when I saw his right index finger flick up. The wheelchair stopped right in front of me. Old Peng slowly and painfully worked the words 'Kung Hei Fat Choy' out of his twisted and drooping mouth.

'Happy New Year,' I said back, smiling.

The nurse reached into her spectacular cleavage and handed me a red envelope. As lucky envelopes went, that was one very lucky envelope. And suddenly the wheelchair was gone, swallowed up in the frantic New Year melee.

Sitting on Jack's terrace I sipped my port then carefully opened the red envelope.

There wasn't any money, just a small, shiny paper sleeve holding a colour negative. Those shiny paper sleeves for storing negatives and postage stamps were called glassine and I hadn't seen one in a very long time.

There were some Chinese characters written on the outside and the single photographic negative inside the sleeve was slightly faded but still in good condition. It was a small square format I also hadn't seen for years, from a Kodak Instamatic, a very popular amateur point-and-shoot camera in the sixties and seventies. There weren't too many GIs in 'Nam who hadn't had a compact little PX-bought Instamatic stuffed in a pocket of their fatigues.

I took the negative out of the sleeve, holding it carefully by the corner. When you've looked at enough negatives you can read them easily. And this one was very interesting.

'Bit of nasty porn, Alby?' Jack asked.

'Something like that, Jack. Any chance Mr Rayes can get me on a flight back home to Sydney first thing in the morning?'

'No worries, mate. But if that means this is a farewell party, maybe we should knock this over and open a bottle of the good stuff.'

'And why the hell not, Jack?' I said.

I didn't see much reason to be rushing upstairs to an empty bed. Especially as I didn't even have that photograph of the lovely Nhu standing naked at the window to console myself with. When I'd picked up my Leica earlier in the day, I'd found the memory card was gone. Miss Nhu Hoang obviously wasn't a trusting soul.

Chapter Thirty-Eight

THE NEXT FEW HOURS WERE A BIT FUZZY BUT WHEN I FINALLY unscrambled my brain I was in an economy-class seat on a plane with its nose pointed south, and with a number of my fellow passengers staring at me.

We'd finished off the port, I remembered, and then Jack had put together a late-night snack of steak sandwiches with tomato relish and shoestring French fries, and he'd opened a '92 Petrus. That was when things got really fuzzy.

I had only the vaguest recollection of getting to the airport and checking in for my flight to Sydney, and now all these people staring in my direction were starting to freak me out. Looking for a distraction, I rummaged through the seat pocket in front of me.

Airline seat-pocket reading material can be pretty ordinary, even on a good day. The laminated safety card isn't too engaging, with its cartoon passengers disembarking in an orderly fashion from a 300-tonne aircraft which the pilot has somehow managed to land neatly in one piece on the gentle bosom of an incredibly smooth ocean. The airsick bags sometimes have instructions like "Insert vomit through open end", with a helpful arrow and thankfully no graphics.

And then there's the airline in-flight magazine. I've been on airlines where the airsick bag makes for more entertaining and engaging reading. However, this magazine was of very superior quality as it contained a photograph of me, which must have been why I was getting the stares. It accompanied an informative article about the WorldPix International photographic agency and upcoming exhibition in Canberra.

WorldPix, the captive reader was informed, grew out of an idea from freelance photographer Alby Murdoch, who was pictured. The Alby Murdoch in the captioned photograph was looking remarkably handsome, if I may say so, and looking a lot more together than the slightly dishevelled bloke crammed into seat 37J. The press release the story was based on had left out the bit about the agency providing cover for certain government agents to carry out their nefarious tasks.

They'd used around a dozen pictures from the exhibition to illustrate the article, including a shot of mine showing a beautiful ten-year-old Balinese girl being taught the graceful and intricate hand movements of the Legong Keraton by an elegant older female dancer. There were actually some pretty confronting photographs in the exhibition, but the magazine's editor had decided to go with the less disturbing ones.

One of these pictures was a shot of the American Ambassador to Australia posing uncomfortably with his three young grandchildren in the grounds of the US Embassy. My mate Harry Wardell had taken that particular picture a few months before getting shot to death in a Double Bay café.

Harry had looked into the eyes of a lot of people over the years, it goes with the job, but after that assignment he'd told me he'd never seen a blacker, deeper, colder and emptier vista than the steel-grey eyes of Vaughan Crockett.

I flicked through the rest of the magazine and stopped at a story about Chinese New Year. The mention of lai see jogged my memory and I took out my wallet and found the red envelope inside. I caught the attention of one of the Asian cabin attendants.

'Any chance you might be able to translate this for me,' I asked, using my very best smile. I showed her the Chinese characters on the outside of the glassine envelope that held the negative.

She looked at the writing and shook her head. 'Sorry, love,' she said,

'I can't read Chinese. I'm actually from Wollongong, but maybe Maxine can help. Hey, Maxine, got a sec? Gentleman in 37J.'

Maxine was blonde and blue-eyed and as gorgeous as the rest of the cabin staff, including the blokes. She was holding a tray of small teacups in one hand and a large Chinese teapot in the other, and deftly managed not to fill my lap with chrysanthemum tea as she leaned over and studied the writing.

'I grew up in Honkers before the handover,' she explained. 'My Chinese is a bit rusty but my old man worked for Lloyds of London and I'm sure that symbol means something like "insurance"', she said, speaking with a slight English accent. 'The other stuff looks like "light" and "cart". Might be symbols phonetically representing a European name. Best I can do, I'm afraid. That help?'

I nodded. 'Might do, thanks.'

She smiled. 'Aren't you a bit old to be getting lucky money?'

'I take my luck where I can get it these days,' I said.

'Sounds fair enough. Would you like some tea?' she asked.

I nodded. 'Thanks.'

She filled one of the cups and I took it from her tray.

'Anything else I might help you with, Mr Murdoch?' she asked. 'To make your trip more pleasant?'

I guessed she must have been reading the in-flight magazine. I shook my head.

'Maybe later then,' she said. 'Just call me.' She paused. 'Anytime. The controls are in your armrest and you look like a man who knows the right buttons to press.'

She was gone before my addled brain could come up with a pithy response.

The aircraft lurched on some turbulence, splashing tea over the lip of the cup. I grabbed up the little red envelope and slipped it back into my wallet. There was no way I was going to let anything happen to Old Peng's insurance policy.

The entertainment screen on the seat-back in front of me displayed updates on our flight time and ETA - seven hours to go. My plan was to do a bit of quick business in Sydney and then grab a City Flyer shuttle to Canberra for the opening of the WorldPix exhibition. There was a nice new dinner suit I wanted to show off and there would be someone at the show I really wanted to bump into.

Maxine was pushing the food service trolley in my direction as I scrolled through to a wildlife channel just in time to see a cobra the size of a python unhinge its jaw and make a meal of a still-twitching rat. For the first time in my life, I considered going for the vegetarian option.

'Would you care for some lunch, Mr Murdoch?' Maxine asked.

'What are my choices?'

'Yes or no, I suppose,' she said with that dazzling smile.

I smiled back. I liked Maxine. Maxine knew what buttons to press, too.

Chapter Thirty-Nine

Bondi was its normal late-summer gorgeous self, and even more welcoming after the long weeks on the film, multiple murder attempts and gruelling flight home. My top-floor apartment in Luxor Mansions on Campbell Parade overlooks the beach, but as much as I wanted to wander down and fall into the waves, I had a lot to do. After making a couple of calls, booking a priority courier pick-up and grabbing a quick shower, I took tea with Mrs Templeton, my elderly widowed neighbour across the hall.

Mrs T had a fresh batch of her oatmeal cookies, still warm from the oven, and we sat and chatted at the table in front of her bay window while I checked through the mail she'd been collecting for me. She grilled me on my love-life, with numerous subtle references to that 'nice wee lass Julie' - it was Mrs T's mission in life to see Julie and me married. While she chatted away in her soft Scottish brogue, Dougal, her ugly, flatulent black pug, snuffled around our feet looking for crumbs. It was nice to return to some sense of normality, even with Dougal's lethal farts polluting the atmosphere.

Normality doesn't last long, especially when you fly into Canberra. The corridors of power in the nation's capital can be a strange place after a change of government. The outgoing politicians are shell-shocked and morose, and even their well-tailored suits seem to hang listlessly on them as they shuffle out of office suites that once had their names on the door, past weeping and soon to be unemployed staffers.

In the weeks following the election, the incoming pollies are ebullient, drunk on victory and the possibility of payback. They delight in asking, 'Aren't you the former member for Woop Woop West who lost his seat in a 9 per cent swing?' You figure if they thought they could get away with it they'd just unzip and piss on the walls to mark their new territory. Perhaps after changes of government the Parliament House caretakers put up temporary signs reading, *You Represent the People of Australia: Please Do Not Urinate in the Hallways!*

Next in the moroseness stakes after the outgoing members come the senior public servants who had unwisely hitched their wagons to the former government's star, and were now being sucked down with the sinking ship. The smarter ones read the signs early and subtly shifted to the middle ground, but the truly faithful found themselves reviewing their superannuation options, abandoning long-term love affairs with personal assistants or undiscriminating journalists, and contemplating buying newsagencies or coffee-shop franchises and the horrifying prospect of reconnecting with their families.

With a bit of time to spare before the exhibition opening, I wanted to get some background information on Detlef Fischer's aquatic enterprise up north so I gritted my teeth and headed for my appointment with Eldon Craddock, the First Assistant Secretary to the new Minister for the Department of Aquaculture Enhancement and Arboreal Export Enterprises. This new department had been quickly nicknamed Fish & Wood Chips and Craddock, despite having worked for the previous Minister, had somehow managed to retain his position under the new owners.

He stood up and walked around from behind his desk as his secretary led me into the office. The room was functional and sparsely furnished, and I noticed a slightly lighter space on the wall where a picture had been recently removed - probably a signed and framed portrait of the former PM, which was now bubble-wrapped and discreetly tucked away under a bed.

Eldon Craddock was about my age, slim but with the beginnings of a potbelly. Disturbingly, rather than the usual suit and tie uniform of public-service apparatchiks, he was wearing a plaid shirt over a black AC/DC 'Dirty Deeds' T-shirt, black skinny-legged Diesel jeans and Vans Johnny Ramone' sneakers. A silver-studded black leather wristband completed the outfit.

'Please have a seat, Mr..' He glanced at the folder his secretary had handed him, and continued,.. 'Murdoch. How can I be of help?'

'It's good of you to take the time,' I said.

'No worries, mate. With any change of government there is always a honeymoon period when we're forced to feign interest.'

No worries, mate?

'We go through this "new broom, things will change, much more accountable, et cetera, et cetera" phase, and then after the appropriate passage of time everything returns to normal.'

"Your honesty is refreshing,' I said.

He nodded and smiled. 'You should enjoy it while it lasts.'

'And how long will it last?'

'Just until everyone in Canberra figures out exactly where they stand.'

A couple of phone calls to Canberra insiders had filled me in on the background of Eldon Craddock. He was a legend in the public service because nobody knew who he was. Craddock had perfected the termite system of career advancement, keeping his head down, staying quiet and relentlessly gnawing away at his opponents' support structures. This approach was combined with a chameleon-like ability to adapt to whatever surroundings he found himself in.

Craddock's new boss was a former rock legend and his chief of staff was an ex-roadie. The Canberra Press Gallery were constantly pissing themselves at how the chief of staff came out before the Minister's press conferences to tap the microphones and chant, 'Two two. Two two.'

Craddock's outfit was a clue to just how far some people in Canberra would go to ingratiate themselves with their new masters.

'But let's get down to tin tacks..' he said, glancing at the folder again,'... Alby. Can I call you Alby?'

I nodded. 'Sure, why not. Should I call you Eldon?'

'Crash,' he said.

'What?'

'Crash,' he repeated. 'Crash Craddock. It's a nickname.'

'Like the sixties pop star? "Knock Three Times." "Dream Lover." "I'm Gonna Knock on Your Door."'

'That's the man. An American, I believe.'

"You're looking for street cred with the Minister?'

He nodded. 'Of course. Not trying too hard, do you think?'

I shook my head. 'Nah,' I said, 'go for it. Maybe you should put up some posters. Abba, Tony Orlando and Dawn, stuff like that.'

'Barry Manilow?'

'Sure, that could work, too.'

He smiled. 'Groovy. Now, I'm a little pressed for time, so how exactly can I assist you? This is to do with Fischer Aquaculture Industries, I believe?

'That's right. I'm looking for whatever background information you have on something called Barrana or JezzaBarrana.'

Craddock studied the folder on his desk. 'A provisional licence was granted to import a test batch of Barrana fingerlings for study and assessment, let me see, around six months ago under the former Minister. You may be aware that expansion of the level of sustainable intensive farming of edible aquatic assets is a priority of this government and this department. Over-exploitation of unregulated non-land-based edible aquatic assets means these assets will soon be approaching a level of non-viability.'

'You mean that pretty soon we'll have pulled all the wild fish out of the oceans, and battered lamb chops and chips isn't going to cut it with the Australian public.'

'Simplistically put, but yes. It's hard to believe, but the oceans off the North American east coast were once jammed with so many giant cod it was thought they could feed the world for eternity. But in less than fifty years of highly mechanised harvesting they were driven almost to extinction.'

'Didn't we have a similar experience down here with the Orange Roughy?'

'Exactly,' Craddock said. 'Fished the little buggers into oblivion. So we were pleased when Fischer Aquaculture Industries sought a licence to establish a secure research facility in the Northern Territory. They're currently testing the viability of an aquatic product that may offer us many long-term advantages.'

Australia has a long history of importing plants and animals to improve the environment, beautify the garden, fill the stew pot or deal with pests, only to have those well-intentioned ideas go belly-up in a very nasty way. Rabbits, foxes, prickly pear, Scotch thistle, the European carp and the cane toad are just some of our ecological management triumphs.

'And you have no concerns about these particular aquatic products escaping into the waterways and breeding with local fish?'

'Mr Murdoch, Alby, the imported fingerlings are all sterile, which was a condition of the licence. Besides which, the fish-farming facility has been assessed as being one hundred per cent secure.'

'Who does the assessing?'

'You might be aware that under the previous government we moved to an extremely high level of self-assessment.'

'So Fischer Aquaculture Industries have conducted a review of the security arrangements of Fischer Aquaculture Industries and Fischer Aquaculture Industries have decided everything about Fischer Aquaculture Industries is just tickety-boo?'

'An interesting turn of phrase but essentially correct.'

'Does self-assessment actually work in the real world?' I asked.

'It would seem so,' Craddock said. 'We have carefully self-assessed our procedures for self-assessment and the advice I get about us from our people is we are doing a fantastic job.'

'So you don't have any reservations about these fish?'

Craddock smiled. 'I always express minor reservations in my reports. It provides a suitable fallback position in the event of the project not going well.'

'By things "not going well" you mean these fish escaping into our nation's rivers and waterways?'

"My, my, Alby, you are a gloomy Gus. These fish are guaranteed to be sterile, as I said, and from what I've been told, quite delicate, having been bred only for pond rearing.'

That didn't sound too much like the fish Cartwright had been forced to incinerate with flamethrowers, Fischer must have left a few things out of his application for the import licence, or maybe he really didn't know what he was getting into.

'Even in the highly unlikely event of one or two Barrana managing to make their way into a creek or river,' Craddock continued, 'we have been assured they would almost certainly die within weeks, if not days, being unused to our robust ecosystem. Imagine if the Department of Aquaculture Enhancement and Arboreal Export Enterprises and other public-service entities spent all their time worrying about worst-case scenarios. With distractions like that, nobody would get any work done. We need to be able to get on with our job.'

'And exactly what job is that?'

'This file of yours seems to indicate an ongoing connection to government, Alby, so I thought you'd understand. The primary task of the public service, simply put, is not to be found out.'

He closed the folder. 'The long-term success of any public-service department lies in its ability to conceal its abject failure. The sociopath expends up to 90 per cent of his energy in trying to appear normal and unremarkable, despite his other proclivities, and I'm sure I could commission a study that would reach the same conclusion about most of my colleagues. I won't, of course, since I would then have to commit vast amounts of my department's resources to concealing those findings.'

I stood up to leave. I'd already self-assessed my visit as a complete waste of time. Still, if the imported Barrana fingerlings were sterile and they tasted as good as Peter Cartwright had said, it was a win-win situation. Just as long as Fischer built very high fences around the ponds and his staff kept away from the water.

'Have you got a location on file for the fish farm?'

Cradock flicked through his folder. 'It appears to be ... ah, somewhere outside of Darwin.'

'That's a lot of territory,' I said. 'You got anything more specific?'

He flicked through the notes again and shook his head.

'Sorry, no,' he said, standing up. 'I hope I've been of some help, Alby. The briefing note that accompanied your request for this meeting indicated you have the highest level of security clearance, which I assume means you are some kind of security operative.' He grinned. 'Of course, I also assume we have one of those situations where you can't confirm this.'

'Can't confirm or deny, Crash, you know how it goes.'

'Because if you did then you'd have to kill me, right?'

I shrugged.

He made a shooting motion with the thumb and index finger of his right hand. 'Gotcha, Alby, stay cool.'

'Thanks, Crash,' I said as I shook his hand.

Deep down, I wanted to kill him anyway, just for the hell of it.

Chapter Forty

I MADE IT DOWN TO OLD PARLIAMENT HOUSE WHILE THERE WAS STILL some finger food left, so maybe my luck was changing. Whoever came up with the idea of using the Old Parliament House building to host exhibitions deserved a pat on the back, as did the design team that had hung the show. The giant photographic prints on display were mounted on the walls or suspended from the ceiling, and already there must have been a couple of hundred people milling about.

Smartly uniformed wait staff were circulating with trays of drinks and hors d'oeuvres. I took a glass of champagne from one bloke and a delicate curry puff from a waitress I knew from attending way too many Canberra receptions.

'Good evening, Kellie,' I said. 'Uni going well?'

She smiled. 'Very well, thank you, Mr Murdoch. One more semester and then hopefully my waitressing days will be over.'

'We'll miss you at these bunfights, I said, 'but God knows the national capital needs as many psychologists as we can get. You remember the plan?'

She smiled. 'Of course, Mr Murdoch. Anything that looks extra tasty comes straight from the kitchen to you.'

'Is the Prime Minister here?'

She nodded. 'He arrived about twenty minutes ago. I'm sure he'll be very understanding about dropping to second place on my list.'

I scooped up another of the curry puffs and headed into the melee. The party was in full swing by this stage, and I couldn't miss Gudrun Arkell because being six foot tall and gorgeous with red curly hair she was pretty un-missable.

'Security around here must be pretty slack,' I said, 'letting people like you in.'

'Lesbians?'

'Journalists.'

'Ouch, Alby,' she said, 'low blow. I'm shattered.'

She bent down and planted a kiss on my cheek after flicking a little something curry-puff-related off my lapel.

'Nice suit,' she said. 'If I wasn't gay, I could go for a man like you. Only younger, and more handsome, and with a little bit of charm, perhaps.'

I guess I'd asked for that. 'So, Goods,' I said, 'you off the clock?'

She held up a glass of champagne.

'Don't get too plastered,' I said, 'and don't leave. I may have a big story for you.'

'How big?'

'Really big.'

She smiled. 'That's nice. A girl can never have too many Walkley Awards.

Queen of the Canberra Press Gallery, Gudrun knew about my double life, but we went way back and I knew she was someone I could trust with a secret. She was also my 'go to girl when I needed to know what was really happening in the corridors of power, or when I wanted to dish a little dirt on anyone who annoyed me. Call me petty and vindictive, and I'll show you my t-shirt that confirms it in bold type.

Gudrun flagged down a passing waiter and switched from champagne to mineral water, and I went Ambassador hunting. I clocked Gwenda Felton smack-bang in the middle of the hubbub. The peroxide, crimson lipstick and chiffon fashion catastrophe was chatting with my target, the US Ambassador. For security reasons, Gwenda had no public link to WorldPix but she couldn't resist showing up at our functions. I'd tried to warn her she was going to get someone killed one day but she wouldn't listen.

Gwenda spotted me at the same time and waved me over.

'Ah, Murdoch,' she said, her smile as white and artificial as her teeth and pearls, 'this is the American Ambassador, the Honourable Vaughan Crockett. Mr Ambassador, this is Alby Murdoch, one of the many talented photographers working for WorldPix.'

We shook hands. I can be polite when I have to, even to people who've been trying very hard to have me killed.

Taller than me by a couple of inches, Crockett was all spray tan, capped teeth, hair plugs and that ersatz bonhomie so beloved of media moguls and powerful politicians. I had the better dinner suit, though.

Just behind the Ambassador were a couple of burly blokes with buzz cuts, loose-fitting suit jackets and discreet ear-pieces. Usually ambassadors bodyguards came from the US government's Diplomatic Protective Service, but there was something about these guys that said they might be freelancers. And not very nice freelancers at that.

'Wonderful show, Murdoch, wonderful show,' Crockett said, gripping my hand for not one second longer than was absolutely necessary. Being the Yank Ambassador, I was pretty sure the CIA had him well briefed on WorldPix and what went on behind the scenes.

Crockett's face was Botoxed smoother than a baby's bottom. Botox is a bad move for actors, since it destroys their ability to show subtle emotion through facial expression, but for politicians this actually works a treat. Together, Crockett and Gwenda looked like a couple of Victorian-era plaster death masks.

'Do you have a favourite picture in the exhibition, Murdoch?' the Ambassador asked.

He had that consummate politician's skill of feigning intense interest while displaying utter contempt.'

'My favourite arrived a little too late to be hung,' I said, 'but I'd love to show it to you when you have a moment. It's in the Cartwright Annexe.'

Even Botox couldn't conceal the change in the Ambassador's expression at the mention of the name Cartwright.

Gwenda was looking at me warily. 'Perhaps the Ambassador – ' she started to say, but I cut her off.

'I think the Prime Minister is looking for you, Gwenda. Last time I saw him he was standing next to the portrait of Lenny de Carlo.'

Gwenda suddenly had that deer-in-the-headlights look I so love to see. Lenny deCarlo was the radio shock jock who'd accidentally left the mike open during a commercial break in an interview with Gwenda while she was still a member of parliament and a minister in the previous government.

A couple of nasty comments about immigrants she thought were off-air had led to her forced resignation, and deCarlo's ratings bump after the incident made you wonder how accidental it really was.

'I wouldn't keep the PM waiting, Gwenda,' I said.

Crockett followed me across the main exhibition room with his bodyguards in tow. The exhibition's curator had made some interesting choices in the hanging of the photographs and we passed through a succession of images of smiling politicians, starving refugees, victims of landmines, famine, deforestation, religious intolerance, political repression and that noble all-too-human desire to become world famous by eating as many hotdogs as possible in just twelve minutes.

I found the doorway I was looking for and suggested that maybe we should have this viewing in private. The Ambassador seemed amused at my suggestion but told his bodyguards to wait outside.

The small anteroom held a couple of armchairs, a side table with a bottle of whisky and two glasses, and a picture on an easel. The picture was about a metre square and covered in bubble wrap.

'You want a drink?' I asked, indicating the whisky

The Ambassador shook his head and glanced at his watch.

'I'm just back from Vietnam,' I said.

'Yes,' he said, 'so I understand. I'm sure things have changed since I was there. It was a very dangerous place back then.'

'Still is. Or maybe I'm just accident-prone. Old Peng and Peter Cartwright send their regards, by the way.'

Crockett tensed up at the names. He was studying the picture on the easel, trying to work out what was under the bubble wrap.

'The past is the past, Murdoch, he said, 'and sometimes people who won't let sleeping dogs lie get bitten.'

'Sometimes those sleeping dogs have rabies, Mr Ambassador, and need to be put down for the common good.'

'I'm not sure your Prime Minister would appreciate someone like you calling the United States Ambassador a mad dog.'

'If the flea collar fits…' I said.

Our discussion was turning out to be more a battle of idioms than a battle of wits.

Crockett glanced at his watch again. 'I have an important dinner to attend. Why don't you just tell me what's on your mind and then we can both go our separate ways.'

'Suits me. All I want is for you to call off your attack dogs and then immediately retire from public life.'

Ambassador Crockett laughed out loud

'I'm serious,' I said.

'What makes you think I have attack dogs to call off? And why would I want to retire from public life?'

'Because I asked nicely. And because if you don't, I'll see that you get charged with multiple counts of murder, war crimes, misuse of government property, fraud, theft and a couple of other incidents that a smart US attorney might reasonably assess as coming under the heading of treason.'

Crockett walked over and stood close to me. We stared at each other for a moment and I knew exactly what Harry had meant about those eyes. It was like looking at a cold, moonless winter midnight sky in Tierra del Fuego, without the stars.

'Listen to me very carefully, you little cocksucker,' Crockett said in a low voice, 'I have a pager in my pocket and my finger is on the button. If I press it, the two men standing outside that door will come in and then we'll all go somewhere private. What happens after that won't be very pleasant - well, not for you at least. I might choose to have them break your fingers, kneecap you, cut out your eyes and perhaps chop off your tongue, and then your cocksucking days will be well and truly over. And given who I am, nobody will be able to do a damn thing about it.'

Standing this close to the Ambassador, I started to wonder if he'd had a chin implant as well as the Botox.

'Then, if you're very lucky,' he continued, 'maybe I'll let you live out your days sitting blind and dumb and crippled in a wheelchair contemplating the wisdom of fucking with people you really shouldn't fuck with.'

The temptation to kick the Ambassador in the balls was overwhelming, but he probably did have a panic button in his pocket. The blokes outside looked both competent and crazy, and I knew Gwenda would never forgive me if I turned our opening night party into a bloodbath before the PM headed back to the Lodge.

'Why don't we compromise then,' I said. 'How about this: you call off your attack dogs and retire from public life, and we'll call it quits.'

'You must be out of your mind,' Crockett said. 'You're talking about ancient history. That was over thirty years ago. And who's going to believe an old Chinese gangster who dribbles or the demented ramblings of a Vietnam vet who was involved in drug running, turned his back on his own country and almost certainly has post-traumatic stress syndrome and early-onset Alzheimer's, or will have by the time my people get through with destroying his credibility in the press. You see, Mr Murdoch, nothing ever happened - there are no reliable witnesses and no proof. End of story.'

I thought that over for a minute. 'It's that old philosophical conundrum so beloved by your sixties hippies, I suppose. If a B-52 drops fifty thousand pounds of high explosives in the forest and no-one survives, did it really happen?'

'Did what happen?' Crockett said with a smile.

'But maybe what we're talking about here isn't some convenient, accidentally off-target arc light strike out in the boonies.'

I wondered if Crockett was thinking about pressing that button.

'Ever get totally wasted at a party, Mr Ambassador, and do something you later regretted?' I asked. 'Speaking for myself, I gave up championship-level drinking a few years back when I realised that if you hang out with photographers and get pissed and do something stupid, some bastard always has a camera handy.'

Crockett looked across at the bubble-wrapped photograph on the easel.

'I was beginning to think you'd never ask,' I said, sliding the protective covering off the photograph.

A picture might be worth a thousand words, but for the Ambassador I reckoned this particular one was worth around seven. Shit creek, barbed-wire canoe, no paddle.

Chapter Forty-One

THE AMBASSADOR STARED AT THE PHOTOGRAPH WITHOUT SPEAKING. Without breathing, too, from the look of things. I knew he wouldn't press his panic button because he couldn't risk anyone else coming in and seeing what we were looking at. Crockett was screwed, and he knew it.

'How do you like it?' I asked. 'The colours in the negative were a bit faded, but that's understandable given its age and the storage conditions. And, of course, colour negative film was pretty crappy back in the sixties but I think the grain adds to the effect.'

Crockett kept on staring and his Botoxed face was very pale.

From the room layout, the photograph might actually have been taken in a suite at the Hotel Indochine Luxe Royale, way back before the renovations. Chloe Ransome, our senior retoucher in the Sydney WorldPix office, had carefully scanned the old negative before cleaning up and sharpening the resulting digital file in Photoshop. She'd brought back most of the original colour and detail, and had done an amazing job considering I'd instructed her to do it with her eyes shut and forget she'd ever seen the image after it was printed and mounted.

In the photograph, several half-empty bottles of Cutty Sark whisky sit on a table amongst bundles of greenbacks and plastic-wrapped packages of compressed white powder with Chinese characters on them. Old Peng had been a good looking man thirty some years back. He was wearing a nicely tailored sharkskin suit and sitting on a couch with several very young Vietnamese girls, all smiling, all topless.

Crockett, probably then in his early twenties, was smoking what appeared an be a very large joint and was naked except for a towel around his waist. He was posing with a Smith & Wesson submachine gun in one hand, a Colt semi-automatic pistol tucked into the towel at his waist and his spare arm around a girl who was also topless and looked about twelve.

I figured Old Peng had organised for an other girl or one of his henchmen to casually take the picture when Crocker was too bloody stoned to care. Old Peng looked as sober as a judge and he was smiling into the camera as someone snapped his insurance policy.

I turned back towards Crockett. 'I'm thinking of titling it, "Future US Ambassador and potential vice-president with booze, under-age Asian hookers, guns, heroin, bundles of cash and nasty Chinese gangster." '

Crockett looked like he might be about to throw up.

'Good thing you were wearing that towel, Mr Ambassador,' I said, 'if they just fuzz out the girl's tits they'll be able to run it on the cover of Time and Newsweek. You want that drink now?'

Crockett nodded. I poured him a triple. The whisky was Cutty Sark, the same brand as the bottles in the photograph. Cutty's a blend, and it isn't something I'd usually drink, but I reckoned a little nostalgic touch might be appropriate.

I studied the picture for a moment, trying to visualise it with the Time or Newsweek logo at the top. If they did run it, they really would fuzz out the tits. That was America for you: they could show a venal politician caught in the act of consorting with criminals, under-age girls, guns, illicit drugs and wads of illegal cash, but the sight of a nipple would bring in millions of letters, phone calls and emails from a morally outraged citizenry.

Crockett had finished off his whisky. 'There was a war on back then, Murdoch, you know.'

'Great,' I said, 'that explains the guns. Now all we have left are the half-naked teenage hookers, the piles of cash and all that heroin. And the Chinese mobster. Even your spinmeisters at MB&F won't be able to help you wriggle your way out of this one. And speaking of MB&F, I hope Brett Tozer's family got a nice little remuneration package after his untimely demise.'

'Brett who?'

'Tozer. He worked for you at MB&F. I'm guessing he was on the movie to look out for your interests.'

Crockett was looking confused and the bluster and bombast was gone. He was even speaking softly.

'My people had instructions to buy off or shut down every attempt to film Cartwright's story because of the questions it might raise, but this production somehow got past us while I was concentrating on securing the vice-presidential nomination. I figured we'd just invest in the film and leverage our position to put someone in to keep an eye on things. I didn't even know the name of our man.'

That was probably true. People like Crockett just issue general instructions to their underlings and then stay well clear, purposely ignorant of the specific dirty work that ensues. Of course qualities like those made Crockett well suited for high government office.

'So what's your price for the negative, Murdoch?' Crockett asked.

I shook my head. The Ambassador thought for a moment and then he decided to go with the approach that usually worked for him.

'You've seen what my people can do. I could set them the task of finding that negative, whatever it takes, no matter who gets hurt.'

'C'mon, Crockett, get with the programme,' I said, 'this is the digital age. The negative means nothing. There are multiple copies of that picture stored all over the world as data files. I'm the only one who knows where they all are and the only person who can make them go away,'

'So you do have a price?'

I nodded. 'And it's a bargain. You go away and they go away. Resign from public life, book a long cruise, start a charitable foundation, try to set a world caviar-eating record, I really don't care. Just fuck off out of politics and never come back, and the picture never sees the light of day.'

He was looking at me again with those dead eyes.

'I'm surprised you are willing to settle for just that, Murdoch. I would have thought a little man like you might want to be known as someone who brought down a potential candidate for vice-president of the United States. What exactly have you got against me, Murdoch? I don't understand. We've never even met.'

I was looking at a bloke who was after the second most powerful position in the world, and he didn't get it.

'Putting aside the fact that you've been trying to kill me and a number of my friends,' I said, 'did you actually look at any of the pictures on the walls out there? People tell me I'm cynical, but my job lets me get up close and personal with what happens when the wrong people start calling the shots - people like you. So let's just call it a pre-emptive surgical strike on behalf of all those poor buggers out there with the potential to be written off as collateral damage.'

I put my glass down on the table. 'Let's say I'll be content to think of you sitting on a yacht somewhere contemplating what could have been, and the wisdom of fucking with people you really shouldn't fuck with.'

"'That makes us sound a little bit alike, doesn't it?

I shook my head. 'Not in the slightest. And the way I can tell is that if I was anything like you, right now you'd be dead.'

'I still have some very powerful friends you know, Murdoch.'

'Bully for you, Mr Ambassador. Sadly, I don't. But I do have a number of very reliable acquaintances who have instructions about what to do should anything unfortunate happen to me, Peter Cartwright and his son, or Jack Stark and his mate VT, and you can be connected to it in any way, shape or form And believe me, that picture will go public and then you'll be able to count your powerful friends on the fingers of no hands. So go take a long boat ride and enjoy your retirement.'

Crockett poured another whisky. 'Okay. Suppose I were to do what you suggest. Can I trust you, Murdoch?

'Nope,' I said, 'not for one bloody second. So I guess that makes us even.'

Chapter Forty-Two

When I got back to the party I was feeling pretty chipper, and my mood got even better when I found there were still some snacks left. I spotted Gudrun in the middle of the hubbub chatting to a photographer visiting from the UK. The bloke was putting in some serious spadework in the charm department so I felt I was actually doing the poor bugger a favour by interrupting.

'Hey, Goods,' I yelled, 'try and grab the Yank Ambassador before he leaves. You might want to ask him if he still plans on throwing his hat in the ring for the Vice-President's job?'

'I owe you, Alby,' she said.

'Always, babe,' I said, and then we split in different directions.

I called over my shoulder to the unhappy-looking Pommy lensman, 'Believe me, mate, you never had a chance.'

Kellie appeared out of the crowd carrying a tray of spring rolls and she seemed to be looking for me.

'Excellent timing,' I said, helping myself to a couple.

'Mr Murdoch,' Kellie said in a low voice, 'there's some one in the kitchen who wants to speak to you. He says it's urgent.'

She led me out to the large kitchen, where two men were waiting.

One of them was another of those bodyguard types who seemed to be cluttering up the evening and the other was Peter Tranh.

"You ought to try one of these cha gio, mate," I said.

Peter Tranh didn't look like a bloke interested in finger food. Peter Tranh looked like a bloke with something to get off his chest.

'Mr Murdoch,' Tranh said, 'I'm here to make a confession.'

'You and your old man don't need to worry about Crockett any more. That's all been taken care of.'

'This is good news, and I know my father will be very grateful, but it's not why I've tracked you down. This is about Project PB, the Barrana.'

'I'll bite,' I said, 'because I know those damned fish do.'

Peter Tranh didn't appear to be in the mood for one of my jokes.

'As you may know, until recently I was a regular visitor at the Manchu Palace Casino's VIP rooms. On several occasions I spoke with Playford Peng on general subjects and sometimes about my research with fish. I mentioned the piranha project and the ensuing difficulties, which seemed to pique his interest. Soon after this, I began to lose heavily at the tables but Playford was more than happy to advance credit.'

As shocking as the concept of a casino running rigged tables was, it was easy to see how the Manchu Palace could afford to hand out ten grand in chips to valued customers.

'When my losses finally reached a level way beyond my ability to repay, Playford suggested that I could eliminate the debt by producing a special batch of fish to his specifications. I'm afraid I wasn't thinking straight, and I was concerned about the shame I might bring on my father, so I gave him what he wanted.'

It was like a car crash you can see coming. Suddenly everything went into slow motion and I knew the spring roll I was holding wasn't going to get eaten. I wasn't even sure I'd be able to keep down the ones I'd already swallowed.

'Peng wanted a batch of fish that weren't sterile, didn't he?'

Peter Tranh nodded. 'Playford Peng now has breeding stock of these dangerous creatures. These particular fish are very enthusiastic at mating time.'

I couldn't fault them on that score, but you just knew the Barrana wouldn't be practising safe sex. In fact, there was nothing safe at all about these bloody fish.

'And if they should escape from captivity,' I asked, 'say,' into our local rivers and perhaps the ocean?'

Peter Tranh looked down at his shoes. 'I'm afraid that would not be a very good thing, Mr Murdoch. That would not be a very good thing at all?'

I was looking around for a bin to dump my spring roll when Kellie came up to me with her silver tray.

'You really need to try these fish balls with lemon and dill mayonnaise, Mr Murdoch,' she said. 'They're straight from the oven and, believe me, they're pretty damned delicious.'

I shook my head. 'Thanks but no thanks, Kellie,' I said. 'I've just discovered there are some other fish balls I need to take care of ASAP.'

Chapter Forty-Three

In my game, I bump into people I know all the time at airports, which can either lead to us having a couple of drinks in the nearest bar or me hiding behind a handy magazine rack until they buzz off. This time, the magazine racks at Darwin airport were tantalisingly just out of reach.

'Hello, Mr Murdoch, fancy meeting you here.'

'Yes,' I said, 'it's a depressingly small world isn't it, Lothar.'

Lothar looked like he was waiting for someone, and thankfully it wasn't me. Last time we'd crossed paths he was hanging out with an ex-con white-collar crim named Priday, born again in prison as pastor to the upwardly mobile. Lothar's job had been to supply guns and muscle, and the relationship hadn't worked out.

'Mr Murdoch, I'd like to say something. I'm sorry about what I done in Sydney and I'm a changed man.'

He did seem different. He was still skinny and seedy-looking, with bad teeth and lank hair, but he now had a tan. The effect was a bit like a first attempt at make-up by an undertaker's apprentice, but at least he was wearing a clean white shirt, neatly pressed chinos and deck shoes.

'Mr Murdoch, I was ensnared by the testicles of organised crime at a young age and now I've finally broken free.'

'Lothar' and 'organised' were two words I'd never put together in one sentence. 'Crime' was a different story. If he was here in Darwin it would be because Sydney was currently too hot for him. He'd probably supplied some heavy dudes with illegal items which weren't exactly as described per the agreement. Besides trading in girls and guns, Lothar sometimes sold counterfeit Viagra that couldn't raise an erection in Long Bay Jail.

'I think you might mean tentacles, Lothar,' I said. 'The things on an octopus.'

'Tentacles? Really? Bugger, that means I'll have to redo all the menus.'

I stared at him and he took a card from his trouser pocket.

Forceps or rubber gloves not being available, I had no option but to take the card with my bare hand, holding it gingerly by one corner. It appeared that Lothar L. Ludovik was now the general manager of Bluey's Backyard BBQ Restaurant, where steak and seafood were a speciality and incredible franchising opportunities were apparently now available. The fine print on the card said the owners, Bluey Operating Systems NL, were a subsidiary of Fischer Aquaculture Industries.

'There's actually no Bluey, Mr Murdoch,' Lothar said, 'that's what we in the biz call a marketing strategy. Darwin's the first branch, but in five years we plan to be open all over the place.'

'Bringing char-grilled marinated octopus testicles to the world is a lofty ambition, Lothar, and it takes balls.'

'Gee, thanks, Mr Murdoch, but I can't take all the credit. Here comes the real brains behind the operation.'

I'd seen Fischer sitting in first class on the flight up from Sydney and I'd spotted him approaching us out of the corner of my eye.

'Mr Murdoch,' Lothar said, 'this is Mr Detlef Fischer of Bluey Operating Systems. Mr Fischer is my CEO.'

Lothar and Fischer were a match made in heaven, if heaven was having a very off day.

'We've already met,' I said.

Fischer was carrying one of those expensive Italian leather overnight bags so popular with the disgustingly rich and the wives of airline baggage handlers. He put his bag down and smiled that million-watt smile again as I shook his hand. The handshake gave me a perfect excuse to drop Lothar's business card.

'I see you're going in for vertical integration with the fish farming, Detlef - hatch 'em, grow 'em, grill 'em, sell 'em.'

'It's the way of the future,' Fischer said. 'You should stop by the restaurant while you're in Darwin, Mr Murdoch, as my guest. Trust me, our seafood is truly excellent and Lothar will take good care of you?'

'Lothar here has tried to take care of me on a number of occasions,' I said, 'and it always ends in tears.'

Lothar smiled uncomfortably and looked down at his feet.

Fischer put one hand on his shoulder. 'Now that seems rather unfair, Mr Murdoch. Mr Ludovik has turned over a new leaf. He has become a vital part of our management team.'

'Do you actually know what CEO stands for, Lothar?' I asked.

He opened and closed his mouth a couple of times.

'Wanna take a crack at spelling it? No? Thought not.'

I looked at Fischer and shook my head. 'Good luck with your plans for world restaurant domination.'

We all left by the same exit, heading towards the car park.

I found my dinky Corolla rental and spotted Lothar stuffing Fischer's gear into a bright red fully restored two-door 1970s Alfa Romeo Montreal. Bastard.

I'd just turned the key in the ignition when everything went red and a heavy throbbing filled my ears. The shiny red Alfa was parked right across the front of my car.

Fischer wound down his window. 'Why don't you let me drive you into town, Mr Murdoch. Lothar can drop the rental at your hotel.'

'Why the hell not?' I said.

Alfa had built less than four thousand of these babies so the offer of a ride in one was too good to pass up. Plus, the trip would give me a chance to find out exactly how much Detlef knew about his new fishy friends, and with any luck discover the location of the fish farm. The Northern Territory is twice the size of Texas and I didn't have time to go wandering around with a fishing rod and a bucket of bait, hoping to stumble over a pond full of feral fish.

Chapter Forty-Four

THE MONTREAL'S INTERIOR WAS LEATHER, THE STEERING WHEEL WAS on the wrong side and Fischer laughed when I reached over my right shoulder for the seatbelt.

'No seatbelts in this baby, Mr Murdoch. No airbags, no pissy unleaded petrol. Just a race-tuned 2.6-litre V8. Cost me sixty grand to get her back into this condition. I've always kept her in Darwin because we had no highway speed limits until recently. Stupid bastards.'

The 'stupid bastards' were the politicians who had decided to scrap the progressive 'go as fast as you like, get as drunk as you like and kill yourselves in record numbers' policy so precious to freedom-loving Territorians. Now they were limited to 130 kph on four major highways and 110 kph on the rest of the open roads. All they had to do now was persuade the locals that a red traffic light actually meant STOP and democracy was all done and dusted up north.

The Montreal's engine started with a low rumble I could feel right down to my socks. Fischer hit the gas and I got that classic V8 rear wheel-drive kick in the pants as we surged forward.

'Nice,' I said.

He nodded. 'Yeah, I've done okay for a boy who started off peeling potatoes in his old man's chip shop at fifteen.'

Now that wasn't what I'd read in the dossier Jimmy Yip had given me in Hong Kong. Rather than this heart-warming rags to riches tale, it'd been more a riches to riches story. One of those 'I started with nothing but a measly twenty million dollar inheritance and with hard work managed to turn it into some serious money'.

For a German, Fischer drove like an Italian. He kept his seat way back, arms outstretched, hands never straying far from the lower half of the steering wheel.

The Montreal's interior was cutting edge in the seventies but it now looked kind of quaint. Still oozed classic Italian design, though. There was a parcel shelf in front of me, and because I'm the inquisitive type I leaned forward and popped open the concealed glove compartment beneath it. A quick glance told me that Fischer might drive Italian, but held true to his German ancestry in the optional extras department. The pistol was a Walther P22 semi-automatic. Ten rounds of .22 ammo in a compact package.

'Wow, just like a real gun, only smaller.'

Fischer leaned across and closed the glove compartment.

'I've got a licence. Just keep it for a bit of target practice when I get bored and to wave at dickheads who annoy me.'

'I'll keep that in mind,' I said.

Lead is lead and ten rounds of dinky .22 long-rifle ammo at close range will put a serious crimp in your life expectancy - just ask any Mafia hit man.

'So what made you decide to expand from importing and wholesaling into the fish-farming business?' I asked.

'The whole thing was Playford's idea. He was willing to take a back seat and bankroll it and give me all the glory, so I thought why not? Jezebel seemed to think it was a great idea - I met her through Peng - and he reckoned the product couldn't miss if we used her profile for marketing.'

'Peng got you and Jezebel involved?'

He nodded. 'Playford dragged me along to a charity dinner in Melbourne a while back and introduced us. We got on like a house on fire.'

Fuelled no doubt by the warm glow of a fifty-grand charitable donation and that romantic dinner for two in her penthouse apartment.

'That was good of him,' I said.

'He was just returning a favour. He owes me big-time.'

'Really?'

'Yeah. Playford and I went to school together at Fairbrothers.'

'I heard.'

'Playford looked up to me at school, still does. I was his protector.'

'Protecting him from what?'

'There are a lot of racist people at a place like Fairbrothers, and a porky little Chink like Playford can have a hard time even if his old man is richer than God. Old Peng used to send me money from Honkers. He wanted me to hang out with Playford, make sure he wasn't lonely. Not much of a socialiser our Playford, even back then. You know I tried to get the bastard his first root when he turned fifteen, but I'm pretty sure he's a bit light on in the tackle department. Never cracked it with any of the chicks I lined up for him. And let me tell you, I had to call in quite a few favours. Playford's no prize, even with all that money.'

'And people say romance is dead.'

'Jezebel was right - you really are a cynical bastard, Murdoch.'

I actually preferred to think of myself as post-cynical but in a hard, cruel world full of nasty pricks like Fischer it wasn't all that easy.

'So how's your fish-farming caper working out so far? I wouldn't mind taking a look at your facilities. Maybe do a WorldPix photo story on the project. We could syndicate it worldwide - great publicity.'

Fischer shook his head. 'Sorry, strictly off limits I'm afraid. Quarantine regulations and all that crap. Playford insists on keeping the location secret until we are sure the first batch has fully acclimatised. We don't want anything leaking out until we're ready to hit the market.'

'No problems so far?'

'Nothing to speak of. We had a few initial glitches, but everything seems fine now. Playford flew some of his people in to keep things under control. The trick apparently is a regular feeding schedule. These babies can get a bit boisterous, shall we say, around meal times. Funny thing is, I always thought sterilising animals tended to make them a bit less rambunctious.'

It was starting to look like Fischer was totally clueless about the whole operation.

'Have any problems with them turning on each other?' I asked. 'I've heard that can happen when vicious predators hang out together.'

Fischer smiled. 'If you are referring to my partnership with Playford, I shouldn't worry too much. Porky little bastard knows exactly how much I did for him at school and, as I said, he looks up to me, sort of like an older brother.'

I guessed the staff at Fairbrothers paid as much attention to teaching their students about irony as they did ethics. And I wondered if Fischer knew what had happened to Playford's last older brother.

Chapter Forty-Five

Bluey's Backyard BBQ was inside one of those massive warehouse structures that usually house hardware stores retailing every tool known to man, or evangelical mega-churches selling DIY stairways to heaven and touting access to divine intervention for the physically ailing or the temporarily cash-strapped: 'All Prayers Now 20% Off - This Sunday Only!' A seventeen-year-old in Dunlop Volley tennis shoes, very short shorts and a tiny bikini top greeted me at the entrance. She was holding a couple of large laminated menus.

'G'day, mate,' she said. 'Bloody great you could make it to Bluey's, where the steaks are awesome, the fish are jumping fresh and the beers are on ice.'

She said it with the unhappy awkwardness common to Aussies forced to act like perky Yanks by a corporate management structure aping some American ideal of a restaurant formula for success. It was almost like being arrested in the US. I expected her to follow up the greeting with, 'You do not have to order anything but anything you do order will be deep-fried to within an inch of its life. If you cannot afford to order anything we have a poor person's special on page seven - also deep-fried and served with extra grease.'

'I've got an appointment with Lothar,' I said, 'and believe me . . .' I bent down to look at her name tag, which put my eyes directly in line with her boobs, '. . . Kylie, I think I'm just as embarrassed to be here as you are.'

Kylie walked over to a podium and spoke into a microphone. 'Lothar to the front gate, please,' boomed out from loudspeakers and echoed around the vast hall. 'Youse have a visitor.'

A joint like Bluey's wasn't high up on my desired culinary experiences list, and there were a hell of a lot better spots to dine in Darwin, but Lothar had a couple of things I needed.

The first was as much information as I could dig out of him on the location and current state of the Barrana project. The second was a little bit of protection for when I went sniffing around said project.

While I waited for Lothar, the full horror of the enterprise became apparent as I looked around the place. Scattered throughout the hall were intersecting sections of your classic Aussie timber-paling backyard fence. At the point where the fences met was a Hills hoist hung with T-shirts, shorts and baseball caps emblazoned with the Bluey's logo, the items being for sale to the restaurant's happy diners. Each of the intersecting fences created four separate dining areas, which were furnished with green plastic grass, an aluminium combo picnic table and seat set, and a gigantic stainless-steel barbecue with gas bottle attached.

The place was packed, even this early in the evening. Above me I could hear the rumble of a ventilation system working overtime to clear the air of smoke and the smell of overcooked beef. The sound system was fighting back with a weird audio mix of didgeridoos, kookaburras, two-stroke lawnmowers and leaf blowers. If you threw in a wading pool full of screaming sunburned kids, a drunken brawl, someone chucking in the oleanders and a boofy bloke having a quick knee-trembler behind the back shed with his best mate's wife, this could all start to look terrifyingly real.

I watched as a young Japanese couple were led to a nearby dining area by Kylie and seated at one of the uncomfortable picnic tables. They had a brief discussion and then pointed to an item on the menu. Kylie keyed something into a small PDA and walked away. Moments later, a pimply teenage boy in board shorts and a Hawaiian shirt walked up pushing an old Victa motor mower. The mower had a steel rack welded to the top and the rack held two eskies.. The boy put one esky near the barbecue and set the other one down by the table.

He took two cans of beer from the esky by the table and plonked them in front of the guests. The beer was followed by several plastic bowls covered with cling wrap - salads, no doubt. The boy then walked back to the barbecue and fired her up. The second esky contained two giant steaks and half a lobster that he held up to show to the young couple. The Japanese girl clapped her hands excitedly. The waiter tossed the steaks and seafood onto the barely warm grill plate with a distinct lack of enthusiasm for his task.

'All set for dinner, Mr Murdoch?'

I turned around. Lothar was wearing board shorts and the same Hawaiian shirt as the waiters, evidently the corporate uniform. On the young waiters it just looked daggy. On Lothar, the ensemble went places you didn't want to think about, but the word paedophile came to mind.

'You definitely out of the gun-running caper, Lothar?'

He looked around to see if anyone had overheard. 'That was my old life, Mr Murdoch,' he whispered, 'you know I'm on the straight and narrow now.'

'Too bad,' I whispered back, 'because if I was deranged enough to even consider dining here I'd order up a nice little Browning so I could blow my fucking brains out.'

'Mr Murdoch, you should keep an open mind to new things. I think you might be surprised. Here at Bluey's we aim to give the customer a real taste of that great classic Aussie backyard barbecue experience. But without the flies.' He paused. 'Or the beetroot.' He looked around again and then whispered conspiratorially, 'The Japs and the other slopes don't seem to like beetroot too much. Wogs neither. I don't know why we let them into this country.'

'Still serving up the xenophobia though, I see.'

Lothar seemed confused. 'No, I don't think we have any Greek dishes on the menu. But I can check with the kitchen if you like.'

'No, don't bother,' I said as I followed Lothar to a picnic table with a reserved sign.

The table was set with disposable plates and cutlery and those cheap paper napkins that leave lint all over your face if you haven't shaved close enough. There was also a plastic squeeze container of tomato ketchup and a tall bottle of HP sauce.

'C'mon, Mr Murdoch, you should try my manager's special,' Lothar said proudly, handing me a plastic laminated menu. 'It's on the house and everything's gratis.'

He leaned over to me. 'That means you don't have to pay,' he said quietly.

To humour him, I took a look at the menu. Like the manager, the manager's special was an unappetising mix of conflicting items. Kangaroo fillet, camel sausages, half a marinated chicken, fried onion rings, oysters Kilpatrick, coleslaw and potato salad, with pavlova to finish. Including a beer or a glass of the house wine and a coffee, it was apparently a bargain at ninety bucks a head.

Further down the menu I noticed that the 'Salt and Chilli Battered Octopus Testicles' had been partly covered by a white label with the word 'Tenticles' hand written on it. I was tempted to say something, but decided to let it go.

I turned the menu over to look at the wine list. 'Might have a drink, though. Does the house red come out of a bottle, a wine cask or a 50,000-gallon railway tanker?'

The look on Lothar's face told me it was the railway tanker, so I opted for an outrageously marked-up bottle of Graveyard Shiraz, which made him wince. He passed the wine order on to a waiter and ordered a steak for himself.

'No Jezza-licious JezzaBarrana on the menu yet?'

Lothar shook his head. 'Mr Fischer expects the first ones to be available very soon. The growing pond at the old Gifford mine outside Gaffney's Creek is up and running.'

So now I had a location. Gaffney's Creek was an old gold-mining town a couple of hours south. It made a lot of sense to use a flooded open-cut mine as a ready-made home for the fish.

'Them Barrana have a hell of an appetite. The abattoirs are having trouble keeping up.'

'What abattoirs?'

'The places that do the kangaroos for pet food. And the beef cattle and camel slaughterhouses. Mr Fischer takes all the waste and the carcasses. We even send our food scraps from here.'

'They're turning all that stuff into fishmeal?'

'Oh no, Mr Murdoch, you don't have to do any of that. You just chuck it all in the pond - heads, feet, fur, everything. The fish do the rest. Every couple of weeks they dredge the bones off the bottom. I've heard some of them fish are already a metre long.'

A waiter poured me a glass of the Graveyard Shiraz, and after giving it a full fifteen seconds to breathe I downed it in one gulp. It wasn't any way to treat a top-notch wine, but the vision of a pond full of Barrana hoeing into truckloads of cow, camel and kangaroo carcasses was really disturbing.

'Here's my dinner, Mr Murdoch,' Lothar said. 'Isn't she a beauty?'

The waiter was proudly displaying the biggest T-bone I'd ever seen. There were smears of blood around the edges of the platter that held the raw meat and I guessed that if I dropped it into a pool of hungry Barrana it would last about two seconds.

The waiter put cutlery including a serrated-edged steak knife on the table in front of Lothar and then set about lighting the barbecue grill.

I poured myself another glass of red.

'Now, you're sure you won't change your mind?' Lothar asked.

I smiled. 'Not in a million years. But there is one little favour I want from you and I'm sure a man of your calibre won't be able to say no?'

I wasn't officially off suspension just yet and didn't have access to the D-E-D armoury. The way things were shaping up, I felt the need for a little protection.

Lothar turned pale. 'No way, Mr Murdoch, no way. I'm out of that game, I told you before. I don't have any inventory no more, you gotta believe me.'

'I'm out of the believing business this week, Lothar. Now we can whack this steak of yours on the barbecue or you can put it on a black eye - you decide.'

It didn't take long for Lothar to make up his mind and while he was gone I toyed with the steak knife the waiter had set down. I'm always bemused by restaurants that offer the most tender of steaks for your dining pleasure and then hand you a knife that could cut through a tree trunk. Talk about mixed messages. The Bluey's logo was branded on the nasty wood-grained plastic handle, but the blade had a nice sharp edge, and since I was kind of missing my balisong I wrapped the knife in a paper napkin and slipped it into my pocket.

Lothar was back from his office in two minutes flat with something concealed in a large envelope. He handed me the envelope under the table and I took a quick peek

'Jesus, mate,' I said, 'haven't we been here before?'

The pistol was a battered little Beretta 25 automatic and it looked way too familiar.

'That gun brought you good luck last time I lent it to you, Mr Murdoch.'

'You didn't lend it to me, you little prick. You took my watch as collateral and then sold me out to the people who wanted me dead. But nothing like that is going to happen this time, is it?'

Lothar shook his head vigorously. 'You can depend on me, Mr Murdoch.'

'No I can't, Lothar. Right now, that's about the only thing I know for certain, which is somehow oddly comforting.'

I slipped the pistol into the same pocket as the knife and stood up.

'Lothar, old buddy, just a bit of friendly advice. If you say anything about any of this to anyone, then that octopus won't be the only thing around this joint with battered testicles.'

Chapter Forty-Six

The menu at Bluey's had taken the edge off my appetite but I was still hungry. While there are some really fantastic restaurants in Darwin, I needed a quiet evening to figure out my next move, so I ordered from the hotel's room service menu.

On very rare occasions hotel room service can surprise you, and when the doorbell rang it turned out to be one of those occasions.

I peered through the peephole and quickly slipped Lothar's geriatric Beretta into my pocket before opening the door.

'I'm not expecting a bloody tip,' Jezebel said, as she wheeled the trolley into the room. I poked my head out into the corridor and saw a room-service waiter standing by the elevators and smiling as he counted cash. When I closed the door and turned around, Jezebel was standing by the trolley with a white napkin draped over one arm.

'Would sir like it on the table or on the bed?'

'We are talking about dinner, right?' I asked. 'You want to join me?'

Jezebel lifted the metal lids off a couple of plates and studied the food. Her nose wrinkled. 'Not even with a bloody gun to my head.'

There was a table near the window, but I pulled the heavy curtains closed before we sat down. Being backlit in a window at night makes for too tempting a target.

Jezebel opened a beer from the trolley and watched as I took a bite of the burger I'd ordered. As hotel burgers go it was a hotel burger, nothing like the Big Bloke's Burger at Soggy Togs in Bondi. Now that was a real burger, but unfortunately the owner had banned me for life after a couple of incidents involving gunplay during the lunchtime rush.

'What brings you to Darwin, Jez?'

'Playford's new 767, as it happens. He had some business to attend to at the casino here so I hitched a ride. Bloody plane's got bidets and gold taps in the dunnies, a pool table, a putting green and in-flight big-screen hi-def porn. Flying private craps all over first class, let me tell you.'

'Eloquently put. And I guess you're in town for a romantic rendezvous with Detlef?'

'Actually, that's why I stopped by. I was supposed to be meeting him for cocktails, but his house at Larrakeyah is locked up, the Montreal's not in the garage and he's not answering his mobile. I checked with that little turd Lothar out at Bluey's and he said Detlef drove you in from the airport.'

I nodded. 'He's in town as far as I know. Maybe he's too embarrassed to show his face in public because of his connection to Bluey's.'

'Jesus, what a dump, eh? I know there has to be a low end to the market, but that bloody place is positively subterranean. I'm trying to get Detlef to let me give it a total makeover and add a bit of class. And the first thing going into the dumpster would be that little prick Lothar, believe me.'

'You're not worried about Detlef are you, Jez? Don't tell me it's true love.'

'Screw you, Alby. Bastard will surface sometime, I guess. I know he's got a meeting with Playford tomorrow to check out the fish.'

'You and Playford aren't a twosome, are you? Or maybe a threesome with Detlef?'

She laughed. 'I'm not exactly sure what lights Playford's fire, but it's not me. I guess some things don't run in the family.'

That piqued my interest. 'You and Old Peng?'

'We might have had a moment, back in the early nineties. I did some cooking on private yachts when I was just starting out and Old Peng had a nice junk that he used for entertaining business clients in Hong Kong. He was a very generous employer. When we parted company, he bankrolled my first restaurant, which was sweet of him.'

'Too bad about the stroke,' I said. 'I hear Playford may have been a contributing factor.'

She shook her head. 'He's been spreading that rumour himself, thinks it might make him sound more like a tough guy if people believe he took out the old man to gain control.'

'Carrying on the proud Peng family tradition of patricide.'

Jezebel shrugged. 'He likes playing the heavy, what can I tell you? Poor bugger had a really awful time as a kid at that shithole Fairbrothers. When I was working for Old Peng he'd come home for school holidays and I'd try to make his life a bit more fun for a few weeks. I'd take him jogging and put him on a more sensible diet after all that boarding-school stodge.'

'Every schoolboy's dream vacation.'

She smiled. "He seemed to enjoy the jogging part.'

'We're not talking your short shorts, no bra and that Hash House Harriers T-shirt I gave you? The one that shrank in the dryer?'

She laughed, glanced down at the Lady Rolex on her wrist and stood up. 'I have to meet Playford in the VIP room at the Darwin Casino. Maybe Detlef's over there with him.'

'Is Playford worried he couldn't get an honest game at his own tables?'

She shook her head. 'He's planning on making a takeover offer for the place and he likes a bit of glam at his elbow during negotiations. Says it keeps the other side from thinking straight.'

I could see Playford's point. I could also see quite a lot of Jezebel through the gauzy top she was wearing.

'That meeting you mentioned, tomorrow at the fish farm, you tagging along by any chance?' I asked.

'No way. I'm not getting up at the crack of dawn. Anyway I'm only interested in getting my name on the label and the money in the bank. Plodding around stinky fishponds out in the boondocks isn't my idea of early-morning fun. And from what I overheard Playford saying, it sounded like it was just going to be him, Detlef and Leroy Fong - boys only.'

'I'm in that club.'

'I remember,' she said, giving me that look I'd seen on the plane.

'Maybe I should stop by tomorrow, offer to take some snaps to introduce the Barrana and its proud parents to the world.'

'That's JezzaBarrana, Alby, and it's trademarked. And seriously, mate, you probably should steer clear of the place. Playford is paranoid about security out there - wouldn't even tell me the exact location. And Leroy Fong is a real nasty bastard, with a very short fuse. The smart move would be not to go snooping around.'

I walked her to the door. 'Smart never was my strong suit, Jez, you know that, but I'm touched by your concern."

I was also touched by her left hand in a fairly intimate spot, and I jumped a little but finally managed to disengage myself from her grasp.

'Can't blame a girl for trying, Alby,' she said, giving me a goodnight kiss, 'not with a lemon meringue pie and a perfectly good hotel bed going to waste.'

When Jezebel had gone, I took the Beretta from my pocket and checked the clip. It was interesting news that Leroy Fong was in town. It was the kind of news that made me wish Lothar had had something with a little more stopping power tucked away in his office.

Chapter Forty-Seven

After stabbing at the lemon meringue pie with a fork to make sure it was as dead as it looked, I poured a cup of room-service coffee, hoping to wash the taste of the hamburger out of my mouth and sharpen up my brain a little.

If Playford and Fischer had an early-morning meeting planned at the fish farm, popping by uninvited might give me some insight into what the hell Playford was up to. Of course, with Leroy Fong in attendance it might also get me dead.

The doorbell rang a couple of minutes later and I looked around the room for any furniture I could use to block the doorway, but there was nothing heavy enough to even slow Jezebel down. But this time it wasn't Jezebel.

Nhu was wearing a floaty dress in a pale grey fabric with a half-moon pattern and contrasting sleeves. There were echoes of the Áo dài in the way it was split rather fetchingly from mid-calf to upper thigh. Red patent-leather sandals finished off the outfit, the red leather accent picked up by the large soft tote bag she carried over one shoulder.

She looked amazing, and no wonder, as everything was brand new and the real deal - none of your night-market knock-offs.

'Very, very nice,' I said. 'Louis Vuitton?'

She smiled. 'It's the new Resort Collection. I'm most impressed, Mr Murdoch.'

'Me too, Miss Hoang.'

She put her bag on the bed and walked across to the room-service trolley. 'Lemon meringue pie, may I?'

'I should warn you that after the burger I just had, I'm not holding out high hopes.'

She took a small taste, grimaced, and put the cover back over the plate.

'So, Miss Hoang, what brings you to our delightful tropical north?'

'My money-laundering investigation has led me to the Darwin Casino, and I am here to make further inquiries.'

'So it's not my fatal charm, then?'

'Your charm is fatal, Mr Murdoch? I'm not sure I understand. Miss Quick appeared to leave your room without suffering injury.'

That was a low blow. I'd noticed her giving the bed a quick once-over before dropping her bag on a chair. Perhaps she was wondering if Jezebel had popped in for more than a chat and was checking the bedspread for signs of recent carnal creasing.

'Fatal charm is just a figure of speech, Miss Hoang - a joke.'

I didn't think it was smart to mention that with Jezebel there was always a chance of suffering a life-threatening injury, and that was certainly no joke.

'And may I ask what brings you to Darwin, Mr Murdoch?'

'I'm here to do a little fishing.'

'How interesting. I enjoy fishing too.'

'I'm partial to the Hardy Angel Smuggler rod with a Sage reel,' I said, 'and maybe a Royal Wulff fly.'

'Oh, trout. I myself prefer going after somewhat bigger fish.'

'And what do you use for a lure, Miss Hoang?'

She smiled that smile.

'I didn't really get the chance to thank you for saving my life back in Hong Kong.'

'I think you showed your appreciation in other ways, Mr Murdoch, in Macau.'

'But I'm not sure I fully expressed my gratitude, Miss Hoang,' I said, moving towards her.

'I still have some things to attend to this evening,' she said, stepping deftly to one side, 'tomorrow might be better. Breakfast perhaps?'

'I'm going fishing tomorrow, early.'

'How unfortunate. A raincheck then.'

Nhu picked up her bag from the bed and I walked her to the door.

'And Mr Murdoch,' she said, 'one more thing. About my early departure in Macau..

'Yes?'

'That urgent business to attend to. You were fast asleep and I didn't want to disturb you.'

'I appreciate that, but you had already disturbed me, Miss Hoang, a great deal.'

I smiled and closed the door behind her.

Miss Hoang had a habit of disturbing me in a very pleasant way, but this time I had a feeling she was keeping tabs on me and I wondered why.

I figured the odds of another hot woman coming to my door that evening had to be pretty slim, so I picked up the remote to see what was on TV. Surprisingly, the doorbell rang a third time. It was Maxine, my friendly and very helpful flight attendant. She was holding a bottle of champagne.

'We overnight in Darwin a couple of times a week,' she said. 'I spotted you in the lobby and talked the girl at reception into giving me your room number. The crew bus is picking me up at five tomorrow morning so we don't have a lot of time to mess around.'

As it turned out, we had exactly the right amount of time to mess around and Maxine really did know exactly which buttons to press.

Chapter Forty-Eight

The drive south from Darwin to the old gold mining town of Gaffney's Creek took a couple of hours. The countryside was mostly flat, with scrubby vegetation and scrawny trees and termite mounds sticking up out of the red dust. The early-morning air was crisp and clear, and traffic was light, with only the odd sparkle reflecting off a vehicle way in the distance behind me.

The open road gave me time to reflect on my situation. I'd just had a night of wild sex with a flight attendant who had several interesting takes on the brace position, and I was on my way to gatecrash a meeting of dodgy fish farmers at a pond full of feral fish, armed only with a plastic-handled steak knife and a museum-piece pistol. And to think my high-school career counsellor had suggested I go into retail banking.

A three-metre-high chain-link fence topped with razor wire surrounded the old Gifford open-cut goldmine a couple of k's outside Gaffneys Creek. The tin sign wired to the fence near the gate read 'Fischer Aquaculture Industries Pilot Project - Definitely No Admittance! Site Under Quarantine!'

The gate was wide open, and since I couldn't spot any roaming guard dogs or off-the-leash Barrana I parked the rented Toyota and wandered in.

There were a dozen or so dilapidated workshop buildings and the odd bulldozer and forklift standing about in the red dust. The only other vehicle I could see was Detlef Fischer's Alfa Montreal parked near one of the sheds. The bonnet was cold to the touch, so the car had obviously been there for some time. Off to my left I could hear water splashing, so I climbed a mullock heap for a look.

The pond was the size of a couple of football fields. An elevated steel-mesh walkway led out to the middle, and the same kind of floating paddlewheel and fountain pump device I'd seen in Vietnam had been anchored at either end of the pond to oxygenate the water. The splashing noise I'd heard wasn't just from the paddlewheels and water jets, though; sleek, silver-grey Barrana were leaping out of the water, and from what I could see they were bloody big fish and there were a hell of a lot of them.

I walked back towards the main building and noticed a large truck-trailer combination parked outside. Even though the smell warned me it was probably a mistake, I climbed up the steps of the driver's compartment and took a peek inside the trailer.

Both truck and trailer were packed with recently butchered kangaroo carcasses, plus heads, tails and skins with the front paws still attached. A gazillion blowflies swarmed over the mess, but they were way too busy to take any notice of me. I was looking at breakfast for the fish and I have to say it really put me off the thought of what I might have for mine.

The blowies had ignored me, but someone else had chosen not to.

'Please step down from the truck, Mr Murdoch, and keep your hands where I can see them.'

Leroy Fong was holding a well-calculated choice of fire-arm. It was a .357 stainless-steel Colt Python Magnum, the one with the eight-inch barrel. I climbed down from the truck, smiling and keeping my hands visible. At this range, a slug from the Python would go through me and both doors of the truck behind me and still have the energy to sail way off into the wild blue yonder. I didn't want to get shot and I definitely didn't want to get shot by an accountant. There are some ways of dying you really can't live down.

'Mr Fischer and I are having a meeting in the workshop building.' Leroy said. 'Perhaps you would like to join us. Please put your gun on the seat of the truck first.'

The muzzle of the Python was pointed at my middle and was rock-steady. I reached slowly under my jacket with my right hand and took out the little Beretta, holding it between thumb and forefinger. Moving slowly and carefully, I placed it on the seat of the truck and then turned back towards Leroy.

'Fourth time's the charm, Leroy?'

He stared at me.

'You haven't had much success so far, have you. Saigon, the bar in Chiang Rai and then the other night in Hong Kong.'

'I was forced to use unreliable local people in Vietnam and Thailand, and in Hong Kong there were complications.'

'You were using local people to keep this quiet from Playford?'

He nodded. 'Old Peng was a very reliable and stabilising influence on our organisation until his unfortunate stroke. Many of our people are feeling less sure of their future under Playford's leadership.'

'So you took on a little outside contract work for Crockett?'

'I was in Vietnam on business for Playford anyway, and the money offered by Crockett's people was very generous. Of course, if I had known how.. difficult you and your friends would turn out to be, I would have negotiated a much higher fee.'

'I hope you got some money upfront,' I said, 'because the firm that contracted you has recently gone into liquidation.'

He smiled. 'Then, of course, in that case my loyalty to Playford remains steadfast.'

'Where is the boss man, by the way?'

'He has been delayed in Darwin. You ask far too many questions, Mr Murdoch. Now, perhaps you would like to join Mr Fischer.'

He indicated with a wave of the Python's long barrel that I should walk ahead of him to the workshop building.

Inside, out of the harsh sunlight, my eyes took a moment to adjust. It looked like a well-equipped workshop with machine tools, welding gear, a lathe and a lot of big steel drums. From the markings, most held diesel or lubricants but I could see a couple stamped with a skull-and-crossbones symbol and the word 'cyanide'. The drums must have been left over from the gold mining days when cyanide was used to extract gold from the pulverised ore. And then I spotted Fischer.

'Good morning, Detlef, how are they hanging?'

The suspensory state of Detlef Fischer's testicles was probably the least of his worries at this particular moment. He was upside down, strung up by his ankles with his head a metre or so above the concrete floor. The rope around his ankles was connected to a winch block attached to one of the shed's steel crossbeams.

'Conducting an overly enthusiastic tax audit, Leroy?' I asked.

'Get me down, Murdoch,' Fischer begged. 'Peng's gone fucking crazy. He got this psycho Chink bastard to tie me up and drive me out here and now the prick reckons he's going to feed me to the Barrana as soon as Peng shows up. Peng kept raving on about what we did to him back in school and the fish not being sterile and how we're all going to pay. Get me down, for God's sake! All these Chinks are fucking crazy.'

'Harm sup gwailo!' Leroy shouted, which is a rather impolite expression in Cantonese. He walked over to Fischer and smacked him in the nuts with the barrel of the Colt, which seemed to be not only impolite but also pretty painful.

Fischer started screaming and Leroy joined in when I stuck the pointy end of Lothar's steak knife into his elbow. The Colt hit the floor and Leroy grabbed for his elbow, then changed his mind and grabbed for his crotch after I kicked him in the groin.

I found some more of the rope Fong had used on Detlef and tied him up. His elbow wound wasn't too serious but it had made him drop the gun, which was my intention.

'I'll kill you, you bastard,' Leroy hissed, as I added a couple more knots for safety. Knots have never been my strong point.

'You're going to have to take a number, mate.'

Behind me, Detlef was moaning softly and I bumped his head on the floor while lowering him from the overhead beam, which probably took his mind off the ache between his legs for a moment. It didn't shut him up, however.

'Cut me loose and let me at that friggin' Chink,' he gasped.

'Not just now,' I said. 'I've got other fish to fry. And you should learn to watch your language, you nasty prick.'

Driving a forklift isn't like riding a bike and it took a while for all the moves to come back. Eventually, I manoeuvred my way into the workshop and managed to get one of the cyanide barrels up on the forks. Then I headed slowly out of the shed and across the yard towards the pond.

The front wheels of the forklift were a dozen or so centimetres from the edge of the pond when I stopped, and that seemed plenty close enough. The barrel was suspended over the water, and the restless surging in the pond indicated that the Barrana must have figured their breakfast was on the way. I switched off the engine and climbed down. All I had to do now was punch a hole in the barrel and bob's your uncle.

A pistol would do the job nicely and it looked like I had two choices; I could grab the Beretta from the truck or I could go back to the workshop for Leroy's Colt. Then a third option presented itself: I could ask Playford Peng for a lend of his pistol.

Peng's Colt Magnum had the two-and-a-half-inch barrel, and from the look in his eye he wasn't about to hand it over, no matter how nicely I asked.

Chapter Forty-Nine

Over Playford's left shoulder I could see a black Lexus. I hadn't heard the vehicle arrive due to the noise of the forklift.

Looking down the barrel of a .357 twice in one morning was two times too many.

'All by yourself, Mr Murdoch?' Peng asked.

'Leroy and Fischer are here, but they're both a little tied up at the moment.'

He nodded. 'I saw them in the shed,' he said. 'Bit of an Aussie funny bugger, aren't you Murdoch?'

I shrugged.

Peng kept smiling but there was no humour in his eyes and I wondered why he hadn't released Leroy.

'I know all about your famous Aussie sense of humour, Murdoch,' Playford continued, 'Fairbrothers was full of Aussie funny buggers.'

'I take it you didn't find them all that amusing.'

'I was the foreigner, the fat boy, eh, Murdoch. I was the Ching-Chong-Chinaman, the Chink, Fat Guts, the Yellow Peril. The kid who ate flied lice.'

'New country, new school, I guess fitting in can be tough..'

'Tough?' Peng almost screamed, 'Tough? It wasn't about fitting in, you idiot, it was about survival. There was a relentless campaign of physical and psychological terror by the whole school against me, you stupid *gwailo.* They stuffed fried rice in my school bag and ganged up to block me from getting to the toilets so I would wet my pants. They put green dye in my shampoo and took my clothes and boiled them in the laundry to shrink them and make me look even more stupid. The teachers ignored the situation and told me to be a man and stand up for myself. I begged and pleaded with my father to take me out of there, but he did nothing.'

'Okay, so it was more than tough, but what have you got against Fischer?' I asked, hoping to buy myself some more time, 'I thought you and he were pals.'

Peng sneered. 'Fischer was the senior boy in my House. He was supposed to be my protector, but he laughed at me behind my back with the rest of them. He took me swimming at Bondi Beach once and spent all day giggling about me with his girlfriends, slutty *gwaii moi* with their tits showing, all sunburnt brown like peasant farmers in the rice paddies They called me the beached whale like I was some stupid Asian who was too thick to understand their taunts.'

'So why the hell would you go into business with Fischer,' I asked, 'if he was that much of an arsehole?'

'Do you know who said, "Keep your friends close and your enemies closer," eh, Murdoch?'

Poor old Sun Tzu. Getting quoted as gospel by every dipshit whack job, life coach, corporate trainer, regional office team-leader, wannabe business executive, advertising-space salesman and real-estate agent with an impostor complex. And not getting royalties.

'So you kept smiling along with Fischer all these years and now it's finally payback time.'

'Revenge is a dish best eaten cold, Murdoch.'

'Like gazpacho?' I suggested.

Playford Peng didn't crack a smile. 'You think you are so funny, eh, Murdoch? Well, Mr Funny Bugger, you see those clouds on the horizon? The wet season is starting and after we bulldoze a channel across to the creek, the first big rain will flood this pond and my Barrana friends will swim down to the sea and have the whole Australian coastline to play on. And when they breed with some of those big wild barramundi, who knows what we'll get? Probably even the sharks and the crocodiles will be fair game.'

Bugger me, the bloke was going totally Columbine, but instead of semi-automatic weapons he was planning on using feral fish.

'All you stinking Aussie bastards love your beaches and you love your seafood. Just wait till you can't dip your toe in the water at Bondi or St Kilda or Cottesloe without getting your leg ripped off by a pack of Barrana. And once your wild fish stocks are decimated by this wonder fish brought to you by Mr Detlef bloody Fischer his name will be mud. Don't you think that's going to be very bloody funny, eh, Mr Murdoch?'

It really didn't sound too funny but it did sound potentially quite bloody.

'Now, why don't we walk over this way,' Peng said. 'I want to show you something. Something that might make you wish you hadn't stuck your nose in where it wasn't wanted.'

I was already way ahead of him on that.

He indicated the path that led to the gantry suspended over the big pond. The idea of strolling over the heads of a pack of man-eating fish had limited appeal but right now Peng had the upper hand. The upper hand is always the one with the gun in it.

Chapter Fifty

THE SOUND OF OUR FOOTSTEPS APPEARED TO ROUSE THE FISH AS WE walked along the metal gangway. I could see them stirring in the pond's muddy water below us. They must have realised it was mealtime about the same moment I woke up to the fact that I was on the menu.

Playford leaned back on the metal balustrade, one hand on the railing while the other kept the Colt pointed at the middle of my chest.

'You're an irritating bastard,' he said. 'I don't know what brought you to my dinner at the Manchu Palace and I don't know what brought you here this morning, but I'll be glad to be rid of you.'

At least while Peng was talking he wasn't shooting.

'What are you, Murdoch, ninety kilos?'

'Give or take a roast dinner or two.'

Peng indicated the pond with a tilt of his head. 'No more than sixty seconds to get you down to the bone, I would estimate. They didn't get breakfast this morning so they're a bit peckish. You'll be the appetiser and then Detlef can be the main course.'

'And Leroy for dessert?' I suggested.

'Leroy has been disloyal to me,' Playford said. 'His actions put my plans in jeopardy, so, yes, the Barrana will be having a three-course breakfast this morning.'

When I took a slow step forward, Peng lifted the pistol and shook his head.

'You're going in, Murdoch. I would prefer it if you were alive when you hit the water, but I'm willing to be flexible on that point.'

I took a step back, and then I saw it. A small red dot was hovering in the middle of Peng's chest. It moved slowly across and travelled down his arm before coming to rest on his left hand, which was gripping the metal railing.

'I hate to be irritating, Playford,' I said, 'but it's been rich and real.'

Playford stared at me quizzically, then his left hand and the guardrail exploded. The impact of the bullet spun Peng around, the Colt flew from his grasp and suddenly he was falling as the shattered rail gave way under his weight.

Playford Peng screamed once as he hit the water. Then the Barrana were on him and their lunging, twisting bodies pushed him under. The pond boiled and bubbled and Playford surfaced for a moment, his arms flailing wildly. Then he was under again and the frothing water turned red. An arm came up momentarily, the fingers already stripped down to the bone, and then it was gone.

Peng really knew his fish. It was all over in less than a minute, and then the swirling pond settled back into stillness.

Something made me look down and I stopped breathing. Right in the middle of my chest was that damned red dot. I knew the rifle was perfectly zeroed to its laser sight from the way the sniper had hit Peng's hand, so it was unlikely they were going to miss.

The dot started to move. It tracked slowly down my chest and across my stomach, paused for one heart-stopping moment on my crotch, then moved out along the walkway.

I followed it with my eyes as it tracked down one of the gantry legs and across the compound to where I'd left the forklift parked beside the pond. The dot travelled upwards and came to rest on the metal drum sitting on the forks. There was a bang and a thin stream of liquid poured out of the punctured drum and into the pond.

Nothing happened for a couple of minutes and I wondered if maybe the drum had been correctly labelled. Then the water began to surge and pulse again as the drifting cyanide reached the oxygenation pumps and was sprayed across the surface of the pond. Barrana began to leap from the water, spinning and twisting, but now their sleek silver bodies were stiff and awkward. Gills flared bright red and mouths with rows of razor-sharp teeth were locked open in one final rictus.

As the wild flurry of activity slowly ebbed away I heard a trail bike start up somewhere behind the outbuildings, the noise of its exhaust dying away in the distance. Now it was just me, Fong and Fischer and a pond full of dead fish.

The Barrana were starting to float to the surface, limp now, their once shiny bodies turning a dull grey. There were hundreds of them, and in the tropical heat they'd soon begin to rot, making the truckload of kangaroo carcasses smell like a rose garden by comparison.

I walked back across the gantry and down the steps to dry land. In the shed Fischer and Fong were still securely bound, just as I'd left them.

'Jesus, thank God it's you,' Fischer said. 'I heard the shooting and thought I was next.'

'You would've been, Detlef, you were meant to be the main course on this morning's menu for the Barrana. And you, Mr Fong, were dessert.'

Both men turned white.

'Untie me, for God's sake, Murdoch,' Fischer pleaded.

'Sorry, I've got to hit the road - but don't worry, I'll send in the cavalry. Why don't you use the time to think about how you got yourself into this little mess, Detlef. And if you're planning on having sons and sending them to Fairbrothers, tell them to be nice to the Asian boys – really, really nice.'

Chapter Fifty-One

'It's Murdoch,' I said when Gwenda answered her phone.

'Alby?' she said. 'Is everything okay?'

Alby? Gwenda had never, ever called me Alby. And she seemed concerned for my wellbeing. It was both touching and extremely disturbing.

'Ambassador Crockett has retired from public life effective immediately and is returning to the US. What did you say to him?'

That was the reason for the concern. A quick chat in an anteroom bringing down an ambassador meant I knew something she didn't, and in a power-crazed town like Canberra that wasn't a good thing.

'The Ambassador and I just chatted about old times.'

'But you're okay?'

The tone of worry in her voice sounded almost genuine. I was toying with asking her to stop by my apartment and water my plants, just to see how far it went.

'I'm in Darwin. Can you get someone to make an anonymous call to the local cops? Tell them that a couple of people are tied up at the Fischer Aquaculture place outside of Gaffney's Creek. And tell them to stay well clear of the pond until they can get a HAZMAT crew to seal it off. It's full of cyanide and dead killer fish.'

'Cyanide? And killer fish?'

'And you'd better make sure the clean-up team is discreet because they are going to find some very odd bones on the bottom of the pond.'

Gwenda was silent on the other end of the phone. Maybe she was trying to figure out an easy way to tell the government it needed to spend several million bucks to clean up a cyanide-polluted pond in the Top End. Still, a couple of million bucks was small change compared to what it would have cost if Playford Peng's carnivorous fish had made it out into the nation's waterways.

Peng's Lexus had all the luxury extras but the keys were in the ignition of the Montreal. Fischer wasn't in any position to object so I fired her up, did a wheelie out of the car park and headed for the highway.

I actually felt a bit sorry for the Barrana, considering the rather unpleasant last meal they'd had. Then I remembered my neighbour, Mrs T. She and I had a bit of a ritual going when I got back from an assignment. If the weather was good, we'd get fish and chips from Bondi Surf Seafoods and eat them under the Norfolk pines on the grassy hillside running down to the beach, while Dougal annoyed the seagulls. Mrs T loved her fish and chips, so how was I going to explain to her that it would be a very long time before I could look a piece of deep-sea perch in the eye again.

I'd been on the highway just long enough to get into top gear when I saw her. Jeans, leather jacket, helmet and a short rectangular case slung over one shoulder. She was standing next to a Yamaha trail bike with a shredded rear tyre, talking on a mobile phone. The bike had shiny chrome handlebars and I wondered if that was what I'd seen glinting in my rear-view mirror on the drive out from Darwin. As I rolled to a stop she snapped the phone shut.

'Miss Hoang, this is an unexpected surprise. Having a problem with your bike?'

She smiled. 'How very fortunate you came along, Mr Murdoch. A baby kangaroo jumped out in front of me and I applied the brakes a little too hard.'

'Wallaby probably,' I said. 'You okay?'

She twisted her body to show me the abrasions on the shoulder and arm of her jacket. 'I just slid down the road a little. Nothing serious.'

'Been hunting?' I asked, indicating the case.

'Fishing, Mr Murdoch.'

'Of course,' I said. 'Me too.'

My money was on Nhu's case holding something other than a rod, a reel and some lures. Probably something chambered for .308 Winchester ammo, judging from the impact with Playford's left hand. Steyr's nifty little Scout Tactical Elite sniper rifle would fit the bill neatly.

'Chuck your...fishing gear in the back and I'll give you a lift into Darwin.'

She nodded. 'I would be most grateful.'

With the case safely in the boot and Nhu in the passenger seat, I fired up the Montreal's V8 and pointed the nose north.

Ten minutes later, I spotted the black Lexus in the rear-view mirror, closing fast. It had to be Leroy Fong, since I figured Fischer wouldn't be in a hurry to see me again.

I suddenly remembered that I'd left Fong's Colt on the bench in the workshop. What jogged my memory was a bullet from a .357 magnum shattering the rear window of the Montreal. That was going to be one very expensive piece of glass to replace.

I floored the accelerator pedal and the power of the Alfa's race-tuned V8 threw us both back in our seats. We surged ahead for a moment and then the Lexus was closing again and another slug from the .357 slammed into the boot. I started swerving in an attempt to spoil Fong's aim.

'Glove compartment,' I said, 'under that shelf.'

Nhu found the latch and it popped it open. 'How very sweet,' she said, taking out the little Walther.

She pulled the magazine and checked the clip. Another bang as a third slug ricocheted off the rear of the Montreal, and I heard Nhu slam the magazine back in and work the slide on the Walther. A .22 against a .357 was no contest, but in this case it would come down to the skill of the operator.

'Please slow down a little and hold as steady as you can,' she instructed. 'I don't have time for a sighting shot and we need to minimise deflection.'

Deflection is the art of firing at a moving object, putting the bullet slightly ahead of the target so they both arrive at the same spot at the same time. If Fong was travelling at around the same speed as us, deflection would be reduced to almost nil and Nhu's chances of doing some damage would be improved. Of course, it would also improve Fong's chances of doing the same thing and he had a lot more muscle going with that .357.

I stopped swerving and moved over to the right-hand lane. In the side mirror I could see the Lexus starting to close up on my left, the driver's window down. Given I was in a left-hand drive vehicle, Fong and I would soon be only a metre apart. Way too close for comfort.

Nhu had twisted around in her seat and was braced with her back against the dash. Fong was almost level now, his right hand on top of the steering wheel and his left holding the Colt across his chest. It was easier for him to steer the car with his damaged right arm, but even with the Colt in his left hand, at this range he couldn't miss.

'Steady, please,' Nhu said quietly, and then she had the Walther up in a firm two-handed grip and it was BANG! BANG! BANG! BANG! right in my face. It sounded like she'd emptied the whole ten-round magazine, and tiny brass shell casings were flying around the inside of the car.

A startled Fong jerked his right hand away from the wheel like he'd been stung, and the Lexus spun off the roadway, tumbling end-over-end into a deep gully in a shower of dust and gravel. Seconds later there was an explosion followed by a giant fireball.

Nhu settled back in her seat and released the Walther's empty magazine. She took a silk handkerchief from her pocket and methodically wiped the pistol and the empty magazine clean before slipping the weapon back in the glove compartment. The latch on the glove compartment got a quick wipe, too. She carefully folded the handkerchief and put it back in her pocket, then looked at the empty strip of bitumen stretching ahead of us to the horizon.

'That makes three.'

'Three, Mr Murdoch?'

'Saigon, Hong Kong and now here. That's three times you've come to my rescue. Or is it four?'

Nhu gave me a look I couldn't quite read and then turned her eyes back to the highway.

I felt something in my hair and when I reached up I found a still-warm empty .22 shell casing. I tossed it out the window.

Chapter Fifty-Two

'It seems poetic somehow that Playford's sleeping with the fishes.'

Nhu looked across at me. 'Excuse me?'

'Old Peng's son, Playford, he's sleeping with the fishes - he's dead.'

'Really?'

I nodded. 'There's been a lot of it going around. You know Old Peng?'

She nodded. 'We've met.'

'I'm surprised Crockett didn't try to have Old Peng killed. He was a very dangerous loose end.'

'Old Peng having a stroke was a lucky break for Crockett,' she said.

'Bit of a lucky break for Old Peng, too. Or maybe a stroke of genius.'

"Stroke of genius, Mr Murdoch? I'm not sure I understand.'

'I think you understand very well, Miss Hoang. Old Peng is obviously a wily old bugger. When he heard that Crockett was angling for a vice-presidential nomination, he must have figured there were loose ends Crockett would need tidied up and he was one of them. Bastard could get himself an Academy Award nomination for his performance in that wheelchair.'

'Old Peng said you were no fool, Mr Murdoch. When did you figure out he had faked his stroke?'

'When he gave me the negative in the casino. He was showing all the classic symptoms of a stroke involving the left side of the brain, you know, difficulty with speech and communication, paralysis of the right side of the body. Problem was, he signalled his nurse to stop next to me by raising his right index finger.'

'You are an expert on strokes, Mr Murdoch?'

'My old man had one,' I said. 'So exactly how did you get involved with Old Peng?'

'I went to Macau to investigate money laundering through the casinos. Out of respect for Old Peng, as the senior member of the family, I requested permission to interview him. Playford had no objections since he believed the stroke had totally destroyed his father's cognitive functions. I didn't expect to find out anything of use - it was purely a courtesy.'

'That's when you realised he was faking?'

'Yes. My grandmother had a stroke. I nursed her for many months after it happened, so I also know the signs, and I called him on it. He liked that and suggested I might possess talents that would be useful to him. He was in the difficult position of having embarrassing information on a rich and dangerous man who was aiming for high government office, and he also had a vicious and amoral son who was becoming increasingly impatient to take over the Peng empire. His position was perilous and he decided drastic and immediate action was needed.'

In Old Peng's world, you first had to figure out who you needed to kill to get power and then who you needed to kill to keep it. It was a full-time job, the kind that kept a bloke awake 24/7, because as soon as you closed your eyes there were people waiting to put a bullet between them.

'But you're a police officer, Miss Hoang.'

'I am also a realist, Mr Murdoch. After the reunification of my country, the traitors in the south - those who had served in the armed forces or who had helped the Americans - were punished for their crimes. Some very harshly and some with long periods in re-education camps.'

'Very harshly' was putting it nicely.

'The extended families of the traitors also suffered,' she continued, 'with many restrictions and with greatly reduced educational and economic opportunities in the new Vietnam. Because of Uncle's involvement, our family was denied many things. Even though I was born long after the war, it was not easy for me to reach the position I now occupy. The financial rewards are not great, and as a woman my chances for further promotion are limited. I felt this was an opportunity to explore other options. And Old Peng is a very generous man.'

'So I've heard.'

'When he told me about the photographic negative of Ambassador Crockett he possessed, I suggested you might be the person to use it to best effect since you had no love for the Ambassador.'

She had that right.

'I contacted Uncle, who said he thought you were in Hong Kong, so I arranged to bump into you.'

'The text message from Jezebel?'

'Yes. But when you came off the Star Ferry I saw that you were being tailed by some very unsavoury characters, so I called in reinforcements from Old Peng's team.'

"And the invitation to dinner with Playford was arranged by Old Peng, so he could bump into me and give me the negative?'

'When you mentioned the WorldPix exhibition, and that Crockett would be in attendance, it seemed the perfect opportunity and it became a matter of urgency.'

'Is that why you took the photograph with my Leica and then lifted the memory card?'

She nodded. 'The photograph was necessary to identify you. Old Peng insisted on putting the negative directly into your hands.'

'Not a very trusting bugger, is he? And here was me thinking you were worried about your naked arse turning up all over the internet.'

'That was definitely another reason to take the card.'

I'd been so busy showing Nhu what a smart bastard I was that I didn't see where she got the gun from. It was a compact little Beretta Tomcat, a semi-automatic with a seven-round magazine. Judging from where she had the muzzle pointed, it looked like all seven rounds might be coming my way.

Miss Hoang was a world-class competition shooter. She'd taken out Playford at long range, hit Leroy Fong firing from a moving vehicle with a dinky .22, and now, sitting just a couple of feet from me, there was no way she was going to miss. This really wasn't working out to be one of my better mornings.

Chapter Fifty-Three

'So what do we do now, Miss Hoang?' It seemed like a fair question.

'I'm considering my options,' she said.

'You weren't calling roadside assistance back there, were you?'

She shook her head.

'Old Peng?'

She nodded.

'And he dislikes loose ends as much as Crockett does.'

'I'm afraid so, Mr Murdoch. I tried to talk him out of it but you know too much. You've outlived your usefulness and have become a liability. I'm very sorry.'

'Not as sorry as I am, Miss Hoang. But, of course, you realise if I'm dead you're the only person left who knows what's been going on, and that also makes you someone with a very short use-by date. The way I see it, as long as I'm alive you're safe, and as long as you're alive I'm okay.'

I didn't know how much sense that actually made, and I didn't really care, as long as it bought me a few extra seconds.

Nhu looked like she was thinking this over and was about to say something when I shouted, 'Kangaroo!' stomped on the brakes, swung the wheel hard left.

Nhu glanced up at the empty road ahead, and as the muzzle of the pistol swung away from me I biffed her one on the jaw.

I'd been brought up not to hit women, but in this instance I figured violence was my only option. Nhu's head snapped back, hitting the side window with a solid thud, and the little Beretta flew out of her hand and landed in my lap.

For a couple of seconds I thought I was going to slide into a three-sixty and lose the Alfa completely, but with both hands on the wheel I managed to get it back on the bitumen and under control, just in time to get waved down by an oncoming Northern Territory police vehicle. The bright blue Commodore with its chequered blue-and-white police livery was probably heading for Gaffney's Creek, following the tipoff from Gwenda. When he flashed his headlights and hit the red-and-blue roof lights, it seemed prudent to stop.

An unconscious Nhu was slumped down in the seat, her back resting against the passenger door. I leaned across and wound the window down, gave Nhu a kiss on the cheek and smiled at the copper, who was leaning out casually through the police vehicle's open window.

'Looked like a bit of pretty dodgy driving back there, mate,' he said. 'Everything okay?'

It seemed like the right moment for a quick bit of self-assessing of the situation. I was in a car that didn't belong to me, with a shattered back window and several large-calibre bullet holes in the rear panels. There was an unconscious, mildly concussed Vietnamese copper next to me sporting a nasty bruise on her chin, I had a semi-automatic pistol in my lap and a sniper's rifle that had taken out a psycho Macau casino operator in the boot. I've been in worse spots before but not many.

'Guess I almost lost her for a minute there,' I said. 'Swerved to avoid a 'roo. But everything's hunky-dory now.' I glanced at Miss Hoang beside me. "Didn't even wake up the lady.'

The cop looked across at me for a few seconds. Aviator sunglasses hid his eyes, making it hard for me to guess what he was thinking.

'You might wanna consider taking things a bit easier for a while,' he suggested, and then he gave me a nod and drove off.

As I watched his dust in the rear-view mirror, it seemed to me to be a very sensible suggestion.

END

About the Author

Melbourne-born author **Geoffrey McGeachin** always secretly wanted to be a writer but deftly avoided the issue by becoming a photographer.

After decades living and working in Asia and the US he settled in Sydney to teach photography and one day decided to sit down and see if he actually had a book in him. The comic caper novel ***Fat Fifty & Fucked!*** was the result, getting him an agent and a publishing deal.

This first book was followed by three tongue-in-check spy novels featuring photographer/secret agent Alby Murdoch: ***D-E-D Dead!, Sensitive New Age Spy*** and ***Dead & Kicking***.

The Charlie Berlin historical crime trilogy came next, with ***The Diggers Rest Hotel, Blackwattle Creek*** and ***St Kilda Blues***. The series, set in 1949, 1959 and 1969, earned him two prestigious Ned Kelly Awards for best Australian crime fiction.

Geoff now lives on the beautiful Central Coast of New South Wales.

Foreward – as an Afterword

The three Alby Murdoch spy novels – ***D-E-D Dead!, Sensitive New Age Spy*** and ***Dead & Kicking*** – are a satirical take on the espionage business, puffed-up politicians, government duplicity, inept public servants, insecure security agencies, and all the poor bastards forced to interact with them.

I originally wrote these books thinking I was being a very tongue-in-cheek and somewhat outrageous storyteller, but recent political developments worldwide have really blurred the line between the funny, the off-kilter and the totally bat-shit crazy. But the good news is politicians are still inept, the security services are still dodgy, football is still a religion and now there are even more areas of Australian life needing to have the piss taken out of them.

Reviewers summed up Alby as, 'a genuine action hero with a truly Australian irreverence' and 'a highly competent larrikin,' descriptions I'm quite happy with.

I considered updating the books for these new editions but decided the originals hold up as written. However, technology has advanced in leaps and bounds over those two decades so *you*, dear reader, will have to deal with a time where fax machines are part of any home office, cassette tapes are still common, homes have landline telephones, there are no smart phones with GPS in people's pockets, and our national coffee obsession is still brewing. I'm sure you can deal with it. Enjoy.

Geoff

Acknowledgements

Many thanks to the amazing Selwa Anthony who set me off on this journey and to Lindy Cameron and Clan Destine Press for giving the Alby Murdoch books a second life in print.

From Geoff McGeachin and Clan Destine Press

www.ingramcontent.com/pod-product-compliance
Lightning Source LLC
LaVergne TN
LVHW091054080826
845145LV00002B/745

* 9 7 8 1 9 2 2 9 0 4 9 6 6 *